力得文化
Leader Culture

MP3

1847　1866　1850

Follow

文學地圖
用英語
造訪世界 40 大景點

Travel Around
the World with
Literature Works

趙婉君 ◎ 著

循著文學故事《咆嘯山莊》、《罪與罰》、《紅字》…的脈絡，
足跡橫跨 **歐**、**美**、**亞** 三大洲，深入了解作品出處及故事背景，
拜訪大文豪的故居、啟發創作靈感之地…

本書引領讀者從
【文學景點巧巧說】、**【揭開序幕小對話】**優雅欣賞文學、悠閒認識景點，
學單字、文學、片語、佳句運用，**附MP3同步學習**，
提升英文閱讀力以及寫作能力　開拓旅遊的**「廣」**度和**「深」**度

特色文學景點搶先看

康諾德《黑暗之心》
【英】倫敦橋、泰晤士河

但丁《神曲地獄篇》
【義大利】佛羅倫斯

霍桑《紅字》
【美國波士頓】女巫博物館

蒙哥馬利《清秀佳人》
【加拿大多倫多】愛德華王子島

無名氏《浦島太郎》
【日本鹿兒島】JR 指宿玉手箱號

作者序

　　學英文，其實是在用另一種語言去了解這個世界，而不只是讀課本、背單字而已。這本《Follow 文學地圖用英語造訪世界 40 大景點》，以歐洲、美洲以及亞洲各區的文學足跡為主題景點，讓你讀書時，好像跟著書中的人物一起旅行，走遍世界文學大家的故居或經典故事的景點，同時也在學英文。

　　如果你覺得故事中的單字有點難，請不要覺得是你的程度不夠，你只是還沒接觸過那個領域的單字。想想小嬰兒的語言的學習，當他接觸到身邊的事物時，才開始發現原來透明的液狀物是「水」，而美國出生的小寶寶，所認識到的透明液狀物則是「water」，所以不管你幾歲開始學英文的，你想要學英文，記住一定要主動增加自己接觸英文的機會（exposure），不管是電視新聞改看 CNN、台灣偶像劇改看美劇，甚至是做筆記開始用一些英文單字註記，語言是拿來用的，不管是透過聽、說、讀、寫，只要多用一點語言，你的英文就會進步一些。

　　本書的文法解析，著重字詞的「功能性」，希望帶領學習者從文法的功能去理解英文這麼語言為什麼有特定的詞序以及用法。

趙婉君

編者序

　　很少有人不愛故事吧？就拿日常生活來說，我們不就常拿演藝圈發生的大小事當作茶餘飯後、閒聊的話題嗎？看電視時，每一個廣告不也是一個短篇故事嗎？隔天一早和朋友、同學碰面，你是不是也有把昨天看的新聞重述一次的經驗呢？這也是一種故事，對吧？那，再問，有人不愛旅遊的嗎？不論你喜歡與否，旅遊不能否認地，總是一個能讓人們好好放鬆、充電的活動，尤其是對於深陷在這個忙、盲、茫生活裡的現代人更是如此啦！

　　《Follow 文學地圖造訪世界 40 大景點》便是希望能透過經典文學的「故事」與大眾熱愛的「旅遊」，幫助讀者能在欣賞文學故事的同時，又能遊歷世界橫跨歐、美、亞洲的景點，並透過景點深入了解故事背景，進而提升英文閱讀能力、加強文法概念；甚至透過作者編寫的對話，學會將文學經典名句實際活用在觀光、旅遊上，探索旅遊的另一種可能和面向。

　　本書以歐、美、亞三大洲為分類，精心整理出各大洲的文學經典故事，先以引言的方式起頭，接著在《文學景點巧巧說》中，納入引言的出處、故事概要、發人深省之處與旅遊景點之間的關係。在《揭開序幕小對話》單元，跟著虛構人物一一走入各大景點，看他們這些文學怪咖「聊」文學、「賞」景點，你才知文學原來也滿親人、可愛、無厘頭的嘛！看完對話看《好好用單字、片語》與《文學佳句怎麼用》，教你輕鬆學會文學單字、片語沒負擔，更教你如何活用文學句型。最後以《文學經典重現》與每個景點必看必去的小提醒收尾，加強文學與景點的連結性。真心期盼讀者讀完每篇單元後，都有意猶味盡、深入其境之感。

　　Ready？別猶豫了，準備好跟著文學地圖「出發囉（Follow）」～

力得文化編輯群

Contents 目次

Part 01 歐洲篇 Europe

Part 02 美洲篇

Part 03 亞洲篇

Part 01

歐洲篇

蘇格蘭
Scotland

莎士比亞《馬克白》 *Macbeth*

" *Come, thick night,*
And pall thee in the dunnest smoke of hell,
That my keen knife see not the wound it makes,
Nor heaven peep through the blanket of the dark
To cry "Hold, hold! "

—— William Shakespeare, *Macbeth*, Act 1, Scene 5

Modern text:

Come, the thick night, making the world shrouded in hell's smoke which is so dark that my sight is blocked from seeing the wounds made by a sharp knife; so dark that heaven can't see through the darkness and cry, "Stop it! Stop!"

- -

　　就讓深夜降臨吧，那黑煙似的深夜，有如地獄；讓深夜遮蔽我的視線，看不清利刃畫下的傷口。

——莎士比亞《馬克白》第一幕，第五景

文學景點巧巧說

　　蘇格蘭（Scotland），位於大不列顛的北部，隸屬於大不列顛及北愛爾蘭聯合王國之下，受大西洋環繞包圍，東部濱臨北海，西南濱臨北海海峽與愛爾蘭海。蘇格蘭以壯麗的地理景觀聞名，湖泊、山岳和海岸線更是不能錯過的旅遊勝地。蘇格蘭同時也是莎士比亞四大悲劇之一《馬克白》的重要場景之一，所以來到蘇格蘭就不能不想到主角馬克白（Macbeth）以及馬克白夫人（Lady Macbeth）為掌握國家大權，不惜背叛鄧肯王（King Duncan）所犯下的滔天大罪，尤其馬克白夫人的野心絲毫不輸其夫，讓人不禁佩服莎士比亞在當時就能刻畫出如此鮮明且能獨立思考的女性腳色，但最令人不寒而慄的，還是人性之險惡是不分性別的吧。本引言與稍後的文學經典重現(英文部分)取自遠東圖書公司印行於1999年發行之莎士比亞叢書《馬克白》。

 揭開序幕小對話

Isaac is a very poetic man; he majored in Western literature in college. In contrast, Hayley is very realistic; she cares more about efficiency due to her management major. On the honeymoon trip, Isaac and Hayley paid a visit to Glamis Castle in Angus, Scotland, and arrived at the castle in the afternoon.

　　伊撒克是一位非常具有詩意的人，他大學時主修西方文學；相反的，海莉是個凡事講求實際的人，她在乎的是效率，典型管理學院的風格。伊撒克與海莉目前正在葛拉米城堡度蜜月，現在正是傍晚時分。

Isaac: I can't believe that I am finally here, the setting of Shakespeare's tragedy, *Macbeth*. Macbeth killed King Duncan and took the throne.

伊撒克：我無法相信我終於到這裡了，莎士比亞悲劇之一，《馬克白》的故事場景。主角馬克白殺了鄧肯王取得王位。

PART 1 歐洲篇

PART 2 美洲篇

PART 3 亞洲篇

Hayley: That's terrible. How did he dare to do that?

Isaac: Macbeth used to be a military officer. Then, three witches foretold that he would become a king. To realize the prophecy, Macbeth's wife encouraged his husband to usurp the throne.

Hayley: That sounds very dramatic.

Isaac: Or in other words, Macbeth's wife provoked his husband by saying he will be a coward if he dares not to kill the king. Finally, he took the throne by murdering the king.

Hayley: The plot is such a cliché. It's like a vicious cycle when it comes to the monarchy.

Isaac: That is so true. And do you know the Song Dynasty was also established in the same way that a previous king was assassinated by his military officer? Also…

Hayley: Issac, please, we are here for the honeymoon, and we should make lots of our memories rather than having litera-

海莉：好可怕！他怎麼敢這麼做？

伊撒克：馬克白原本是一位軍官。後來，三位女巫預言他將為成為國王。為了加速預言的發生，馬克白夫人鼓勵他加緊篡位。

海莉：聽起來非常戲劇化。

伊撒克：也就是説，馬克白夫人以膽小鬼之名刺激自己的丈夫把國王殺了。最後，馬克白謀殺成功，接下王位。

海莉：這種劇情好老套喔。有君主專制的地方總是有這種故事流傳。

伊撒克：沒錯。你知道中國的宋朝也是因為軍官謀殺帝王而建立的嗎？而且啊…

海莉：拜託，伊撒克，我們是來這度蜜月並創造兩人的共同回憶，而不是在這裡做文學跟

ture reviews or history discussions.

Isaac: All right. (After a short silence, Isaac starts to imitate Lady Macbeth) Hey, it's getting dark. **Come the thick night, making the world shrouded in hell's smoke which is so dark that my sight is blocked from seeing the wounds made by a sharp knife.**

Hayley: Issac, that is enough. (Hayley pouts her lips and stares at him angrily.)

Isaac: Honey. (Isaac hugs her and says no more.)

歷史探討的。

伊撒克：好吧。（一陣沉默後，伊撒克開始模仿馬克白夫人）嘿，天色漸漸晚了。就讓深夜降臨吧，那黑煙似的深夜，有如地獄；讓深夜遮蔽我的視線，看不清利刃畫下的傷口。

海莉：伊撒克，夠了喔！（海莉嘟著唇嬌嗔的看著他。）

伊撒克：我的甜心。（伊撒克不發一語緊緊抱著她。）

 好好用單字、片語

1. major *v./n.* 主修
2. realistic *adj.* 實際的
3. encourage *v.* 鼓勵
4. usurp *v.* 篡奪
5. throne *v.* 王權
6. establish *v.* 建立
7. imitate *v.* 模仿
8. shroud *v.* 遮蔽
9. .block *v.* 阻擋

10. in contrast *phr.* 相對的比較：contrast *v.* 對比 *n.* 對照　解析：contrast 的英文解釋為 to be different especially in a way that is very obvious，也就是在某方面有明顯的不同，字義的核心為異 different，而不同之處，需要經過相比 compare，所以在使用 compare 時，需要比較兩個人或兩種事物。

例 ❶ The teacher asks his student to compare and contrast the weathers in Asia, Europe, and Africa.

老師要求學生比較亞洲、歐洲、及非洲的天氣。

❷ Tina can sing very well. Her beautiful voice is gifted. In contrast, Rob's singing skill comes from constant practice.

蒂娜歌唱得很好，她有著天生的好聲音。相對的，羅伯的歌唱技巧，來自他不斷的練習。

文學佳句怎麼用

Come, the thick night, making the world shrouded in hell's smoke which is so dark that my sight is blocked from seeing wounds made by a sharp knife.

就讓深夜降臨吧，那黑煙似的深夜，有如地獄；讓深夜遮蔽我的視線，看不清利刃畫下的傷口。

句型 1 分詞構句怎麼用？分詞構句為連接兩個句子的概念，當兩個句子有相同的主詞時，可以去掉其中一個主詞，將兩個句子連在一起，此類較為精簡的變化即為「分詞構句」。

首先我們先從兩個句子的合併開始。

❶ 兩個有相同主詞的句子：

Come, the thick night. The thick night makes the world shrouded in hell's smoke which is so dark that my sight is blocked from seeing wounds made by a sharp knife.

❷ 將後面的主詞，改為關係代名詞 which，合併為一句。

Come, the thick night, which makes the world shrouded in hell's smoke which is so dark that my sight is blocked from seeing wounds made by a sharp knife.

句型 2 be blocked from 妨礙，阻止 to be placed in front of something so that people or things cannot pass through

例 ❶ Hayley's facebook account is mistakenly blocked from her posting.

海莉的臉書帳戶出錯，讓她無法刊登消息。

❷ More and more skyscrapers are built, blocking the view from the window.

摩天大樓蓋的越來越多，擋住了窗外的視線。

其它補充

blocked up *v.* 完全阻塞　例：My nose is blocked up. 我的鼻子塞住了。

 文學經典重現 Track02

The raven himself is hoarse

That croaks the fatal entrance of Duncan

Under my battlements. Come, you spirits

That tend on mortal thoughts, unsex me here,

And fill me from the crown to the toe top-full

Of direst cruelty. Make thick my blood.

Stop up the access and passage to remorse,

That no compunctious visitings of nature

Shake my fell purpose, nor keep peace between

The effect and it! Come to my woman's breasts,

And take my milk for gall, you murd'ring ministers,

Wherever in your sightless substances

You wait on nature's mischief. Come, thick night,

And pall thee in the dunnest smoke of hell,

That my keen knife see not the wound it makes,

Nor heaven peep through the blanket of the dark

To cry "Hold, hold!"

Modern text:

The raven made a hoarse croak that sounded as a deadly omen for Duncan entering my castle. Come, you spirit of violent thoughts, do not think me as a woman but instead, turn me into the cruelest human in the world. Make my blood thick and stop it from flowing and thus from feeling guilty. Come into my arms, and make my milk poisonous you murdering demons whenever you are lurking behind, waiting for doing something evil. **Come, the thick night, making the world shrouded in hell's smoke which is so dark that my sight is blocked from seeing wounds made by a sharp knife;** so dark that heaven can't see through the darkness and cry, "Stop it! Stop!"

鄧肯走進城堡之時，烏鴉呱叫，像是不祥預兆。來吧，邪惡的幽魂，別把我當成女人，而是讓我成為全世界最狠毒的人類。凝結我的血液，不讓它流動，讓我不知罪惡感為何物。你這殺氣騰騰的惡靈，來吧到我懷裡，儘管伺機而動圖謀不軌，並讓我變成最邪惡的人。就讓深夜降臨吧，那黑煙似的深夜，有如地獄；讓深夜遮蔽我的視線，看不清利刃畫下的傷口，連上天都看不穿這黑暗，還不禁叫道：「住手！住手吧！」

單字小解

1. omen *n.* 惡兆
2. lurk *v.* 潛伏

 來到蘇格蘭必看必去

　　葛拉米城堡位於安格斯（編註：英國蘇格蘭 32 個一級行政區之一），也是莎士比亞作品裡馬克白獲封為葛拉姆斯領主的地方。這裡有步道可走，當時建立此步道是為了吸引觀光客來訪蘇格蘭東北區，同時也能讓大眾更加了解中古時期的蘇格蘭。

　　VisitScotland 歡迎遊客來步道走走，這裡除了「提供包括傳單和標示等傳統方式來宣傳步道的資訊，也會使用新科技，如 QR 條碼、Android 和 iPhone 系統；掃下條碼後，使用者就能取得更多資訊。」

　　關於票價等參觀資訊，請進入他們的官方網站：http://www.glamis-castle.co.uk/index.cfm

PART 1 歐洲篇

PART 2 美洲篇

PART 3 亞洲篇

Unit 02

威爾斯 蒙茅斯郡廷騰村
Tintern in Monmouthshire, Wales

華茲華斯《廷騰寺》 *Tintern Abbey* Track03

> *Do I behold these steep and lofty cliffs,*
> *That on a wild secluded scene impress*
> *Thoughts of more deep seclusion; and connect*
> *The landscape with the quiet of the sky.*

—— William Wordsworth, *Tintern Abbey*

Modern text：

Once again, I see a wild and secluded scene with these steep and lofty cliffs. And from such scene, thoughts of being solitary are more determined. Also such scene connects the landscape with the quiet sky.

再一次，有著陡峭和險峻懸崖的這般寂寥絕景又映入我眼簾，讓我想要獨處的念頭又更堅定了。這般景色也和寂靜的天空連成一氣。

—— 華茲華斯《廷騰寺》

文學景點巧巧說

　　威廉・華茲華斯（William Wordsworth）是英國浪漫時期的詩人，詩作總是表現出對自然深厚的情感，《廷騰寺》這首詩也不例外，本詩全名為《1798 年七月 13 日再訪威河沿岸之旅，於廷騰寺前方幾里處所做詩句》（"Lines Composed a Few Miles above Tintern Abbey, on Revisiting the Banks of Wye during a during. July 13, 1978"），詩中描述主角，也就是華茲華斯本人，睽違五年後再次來到廷騰寺的心情，眼前的威河村、廷騰寺的遺跡與當地的壯麗山色在眼前開展，詩人也不禁陷入沉思，再次檢視自己的過往，想想當下以及對未來的期待。廷騰村位於蒙茅斯郡（Monmouthshire），是威爾斯東南部的一個郡，此地的觀光業最早始於 18 世紀，來到此地絕對不能錯過"如畫"（picturesque）般的天然美景，學學華滋華斯，來趟思古幽情、自我探索之旅吧。本引言與稍後的文學經典重現（英文部分）取自 Norton 所出版之 *The Norton Anthology of English Literature*，第七版、第二輯。

 揭開序幕小對話

　　Isaac is very versatile. He is a novelist, a poet as well as a columnist. He is now sitting on a rock alone with his laptop in front of Tintern Abbey. He is complaining to his friend, Carlos online.

　　伊撒克非常多才多藝，他寫小說、詩集、有時寫些專欄。現在他在廷騰寺前，坐在石頭上，用筆電跟朋友卡洛斯在線上發牢騷。

Isaac: I am totally out of inspiration!

伊撒克：我完全沒有靈感啊！

Carlos: You should relax. Let's go for a drink tonight.

卡洛斯：你真該放鬆一下，今天晚上一起去喝一杯吧？

Isaac: Not tonight. I am not in town. I am at Tintern Abbey, the village of Tintern in Monmouthshire.

伊撒克：今晚不行，我不在城內。我在廷騰村的廷騰寺，這裡位在蒙茅斯郡。

Carlos: Where is it? Sounds like a very far away mountain area.

卡洛斯：這是哪裡啊？聽起來像是非常偏遠的山區。

Isaac: Don't belittle this Tintern Abbey. Although Tintern Abbey is located in a rural area, it is the place where William Wordsworth, one of representative English Romantic poets, praised a lot about. I think I've so immersed myself into the natural and historical atmosphere here. I am full of inspiration now.

伊撒克：別小看延騰寺，這個鄉下地方可是英國浪漫詩人之一的威廉·華茲華斯所大大讚頌的地方呢。現在，感受著這邊的自然景觀及歷史氛圍，我的靈感泉湧啊。

(Isaac is opening his video camera on his laptop in order to show the scenery of Tintern Abbey to Carlos.)

（伊撒克打開筆電的視訊，讓卡洛斯看看延騰寺的美景。）

Carlos: What a beautiful abbey. I can feel peace around there.

卡洛斯：好漂亮的寺廟啊，我感受到這裡的寧靜以及平和。

Isaac: I know. Once again, I see a wild and secluded scene with these steep and lofty cliffs. And from such scene, thoughts of being solitary are more determined. Also such scene connects the

伊撒克：是吧！再一次，有著陡峭和險峻懸崖的這般寂寥絕景又映入我眼簾，讓我想要獨處的念頭又更堅定了。這般景色也和寂靜的天空連成一氣。

landscape with the quiet sky.

Carlos: That's very poetic of you. It seems you have found your flow in writing again.

卡洛斯：你真的是詩意盎然的一個人。感覺你找回你的寫作靈感了。

Isaac: Hehe, I just imaitated William Wordsworth's style. I am a big fan of him.

伊撒克：呵呵，我只是要模仿威廉・華茲華斯的風格而已。我是他的大粉絲。

 好好用單字、片語

1. column *n.* 專欄
2. complain *v.* 抱怨
3. area *n.* 區域
4. praise *v.* 稱讚
5. secluded *adj.* 與世隔絕的
6. solitary *adj.* 孤獨的、隱居的
7. determined *adj.* 堅定的
8. flow *n.* 想法的連貫、靈感
9. belittle something/somebody *phr.* 小看某事或某人，英文意思是 to make what others' doseem unimportant，也就是覺得某人的所作所為沒有什麼了不起的。

例 ❶ Renee is an inspiring teacher who never belittles her students' goals, dreams, or even their little achievements.
芮妮很會鼓勵學生，她從不會小看學生的目標、理想、甚至是它們小小的成就。

❷ Don't feel disappointed. Other people do not have the right to belittle your choices.

PART 1 歐洲篇

PART 2 美洲篇

PART 3 亞洲篇

別難過，其他人沒有權利小看你的選擇。

10. be full of something *phr.* 充滿，英文意思為 having a lot of something，可以指空間上沒有空隙，或是抽象的心靈層面被某些情緒占滿。

例 ❶ When I walked into Leah's room, I was amazed. Her room was full of bookshelves and books.

當我走進莉亞的房間，我感到驚奇，她的房間充滿書櫃還有書。

❷ In Claire's opinion, life is full of many unpredictable changes and at the same time happiness.

對克萊兒來説，生命中充滿無數難以預測的變局，但同時也洋溢著幸福。

文學佳句怎麼用

Once again, I see a wild and secluded scene with these steep and lofty cliffs. And from such scene, thoughts of being solitary are more determined. Also such scene connects the landscape with the quiet sky.

再一次，有著陡峭和險峻懸崖的這般寂寥絕景又映入我眼簾，讓我想要獨處的念頭又更堅定了。這般景色也和寂靜的天空連成一氣。

句型 1 such *adj.* 這樣的，為形容詞，為加強語氣之義，such 如其他形容詞一樣後接名詞，形成一個語氣加強的名詞片語。

例 ❶ It is such **a wonderful world.**（當補語）

❷ Such **scene**（當主詞）connects the landscape with the quiet sky.
句子中的 **such**（這樣的）＋**scene**（景物）為句子的主詞。

❸ Fiona is such **an adorable girl**（當受詞）；I will surely talk to her again. 這時 **such** 加上名詞片語，**an adorable girl**，為句中的受詞。

句型 2 with *prep.* 伴隨著、有著，為介系詞，後面接名詞。

例 ❶ I see a wild and secluded scene with these steep and lofty cliffs.

我看見有著陡峭險峻的岩壁的寂寥絕景。（這邊是有著…的…的概念。）

❷ Also such scene connects the landscape with the quiet sky.

另外，這樣的景色與寂靜的天空連成一氣。（這邊是 A 伴隨 B 的概念。）

文法概念

名詞在英語文法中，可以當主詞、當受詞、也可以當補語，要注意名詞不只是你認識的 a dog，以下畫底線的片語看似很長，卻是屬於名詞的名詞片語：

thoughts of being solitary are more determined。

文學經典重現 Track04

"FIVE years have past; five summers, with the length
Of five long winters! and again I hear
These waters, rolling from their mountain-springs
With a soft inland murmur.

--Once again
Do I behold these steep and lofty cliffs,
That on a wild secluded scene impress
Thoughts of more deep seclusion;
and connect
The landscape with the quiet of the sky."

　　又是一個五年過去了，歷經五年的冬夏，再一次，我的耳邊又響起山澗潺潺的流水聲，還有大地溫柔的呢喃。再一次，有著陡峭和險峻懸崖的這般寂寥絕景又映入我眼簾，讓我想要獨處的念頭又更堅定了。這般景色也和寂靜的天空連成一氣。

來到威爾斯 蒙茅斯郡廷騰村必看必去

　　廷騰寺由石磚堆砌而成，讓人不禁讚嘆當時的建物之美，這裡曾經做為修道院，因此可以想像僧侶誦經聲迴盪在空氣與室內中。這裡同時也是威爾斯保存最完善的中古時期修道院，有修繕過的記錄，但修道院的風格基本上維持原來的樣子。來這看得到悠久的歷史遺跡，有興趣可到威河谷地（Wye Valley）的博福特小屋（Beaufort Cottage）渡假，選一處能將廷騰寺美景一覽無遺的窗口，好好欣賞放鬆一下。關於威河谷地度假村的詳細資料，可至以下連結：http://www.wyevalleyholidaycottages.co.uk/beaufort-cottage-tintern-abbey

MEMO

英國肯特郡 多佛海峽
Dover, Kent in South East England

莎士比亞《李爾王》 *King Lear* Track05

> *Come on, sir; here's the place. Stand still. How fearful*
> *And dizzy 'tis to cast one's eyes so low!*
> *The crows and choughs that wing the midway air*
> *Show scarce so gross as beetles.*

—— William Shakespeare, *King Lear*, Act 4, Scene 6

Modern text:

"Come here with me, sir. Here we are. Stand still. So terrifying here. It's so dizzy if you lower your eyes. Flying in the sky, crows and choughs are no bigger than beetles."

· ·

　　我的主人，請跟我來。就是這裡，站穩了。這裡真是嚇人阿，往那懸崖底一看頭都要昏了。烏鴉山鴉飛在空中，從這看還沒有甲蟲般大阿。

—— 莎士比亞《李爾王》第四幕，第六景

文學景點巧巧說

多佛（Dover），是座位於英國東南方肯特郡的城鎮，也是主要的渡輪港口。多佛海峽出海口與英吉利海峽交接處極為狹窄，擁有世界第一的貿易量。靠海的多佛海峽還有個非常有名的多佛懸崖（the white cliffs of Dover），遠看或近看都有撼動人心之感。這裡也是莎士比亞四大悲劇之一《李爾王》（King Lear）中的一個重要場景。想像那個風雨交加的夜晚，場景就在多佛附近，孝子愛德格（Edgar）假扮乞丐湯姆，攙扶著他失明的父親葛羅斯特伯爵（the Earl of Gloucester）；他了解他的父親身陷誤解親兒，也就是自己的懊悔之中，一心求死，於是順著他的意，對著他描述他們正身處在懸崖邊，地勢險峻，還演出一齣"死而復生"的戲碼。本引言與稍後的文學經典重現（英文部分）取自 Norton 所出版之 *The Norton Anthology of English Literature*，第七版、第一輯。

揭開序幕小對話

Fiona and Ashley are at a travel fair where many travel agencies are promoting their package tours with special prices.

費歐娜與艾希莉在逛旅遊展，各家旅行社正努力推銷販售折扣旅遊行程。

Fiona: Let's find a perfect package tour for our summer trip. I want to take a trip to Europe.

費歐娜：我們來找出這個夏天最棒的旅遊行程吧，我想要去歐洲。

Ashley: Europe is a good choice if you like to visit historical sites.

艾希莉：如果你喜歡造訪古蹟，歐洲是很棒的選擇。

Fiona: You are such a mind reader. I am

費歐娜：你真懂我，其實我計

actually planning to go to Dover, England. Dover is a harbor city, which is famous for Dover Castle and White Cliffs.

(Ashley are so much distracted by a variety of booths rather than listening to Fiona. Then, Ashley stopped in front of a screen showing a video now.)

Ashley: Look! The white cliff is stunningly beautiful.

Fiona: This is exactly the place I was talking about.

(Fiona and Ashley stopped and watched the video, and in it there is a tour guide introducing why White Cliffs of Dover is a best choice for a day out.)

Guide: The best way to get a great view of the cliffs is to take a walk along the coastal path. The cliffs were not only used for defense in World Wars, but also a setting for one of Shakespeare's tragedy plays, *King Lear.* And now, let's watch and imagine how the characters from *King Lear* appreciated the magnificent

畫要去英國的多佛，一個以多佛城堡及白色峭壁聞名的海港城市。

（艾希莉沒仔細聽費歐娜說話，更專注於各式各樣的攤位。後來，她將注意力放在撥放影片的一個螢幕上。）

艾希莉：看！這白色峭壁真是太美了。

費歐娜：這就是我剛剛說的地方啊。

（費歐娜與艾希莉駐足觀賞影片，影片中，一位導遊在介紹白色峭壁，並說明這是一個外出的好去處。）

導遊：沿著海岸線散步是欣賞白色峭壁的最佳選項。這沿海的峭壁，不僅是世界大戰時重要的防線，也是莎士比亞著名悲劇，李爾王，的故事場景。現在，讓我們來看看並想像故事中的角色是如何欣賞白色峭壁的壯闊吧。

scenery of White Cliffs.

The actor: Come here with me, sir. Here we are. Stand still. So terrifying here. It's so dizzy if you lower your eyes. Flying in the sky, crows and choughs are no bigger than beetles.

角色演員：我的主人，請跟我來。就是這裡，站穩了。這裡真是嚇人啊，往那懸崖底一看頭都要昏了。烏鴉山鴉飛在空中，從這看還沒有甲蟲般大阿。

Ashley: This is where I want to have my vacation.

艾希莉：這就是我休假時想去的地方。

Fiona: Good idea. Let's go and check the agency's package tours.

費歐娜：好主意，我們來看看旅行社有什麼套裝行程吧。

Ashley: And we can also invite Isaac and Hayley. They are travel enthusiasts.

艾希莉：我們也可以約伊撒克跟海莉去，他們那麼熱愛旅遊。

 好好用單字、片語

1. travel agencies *n.* 旅行社
2. historical site *n.* 古蹟
3. stunningly *adv.* 震驚地
4. defense *n.* 防禦
5. character *n.* 角色
6. magnificent *adj.* 壯麗的
7. dizzy *adj.* 暈眩的

PART 1 歐洲篇

PART 2 美洲篇

PART 3 亞洲篇

8. travel enthusiast *n.* 熱愛旅行的人

9. A is famous for B *phr.* A 以 B 聞名。famous *adj.* 為 widely known，廣泛地被知道，即有名的意思。字根為 fame *n.* 聲望。

　　例：J.K. Rowling is internationally famous for her novels.

　　　　J‧K‧羅琳以她的小說聞名世界。

　　補充：字首 in＋ famous＝infamous *adj.* 聲名狼藉的，句型同樣為 A is infamous for B，但是接在 for 後面的名詞，必須為負面的，英文意思為 something is well known for being bad or evil。

10. A rather than B *phr.* 是 A 而不是 B。語意的重點強調說話者選擇的為 A 而不是 B。

　　例：Every time when Isaac encounters an adversity, he tries to overcome it on his own rather than asking for help.

　　　　每當伊撒克遇到困難時，他總是自己解決而不去求助他人。

文學佳句怎麼用

　　Come here with me, sir. Here we are. Stand still. So terrifying here. It's so dizzy if you lower your eyes. Flying in the air, crows and choughs are no bigger than beetles.

　　我的主人，請跟我來。就是這裡，站穩了。這裡真是嚇人啊，往那懸崖底一看頭都要昏了。烏鴉山鴉飛在空中，從這看還沒有甲蟲般大啊。

句型 1　be no bigger than *phr.* 用於比較兩者間的差異，文法上稱之為「比較級」的用法。基本句型為 A＋be＋比較級形容詞＋than＋B。

　　例：How amazing! The tiny box is heavier than the big box.

　　　　好驚人！這個小盒子竟然比大盒子還要重。

　　　　若想要加強形容詞的語氣，可加入 much 或 even。另外，前面提到的名詞 box，第二次在句中提到時，可以用代名詞 one 來取代 box。

例：How amazing! The tiny box is much heavier than the big one.

好驚人！這個小盒子竟然遠比大盒子還要重。〔強調小盒子重量之重〕

而在佳句中的 be no bigger than，也可以這樣應用。其實本句與上列例句要表達的意思一樣，端看説話著要強調大盒子的重量之輕，還是小盒子重量之重。

例：How amazing! The big box is no heavier than the tiny one.

好驚人！這個大盒子竟然不比小盒子還要重。〔強調大盒子的重量之輕〕

補充：所謂比較級的形容詞，有兩個特徵：er 或是 more。

(1) 一般來説，在形容詞的字尾＋er 即可，例如：tall->taller。

(2) 字尾是母音＋子音時（口訣：母子生孩子），重複字為子音＋er，例如：big->bigger。

(3) 當遇到字尾為 y 時，必須去 y＋ier，例如: heavy->heavier

若形容詞的發音有三個音節，則於形容詞前＋more。例如：difficult->more difficult。

名言中，我們還可以學習如何用感覺或比喻來描述所見之美景，而不僅僅只是用 amazing（驚人的）、magnificent（壯麗的）、或是 beautiful（美麗的）來描述。

(1) 以身體的感受，暈眩（dizzy），來描述風景之壯麗，如編寫文中的：
It's so dizzy if you lower your eyes.

(2) 運用比較級，以烏鴉小如甲蟲之感來對比美景之廣闊，如編寫文中的：Crows and choughs are no bigger than beetles.

 文學經典重現 Track06

Edgar : **Come on, sir; here's the place. Stand still. How fearful
And dizzy 'tis to cast one's eyes so low!
The crows and choughs that wing the midway air
Show scarce so gross as beetles.** Halfway down

Hangs one that gathers sampire- dreadful trade!

Methinks he seems no bigger than his head.

The fishermen that walk upon the beach

Appear like mice; and yond tall anchoring bark,

Diminish'd to her cock; her cock, a buoy

Almost too small for sight.

The murmuring surge That on th' unnumbered idle pebbles chafes

Cannot be heard so high. I'll look no more

Lest my brain turn and the deficient sight

Topple down headlong.

Modern text:

Come here with me, sir. Here we are. Stand still. So terrifying here. It's so dizzy if you lower your eyes. Flying in the sky, crows and choughs are no bigger than beetles. Halfway down the cliff there's somebody clinging to the rock and gathering wild herbs—a risky business! He is no bigger than his head to me.

. . . .

我的主人，請跟我來。就是這裡，站穩了。這裡真是嚇人阿，往那懸崖底一看頭都要昏了。烏鴉山鴉飛在空中，從這看還沒有甲蟲般大阿。還有個人爬在懸崖上，採集石料和草藥，真是危險的工作，對我來説，他整個人看起來大概就剩下一顆頭那樣的大小了吧。

單字小解

1. choughs [tʃʌf] *n.* 歐洲的紅嘴山鴉

2. sampire *n.* 草藥

3. yond [jand] *adv.* 在那邊

來到多佛海峽必看必去

　　來到多佛懸崖，除了要到海邊走走，來個水上活動。多佛博物館（Dover Museum）位於英格蘭東南方的肯特郡（Kent），館藏有源自於銅器時代的沈船遺跡，還有許多考古文物，有機會一定要來看看。另外來這裡還能參觀多佛城堡（Dover Castle），感受中古世紀的氛圍與皇室亨利二世（King Henry II）的宮庭生活，看宮廷擺設如實在眼前呈現，就像穿越時空，有身歷其境之感。多佛城堡還成了多部電影的場景，最有名的是 1990 年由梅爾吉勃遜（Mel Gibson）主演的《哈姆雷特》（Hamlet），近期則有 2014 年的《黑魔法森林》（Into the Woods）。

MEMO

英國倫敦威廉王街、伍爾諾斯聖馬利亞堂

King William Street and St Mary Woolnoth, London, England

艾略特《荒原》 *The Waste Land*

 Track07

66 *Unreal City,*
Under the brown fog of a winter dawn,
A crowd flowed over London Bridge, so many,
I had not thought death had undone so many. 99

—— T.S. Eliot, *The Waste Land*

Modern text:

This is an unreal city. Under the brown fog of a winter dawn is a crowd flowed over London Bridge. They are so many and I had not thought the dead men could be so many.

這是座虛幻之城。冬天凌晨的濛濛霧氣中，倫敦橋上都是人，我從來沒想過亡者居然能有這麼多。

——艾略特《荒原》

文學景點巧巧說

　　第一次世界大戰後，西方世界中的文化、建設都面臨一連串的挑戰，對進步、對探索、對自我成就等價值的積累，也在戰亂後瓦解崩毀，人們開始質疑過去自我能不斷擴張、成長的價值，轉而走入一段失落、無力的時期，當時的許多文學作品、藝術都瀰漫一股頹喪的風格，而艾略特的這首詩《荒原》也呼應了這段背景，整首詩處處充滿超現實又虛幻的景象：冬天清晨霧氣朦朧，倫敦橋上擠滿了亡者，這不是什麼靈異故事；而詩的詮釋也不盡相同，但可以聯想的，作者想要表達的，是種空有軀殼而無靈魂的生命和價值。英國果然是文化歷史濃厚的國家，每個景點都有它的故事，下次來到倫敦橋除了拍拍美景外，也想想詩人艾略特那段時期的感受，還要學會說：「多麼虛幻的世界啊（This is an unreal city）。」，或許能激發你的詩人靈魂呢。本引言取自 Houghton Mifflin Harcourt, 2014 所出版之 *The Waste Land and Other Poems*。

✈ **揭開序幕小對話**

　　Isaac and Hayley decided to move to a bigger apartment after their marriage. All the stuff should be packed before tomorrow. However, it is hard for Isaac to focus on packing, for there are so many old things that brought him back to his childhood. He found one of his favorite computer games, *The Waste Land.*

　　伊薩克和海莉決定結婚後就搬到大一點的公寓去。很多東西需要在明天前打包好，但伊薩克實在無法專心打包，有太多老東西帶他回到孩童時光。他找到他以前最愛的電腦遊戲之一《荒原》。

Isaac: I can't believe that I still keep it. I used to play the game with Carlos when we were junior high school students.

伊撒克：真不敢相信我還留著它。我和卡洛斯在國中當同學的時候，曾經玩過這個遊戲。

(While Isaac is immersing in his happy childhood, the doorbell rings.)

（伊薩克還沉浸在他快樂的孩童時光時，門鈴響了。）

Carlos: Hey, Isaac, it's me. What's up?

卡洛斯：嘿，伊撒克，是我。你在幹麼？

Isaac: You are just in time. Do you remember this?

伊撒克：你來的正是時候。你還記得這個嗎？

Carlos: Of course. We used to play the game after school. It's not easy to clear every mission.

卡洛斯：當然。我們以前下課後都會玩這個遊戲，要破關不是那麼容易。

Isaac: Let's play it again.

伊撒克：讓我們再玩一次吧。

(The CD-Rom still works. The game is on, and it begins with a short animation of the war scene.)

（光碟還能跑。遊戲一開始先播放以戰爭場面為背景的小動畫。）

Narrator in the video: Unreal City, Under the brown fog of a winter dawn, A crowd flowed over London Bridge, so many, I had not thought death had undone so many. You will be doomed if

遊戲中的旁白：這是座虛幻之城。冬天凌晨的濛濛霧氣中，倫敦橋上都是人，我從來沒想過亡者居然能有這麼多。沒破關，就等著受詛咒吧。現在準

you fail to clear the mission. Now, are you ready to save the city?

備好拯救這個城市了嗎？

(Carlos is not in the mood to play the game; instead, he stands still, deep in thought.)

（但卡洛斯沒心情玩遊戲，他只是站著，陷入沉思。）

Carlos: It was not until I became a Western literature major did I know that the introduction of the game originated from Eliot's poem, *The Waste Land*. This poem delineates the fragile psychological state of humanity after World War I. Look! It is King William Street. It is where the dead walking in the poem. And at the corner of the street locates St Mary Woolnoth, a church that has been used for worship for at least 2,000 years. And now, the street houses a number of investment banks and firms.

卡洛斯：我在主修西洋文學前，都不知道這遊戲的開場白源自艾略特的詩《荒原》。這首詩描述世界一戰後，人性脆弱的精神狀態。看，這是威廉王街，也是詩裡面亡者走動的地方。這條街的轉角還有伍爾諾斯聖馬利亞堂，這座用來禮拜的教堂至少有 2000 年的歷史。時至今日，這條街上有許多投資銀行和公司。

 好好用單字、片語

1. apartment *n.* 公寓
2. stuff *n.* 東西
3. pack *v.* 打包
4. favorite *adj.* 特別喜愛的

5. challenge *n.* 挑戰

6. animation *n.* 卡通片

7. doomed *adj* 受詛咒的

8. delineate *v.* 描述

9. fragile *adj.* 脆弱的

10. immerse in *phr.* 沉浸在，英文意思為 become completely involved in something，也就是投入於某事之中。

例 ❶ For eight months, Fiona totally immersed herself in her work.

八個月以來，費歐娜完全沉浸於工作之中。

11. originate from *phr.* 源自於，英文意思為 begin to exist，也就是開始存在之意。

例 ❶ God and his angels don't originate from Earth. By definition, they're extraterrestrial.

上帝跟天使們不是來自地球的。依定義來説，他們是外星人。

文學佳句怎麼用

This is an unreal city. Under the brown fog of a winter dawn is a crowd flowed over London Bridge. There are so many and I had not thought the dead men could be so many.

這是做虛幻之城。冬天凌晨的濛濛霧氣中，倫敦橋上都是人，我從來沒想過亡者居然能有這麼多

片語解析

1. flow over *phr.* 流過，英文意思為 move over someone，這邊的 flow over 有像液體一樣淹蓋過某物之意，除了可以表是實體的事物淹沒般的湧入，也可以指心靈上被某事物淹沒的感受。

例 ❶ The water flowed over the land, covering everything.

洪水沖刷過土地，淹沒了所有東西。

❷ Standing in front of the natural scene, Austin lets all the voices and colorful images flow over him.

站在自然景觀前，奧斯丁讓所有聲音及多彩的景色湧上心頭。

2. [某某地方存在著某物的句型]

➤ There is/are +名詞+地方。本句型中文翻譯為「某地有…」，這個有不是擁有的意思，而是要表達某物某人存在著。

➤ 當名詞為單數時，be 動詞使用 is，當名詞為負數時，動詞使用 are。

例 ❶ There is no accurate count of English teachers all over the world. 全世界的英文老師的數量並不清楚。

❷ I like to go shopping in Taipei because there are so many malls. 我喜歡在台北購物，因為那裡商場林立。

3. [數量形容詞的使用]

➤ many *adj.* 很多的，英文意思為 numerous，為數眾多之意。

➤ many+複數動詞，形成一個名詞片語，名詞片語的本質還是名詞，因此可以放在句首當主詞（如例 1），或是當動詞的受詞（如例 2）。

例 ❶ Inspired by Steve Jobs, many mangers changed their way to run the company.

受到賈伯斯的啟發，很多管理者改變他們經營公司的模式。

來到倫敦威廉王街、伍爾諾斯聖馬利亞堂必看必去

倫敦威廉王街正處於熱鬧繁華的倫敦市中心，離倫敦威廉王街最近的地鐵站為 Monument Tube Station，不遠處有倫敦塔（Tower of London）、羅斯劇院（Rose Theatre）還有波特草原公園（Potters Fields Park），坐在綠草茵茵的公園裡，看得到倫敦市政廳（City Hall）（也就是倫敦市長辦公的地方）還有倫敦塔橋（Tower Bridge）。公園前方就是泰晤士河南岸，每到一年一度的九月泰晤士河節，這裡就會舉辦許多活動，熱鬧不已。

英國倫敦橋、泰晤士河
London Bridge and River Thames, England

 Track08

約瑟夫康拉德的《黑暗之心》 *Heart of Darkness*

" *The sea-reach of the Thames stretched before us like the beginning of an interminable waterway.* "

—— Joseph Conrad, *Heart of Darkness*

Modern text :

Reaching the sea, the river of Thames before us was marked as the start of a journey on the sea stretching all the way without an end.

．．．

　　泰晤士河緊接著海口，在眼前拓展開來，就要出海了，旅程即將展開，航向漫無邊際的大海。

——約瑟夫康拉德的《黑暗之心》

文學景點巧巧說

　　說到倫敦橋，就會想到泰晤士河（River Thames），該河位於英格蘭的東南方，是流經倫敦的重要都市河流，水面交通繁忙，也是倫敦重要的地標之一。不少文學作品也都有提及泰晤士河，約瑟夫康拉德的《黑暗之心》（Joseph Conrad's *Heart of Darkness*）就是一個例子。在那樣的地理擴張時期，西方國家經常出海至其他非白人國家做生意上（trade）的往來，實際上卻是強行（by force）掠奪當地的資源，就像是《黑暗之心》所提到的象牙（ivory）交易，故事一開始就在繁忙的泰晤士河展開，由主角馬洛細細道來他受象牙貿易公司的命令，擔任內河蒸汽船船長後的事情。泰晤士河和剛果河（Congo River）則在這部作品呈現對比，在諸多文學分析中都有討論，也就是英國面對剛果河的姿態，就像當初羅馬人抵達英國泰晤士河那樣，都帶著一種文明世界想要教化元仍原始、待開發地區的使命，但實際上這樣的教化使命卻更為蠻橫、無理也可笑。不過回到現實，引言中的情境倒也能貼切形容泰晤士河的壯觀景象，滔滔不絕地河流向大海（it stretches all the way to the sea.），好像沒有盡頭一樣（interminable; without an end）。本引言與稍後的文學經典重現（英文部分）取自 Taylor&Francis, 2010 所出版之 *Heart of Darkness*。

揭開序幕小對話

　　Alisa has had a crush on Carlos since she was in the elementary school. Ten years go by, her feeling towards Carolos remains the same. Their friendship doesn't turn into a romance; instead, they have become good friends. She always knows where she can find Carlos.

　　愛麗莎還是小學生的時候，就暗戀卡洛斯了。十年過去了，她對卡洛斯的感受依然不變。他們還是很好的朋友，並沒有變成情人的關係。她總是知道去哪找得到卡洛斯。

Alisa: If Carlos wis not at home, then he must be in the coffee shop, thinking and writing.

愛麗莎：如果卡洛斯不在家，那他一定在咖啡店思考和寫作吧。

(Alisa walked into a neat coffee shop, and she found a tall figure sitting in the corner.)

（愛麗莎走進一間整潔的咖啡店，並在角落發現坐著一位身材高大的人。）

Alisa: Hey, Carlos, how are you doing?

愛麗莎：嘿，卡洛斯，你好嗎？

Carlos: I am searching for the history of River Thames. London's fame and fortune has much to do with the river, which has been an important trade and transport route centuries ago.

卡洛斯：我正在搜尋泰晤士河的歷史。倫敦的聲望和財富都和這條河脫離不了關係，數百年來，這條河一直是重要的貿易和交通路線。

Alisa: Riverside is my favorite spot for a day out. How about taking a boat trip next month?

愛麗莎：河邊是出門走走最愛去的地點，下個月我們何不一起搭船去玩呢？

Carlos: Sounds like a good plan.

卡洛斯：聽起來是個好點子。

(Alisa is preparing to show a video that introduces London's most famous waterway, River Thames.)

（愛麗莎正準備播放介紹倫敦最有名的水道，泰晤士河的影片。）

Alisa: Let's check the video of attractions London.

愛麗莎：讓我們來看看倫敦景點的影片吧。

Narrator in the video: Reaching the sea, the river of Thames before us was marked as the start of a journey on the sea stretching all the way without an end. It spans 215 miles, flowing straight through the heart of the city. You can take pictures of the most iconic landmark along the river by taking a cruise, traveling east down the River to the National Maritime Museum, or getting off the cruise to visit Tower Bridge.

Carlos: Let's book a flight to London now.

影片中的旁白：泰晤士河緊接著海口，在眼前拓展開來，就要出海了，旅程即將展開，航向漫無邊際的大海。這條河全長 215 英里，穿透流經城市的中心。您可以搭乘遊艇，並幫佇立河邊的知名地標拍幾張照，接著沿著河的東邊過去有座國家航海博物館，您可以去那邊看看，或者下船看看倫敦橋。

卡洛斯：我們現在趕緊訂機票去倫敦吧。

 好好用單字、片語

1. neat *adj.* 整潔的
2. fortune *n.* 財富
3. century *n.* 世紀
4. spot *n.* 地點
5. waterway *n.* 水路；航道
6. span *v.* 橫跨，跨越
7. iconic *adj* 具指標性的
8. landmark *n.* 地標
9. have a crush on *phr.* 迷戀，crush 英文意思為 a strong but temporary feeling of liking someone，即一種強烈卻短暫的迷戀之情。

例 ❶ Renee has a crush on one of her teachers at school.

芮妮迷戀學校的一位老師。

❷ Renee's mother asks her to get over the crush because it is un-likely to work.

芮妮的媽媽要求她不要再迷戀老師了，因為不會有好結果的。

10. turn into *phr.* 轉變、變成。

例 ❶ The sounds of chewing gum can really enrage me. I feel like I would turn into the Hulk sometimes.

嚼口香糖的聲音真的很惱人，有時候我真的會變成綠巨人浩克（比喻暴怒）。

❷ If you really want your first date to turn into something more, you should remain mysterious.

如果你希望在第一次約會後有更多進展，你得保持神祕感。

文學佳句怎麼用

Reaching the sea, the river of Thames before us was marked as the start of a journey on the sea stretching all the way without an end.

泰晤士河緊接著海口，就要出海了，旅程即將展開，航向漫無邊際的大海。

單字解析

➤ mark *v.* 標記，英文解釋為 to be a distinguishing feature of，即為有顯著特色之意。

片與 be marked as *phr.* 有「被標記為…」之意。

文法重點

➤ 被動式（passive voice）的用法：

句型：受詞（接受動作者）＋be 動詞＋ p.p.（動詞的過去分詞）＋by＋主詞（動作執行者）。

❖ 也就是說被動語態的形成需要藉由及物動詞的幫助，所謂及物動詞就是動詞後面需有一個接受者，例如：love（愛），I love you，一定要寫出受詞 you，語意才能完整。

❖ 有些動詞是沒有被動語態的，例如：swim（游泳）、succeed（成功）等等的不及物動詞。

❖ 使用時機被動式的用法，語意為某人或某物被怎麼樣了，後面可以用 by 接明確的執行者，或是不用也可以表達完整語意，例如：

1. Mary is killed by Tom.

   瑪莉被湯姆殺了。〔說話者若想強調動作的執行者，可於介係詞 by 後面加上明確執行者。〕

2. Mary is killed.

   瑪莉被殺了。〔說話者若不清楚動作的執行者是誰，或是不希望暴露殺人犯的名稱，不需加 by。〕

佳句解析

➢ The river of Thames before us was marked as the start of a journey on the sea stretching all the way without an end.

❖mark 一字較為特殊，使用與被動語態時需在加上介係詞，即 be＋p.p.＋as。

❖ 本句省略 by＋動作執行者，可以顯示出「我們面前的泰晤十運河被標示為無際大海的起點」沒有明確的執行者，原因是這件事是眾所公認的，因此不需特地寫成：

The river of Thames before us was marked as the start of a journey on the sea stretching all the way without an end by the public.

佳句應用

➢ 當你走訪風景名勝時，可以這樣用

Taipei 101 was once regarded as the tallest building in the world.

台北 101 曾經是世界上最高的建築物。

➢ Now, Khalifa tower in Dubai is known as the tallest structure in the world.

現在杜拜的哈里發塔被認為是世界上最高的建築物。

 文學經典重現 Track09

The Nellie, a cruising yawl, swung to her anchor without a flutter of the sails, and was at rest. The flood had made, the wind was nearly calm, and being bound down the river, the only thing for it was to come to and wait for the turn of the tide. **The sea-reach of the Thames stretched before us like the beginning of an interminable waterway.** In the offing the sea and the sky were welded together without a joint, and in the luminous space the tanned sails of the barges drifting up with the tide seemed to stand still in red clusters of canvas sharply peaked, with gleams of varnished spirits. A haze rested on the low shores that ran out to sea in vanishing flatness. The air was dark above Gravesend, and farther back still seemed condensed into a mournful gloom, brooding motionless over the biggest, and the greatest, town on earth.

奈莉號小艇不動聲色地搖晃幾下後，拋錨停船。海水高漲，風勢幾乎平息下來。船正沿著河水而下，我們能做的就是等待潮水退去。

泰晤士河緊接著河口，在眼前拓展開來，就要出海了，旅程即將展開，航向漫無邊際的大海。海天在遠處連成一片，黑色的風帆配上尖尖的紅布，好像鬼魂上色般釋放著幽光。烟霧籠罩在海灘上，平坦地往大海那蔓延，消失在遠處。格雷夫森港的天色昏暗，越往裡處越幽暗，凝結成一團，徘迴在這最偉大的城市之上。

單字小解

1. luminous *adj.* 發光的
2. varnish *v.* 上漆

3. vanish *v.* 消失

4. condense *v.* 凝結

 來到倫敦泰晤士河必看必去

　　説到倫敦塔橋（London Bridge），就會讓人聯想到那首《倫敦塔橋塌下來》的兒歌，這座橋的歷史悠久，橫跨泰晤士河，除了曾經出現在康諾德的《黑暗之心》中，也曾出現柯南道爾的《福爾摩斯》裡，也就是福爾摩斯與華生乘坐馬車經過的那條橋。倫敦塔橋下方設有倫敦塔橋博物館（The London Bridge Museum & Educational Trust），是可以深入了解倫敦塔橋歷史的地方。倫敦塔橋每天會在固定時間開啟，場面很新鮮有趣，幾乎是第一次去倫敦的遊客必去的景點之一啊。

英格蘭諾丁漢
Nottingham, the East Midlands of England

勞倫斯《兒子與情人》 *Sons and Lovers* Track 10

"*Her grandfather had gone bankrupt in the lace-market at a time when so many lace-manufacturers were ruined in Nottingham. Her father, George Coppard, was an engineer—a large, handsome, haughty man, proud of his fair skin and blue eyes, but more proud still of his integrity.*"

—— D.H. Lawrence, *Sons and Lovers*

　　諾丁漢內多家蕾絲工廠倒閉的同時,她祖父在蕾絲市場的經商也宣告失敗;而她的父親,喬治卡柏,則是一名工程師,身材高大帥氣,很滿意自己的膚色和藍色雙眼,但最讓他引以為傲的,還是他正義凜然的個性。

——勞倫斯《兒子與情人》

文學景點巧巧說

　　諾丁漢位於英國的諾丁漢郡，歷史悠久，是英國重要的工商業城市，工業革命時代有許多紡織廠在此設立，《兒子與情人》作家勞倫斯（DH Lawrence）的故鄉也在這，伊斯特伍德（Eastwood）還有勞倫斯遺產中心（DH Lawrence Heritage Center），是當地知名的景點。《兒子與情人》一作最讓讀者印象深刻的，就是兒子與母親間的關係，源頭則是母親與父親的婚姻，情感此消彼長，母親不滿做礦工的丈夫成天酗酒，種種失望情緒積累下，母親將情感投注在自己的兒子身上，最後對兒子的生命產生了不少影響。作品裡在介紹母親（Mrs. Morel）時，提及母親的祖父曾經營蕾絲工廠（lace-manufacturer），可見母親的出生環境不錯，或多或少也突顯對現實生活的不滿與和過去的落差。本引言與稍後的文學經典重現(英文部分)取自 Cambridge University Press, 2002 所出版之 *The Cambridge Edition of the Works of D. H. Lawrence: The Complete Novels of D. H. Lawrence 11 Volume Paperback Set*。

揭開序幕小對話

　　In the coffee shop, Carlos and Alisa are still planning their trip to England. Throughout their conversation, Carlos can't help but link some of the tourist destinations to classic literary works.

　　在咖啡店裡，卡洛斯與愛麗莎仍在計畫他們的英國行。在他們討論時，卡洛斯總是會把旅遊景點和經典文學作品連結在一起。

Carlos: Have you read *Sons and Lovers*, a novel written by D. H. Lawrence? Nottingham is his hometown. If we go to England, we should definitely pay a visit there since it's a must-see site. There are

卡洛斯：你有看過大衛‧赫伯特‧勞倫斯寫的小説《兒子與情人》嗎？諾丁漢鎮是他的家鄉，如果我們到了英格蘭，一定要去那兒看看，因為那可是

numerous **museums** and art galleries.

必去的名勝呢。那裡有許多博物館及藝廊。

Alisa: Go backpacking there will be nice. I heard that the public transport system in Nottingham is very convenient. Buses, railways, and the modern Nottingham Express Transit are available.

愛麗莎：去那自由行很不錯。我聽說那邊的交通很方便，有公車、火車和現代諾丁漢捷運系統可以選擇。

Carlos: So, are you in?

卡洛斯：所以你要去囉？

Alisa: Yes, I am in. Tell me more about the story in *Sons and Lovers*.

愛麗莎：是的，算我一份。再多告訴我《兒子與情人》的故事吧。

Carlos: The story is about the unfortunate marriage of Gertrude, Mrs. Morel who argues a lot with her husband. Thus, Mrs. Morel takes comfort in her children, especially her oldest son, William.

卡洛斯：故事和葛特璐不幸的婚姻有關，葛特璐，也就是莫瑞爾太太經常和先生吵架，因此常從孩子身上尋求慰藉，特別是他的大兒子，威廉。

Alisa: Why didn't she try to solve the problem?

愛麗莎：那她怎麼不試著解決問題呢？

Carlos: Everything happens for a reason. Gertrude married to Walter Morel with the belief of being well provided with housing, clothing, and food. However,

卡洛斯：事情發生自有他的道理。葛特璐抱著衣食無缺的心情嫁給墨瑞爾先生的，可是很快地她便發現事情不是她想的

she soon realized that she's wrong. In fact, Gertrude's family makes a living from lace-manufacturing, indicating a wealthy life. Although **her grandfather finally failed in the lace-market when so many lace-manufacturers were destroyed in Nottingham,** she just couldn't get used to live poorly.

那樣。其實葛特璐的家族經營蕾絲工廠，意味家境富裕。雖然最後她的祖父經營工廠失敗，當時有許多在諾丁漢的蕾絲工廠也倒閉了，她還是無法習慣貧困的生活。

Alisa: I almost can picture Gertrude's gloomy expression. I like the story. I think I will get the book and read it.

愛麗莎：我幾乎可以看到葛特璐的抑鬱神情。我喜歡這個故事，我會找來看看的。

Carlos: By the way, Gertrude's **father, George Coppard, was an engineer. He is tall and handsome; proud of his fair skin and blue eyes, but more proud of his integrity.** It must somehow influence her when choosing a partner in marriage.

卡洛斯：順帶一提，她的父親喬治卡伯以前是位工程師，身材高大帥氣，很滿意自己的膚色和藍色雙眼，同時他也以自己正義凜然的個性為傲。也許父親的個性也影響了她選擇伴侶的決定吧。

 好好用單字、片語

1. definitely *adv.* 肯定地
2. must-see *n./adj.* 影片、景點等必須看的東西
3. numerous *adj.* 為數眾多的
4. gallery *n.* 畫廊、美術館
5. available *adj.* 可取得的、可用的

6. argue *v.* 爭執

7. realize *v.* 了解到、領悟

8. indicate *v.* 指出、顯示出

9. takes comfort in *phr.* 在…方面找到慰藉、心情輕鬆。comfort *n.* 英文意思為 a feeling of being less worried and upset，一種比較不擔心或煩躁的感受。另外，in 為介係詞，後面需接名詞或動名詞。

　例 ❶ Students take comfort in knowing that the teacher won't punish them.

　　　學生知道老師不會處罰他們而感到輕鬆。〔in＋動名詞〕

　　❷ Losing his beloved daughter, the father can only take comfort in his memories about her.

　　　失去了至愛的女兒，這位父親只能從記憶中尋找慰藉了。〔in＋名詞〕

10. be provided with *phr.* 被提供…。provide *v.* 提供，英文意思為 give something to somebody，將「某某東西給某人」。本句若以被動式呈現，則句型為 be 動詞＋p.p.（動詞的過去分詞）＋with。

　例 ❶ Employees should be provided with support and advice from employers.

　　　員工應該要得到雇主所提供的支持與建議。

　　❷ If you want to find participants for your study, they should first be provided with useful information, issues, and methods.

　　　如果你想要為你的研究找受試者，你應該提供給他們有用的資訊、議題以及研究方法。

📖 **文學佳句怎麼用**

Her grandfather failed in the lace-market when so many lace-manu-facturers were destroyed in Nottingham. Her father, George Coppard, was an engineer. He is tall and handsome; proud of his fair skin and blue eyes, but more proud of his integrity.

諾丁漢內多家蕾絲工廠遭破壞的同時，她祖父在蕾絲市場的經商也宣告失敗；而她的父親，喬治卡柏，則是一名工程師，身材高大帥氣，很滿意自己的膚色和藍色雙眼，但最讓他引以為傲的，還是他正義凜然的個性。

句型 1 fail in *phr.* 在…方面失敗，無法於…方面成功。fail *v.* 英文意思為 not be successful in achieving something，介係詞 in 後面需加名詞，即在某某方面失敗了。

例 ❶ Lori failed in his first attempt, but succeeded in her second attempt.

羅莉在第一次的嘗試中失敗，卻在第二次的嘗試中成功了。

❷ People all fail in their lives, and they make mistakes.

人生中總是有失敗及失誤的。

句型 2 be proud of *adj.* 對…感到驕傲，proud *adj.* 英义為 showing pride，展現出自豪及自信之意。

例 ❶ Don't be depressed, you should be proud of your accomplishment.

別沮喪，你應該對自己的成就感到驕傲。

❷ There is nothing to be proud of.

沒有什麼值得驕傲的。

句型 3 when *conj.* 當，英文意思為 during the time that，when 當連接詞時須連結兩個句子。連接詞的位置可放在句首，但須於兩個句子中間加上逗號，亦可置於句中，不需加上逗號。

例 ❶ I believe life will be better when I get a job.

我相信當我找工作時，生活會好轉的。

❷ When Carlos finally showed up, he was drunk. Everyone worries about him.

當卡洛斯終於出現時，他卻醉了，大家都為他擔心。

 文學經典重現 Track11

Mrs. Morel came of a good old burgher family, famous independents who had fought with Colonel Hutchinson, and who remained stout Congregationalists. **Her grandfather had gone bankrupt in the lace-market at a time when so many lace-manufacturers were ruined in Nottingham. Her father, George Coppard, was an engineer-a large, handsome, haughty man, proud of his fair skin and blue eyes, but more proud still of his integrity.** Gertrude resembled her mother in her small build. But her temper, proud and unyielding, she had from the Coppards.

莫瑞爾太太來自一個古老且優良的市民家庭，祖先曾與哈欽森上一同作戰，世代以來一直是公理會的虔誠教徒。有一年，諾丁漢內多家蕾絲工廠遭破壞的同時，她祖父在蕾絲市場的經商也宣告失敗；而她的父親，喬治卡柏，則是一名工程師，身材高大帥氣，很滿意自己的膚色和藍色眼睛，但最讓他引以為傲的，還是他正義凜然的個性。格特魯德身材像母親一樣嬌小，但她卻有科珀德家族特有的高傲與倔強的性格。

單字小解

1. burgher [ˋbɝgə] *n.* 城鎮居民
2. Congregationalist [ˌkɑŋ grɪˋgeɪʃənəlɪst] *n.* 公理會之教友
3. resemble *v.* 相像

來到英格蘭諾丁漢必看必去

　　來到勞倫斯文化遺產中心（D.H. Lawrence Heritage Centre），除了看看勞倫斯的手稿和他的生平背景，還能參加相關活動。另外這裡還設有藍線步道（The Blue Line Trail），沿途除了有勞倫斯遺產中心，還有王子街、教堂學校、峽谷區等景點，想要來趟深度勞倫斯之旅的遊客和書迷，絕對不能錯過。關於勞倫斯遺產中心與藍線步道的相關資訊，請至以下連結：http://www.nottingham.ac.uk/dhlheritage/in-dex.aspx

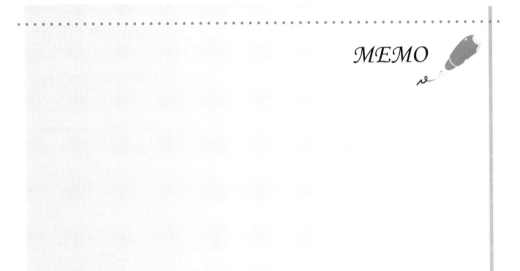

MEMO

英格蘭北約克國家公園
The North York Moors National Park-England

 Track12

艾蜜莉布朗特《咆嘯山莊》 *Wuthering Heights*

" *Heathcliff bore his degradation pretty well at first, because Cathy taught him what she learnt, and worked or played with him in the fields. They both promised fair to grow up as rude as savages.* "

—— Emily Bronte, Wuthering Heights

　　遭到如此不受尊重的對待，希斯克利夫起先還能接受，那是因為有凱西把她會的都教給他，也和他一起在田地裡工作或玩耍。他們答應對方要像野人一樣長大。

—— 艾蜜莉布朗特《咆嘯山莊》

文學景點巧巧說

《咆嘯山莊》（*Wuthering Heights*）原著由艾蜜莉布朗特（Emily Bronte）所著，原著主要場景正如書名所呈現，說的正是名為咆嘯山莊所發生的故事，英文的 Wuthering 形容凜冽、多風雨的氣候環境，為故事增添一種不平靜的氣氛，故事的角色彷彿也沾染了約克夏荒地（Yorkshire Moors）的性格，有人狂放不羈，就像悲劇主角希斯克利夫（Heathcliff），也有人無拘無束，就像希斯克利夫的兒時玩伴凱薩琳（Catherine），可當社會禮教（doctrines）和本性相互產生矛盾、衝突時，一齣齣情感糾葛，有如呼應陰晴不定的荒地氣候般，就此展開。說到約克夏荒地，就不能不提到北約克國家公園（The North York Moors），這裡位於英格蘭北部，景色優美，看得到一望無際的高地荒原，心胸也不禁感到開闊。本引言與稍後的文學經典重現（英文部分）取自 Ignatius Press, 2008 所出版的 *Ignatius Critical Editions: Wuthering Heights*。

揭開序幕小對話

　　Isaac and Hayley have dated for nine years before they get married. They have many habits in common, and seeing movies is one of their favorite activities for weekends. In front of a movie theater, Isaac and Hayley are talking about the movie, *Wuthering Heights.*

　　伊薩克和海莉交往九年後才結婚。他們有很多類似的習慣，看電影就是他們週末最愛的活動之一。這回兩人在電影院前，討論電影《咆嘯山莊》。

Hayley: The movie depicts Heathcliff and Catherine's passionate and ungovernable love for each other.

海莉：這部電影描述希斯克利夫和凱瑟琳對彼此深厚、難以掌控的愛戀。

Isaac: That's fascinating. Healthcliff was once an orphan and then raised by Mr. Earnshaw. Catherine, the young daughter soon grew inseparable with Heathcliff, who was beloved in the Earnshaw family. They spent their days playing on the moors. Things became different after the death of Mr. Earnshaw. Heathcliff was treated as a servant, and he had to work on the field. **But Heathcliff was fine to be treated in a less respected way at first because Catherine taught him what she learnt, and worked or played with him in the fields. They promised each other to grow up as savages. Do you feel the passion between them, Hayley?**

伊薩克：他們之間的關係很吸引人，希斯克利夫是孤兒，是老恩肖把他養大。凱瑟琳是老恩肖的小女兒，她很快地便和在老恩肖家討人喜歡的希斯克利夫形影不離，成天在原野上一起玩耍。但老恩肖過世後，事情就全變調了。希斯克利夫被當成下人對待，還要到田裡工作，但他一開始並不在乎受到這樣不受尊重的對待，因為凱薩琳會教他她學會的，也會和他一起在原野上工作和玩耍。兩人還答應對方要樣野人一樣地長大。妳有感受到他們之間的感情嗎，海莉？

Hayley: You are always so talkative when it comes to literature.

海莉：每回提到文學，你就講不停耶。

Isaac: You know me so well, my dear.

伊薩克：你真是了解我，親愛的。

Hayley: I like the story, but not as much as you do. My favorite part of the movie is when they spent their days running together on the Moors, a wet and wild land.

海莉：我很喜歡這個故事，但沒你那麼喜歡。這部電影我最愛的地方，是他們在潮濕、天然原野上奔跑的日子，那裡就

It's like a secret base.

Isaac: We can plan a trip there, North York Moors National Park, and that will be ours.

Hayley: I want to be there in early summer and watch the flowering heather turning the moors into a purple carpet that stretches for mile after mile.

Isaac: You are always so imaginative when talking about traveling.

好像他們的秘密基地。

伊薩克：我們可以來趟北約克國家公園之旅，那就會是我們的秘密基地。

海莉：那我想在初夏的時候去，然後欣賞盛開的石南花把原野變成一大片連綿不絕的紫色地毯。

伊薩克：每次一聊到旅遊，你總是充滿想像力呀。

 好好用單字、片語

1. depict *v.* 描述

2. passionate *adj.* 熱情的

3. ungovernable *adj.* 任性的

4. orphan *n.* 孤兒

5. servant *n.* 僕人

6. carpet *n.* 地毯

7. stretch *v.* 鋪開

8. imaginative *adj.* 富有想像力的

9. when it comes to+N *phr.* 英文意思為 speaking about something，一說到…；一碰上…。

   例 ❶ When it comes to trouble, my naughty nephew really knows how to cause it.

   一說到麻煩，我的頑皮的小姪女真的是製造專家。

❷ Rita is always well prepared when it comes to celebrating Chinese New Year.

一碰上慶祝中國的新年，瑞塔總是準備的很周全。

10. spend + N + Ving *phr.* 花某特定時間做某事，英文意思為 to allow (time) to pass in a particular place or while doing a particular activity，也就是 spend＋一段特定時間＋（on）＋做某事。

例 ❶ Carlos spent eleven months traveling around the world.

卡洛斯花了 11 個月的時間環遊世界。

❷ The diligent student spends 10 hours studying for tomorrow's test.

這位用功的學生花了十小時準備明天的考試。

文學佳句怎麼用

Heathcliff was fine to be treated in a less respected way at first, because Catherine taught him what she learnt, and worked or played with him in the fields. They promised each other to grow up as savages.

遭到如此不受尊重的對待，希斯克利夫起先還能接受，那是因為有凱西把她會的都教給他，也和他一起在田地裡工作或玩耍。他們答應對方要像野人一樣長大。

連接詞的句型

字詞解析

because *conj.* 因為。使用 because 作為連接詞時，主要連接兩個句子具有因果關係的句子。because 的英文解釋為 for the reason that，可以替換為 for。

and *conj.* 也、並且。and 可連接兩個句子，也可連接兩個詞性相同的片語。

連接詞是什麼

　　你是否常常覺得疑惑，為什麼英文句子有時候那麼長？明明課本裡學的，I love you，只有三個字就句點了，但是實際的文章卻不是如此？關鍵就是連接詞。

　　連接詞連接兩個句子，首先需要了解句子的組成要素：一個句子必須要有主詞、動詞、受詞（依照動詞的屬性決定加不加受詞）。

➤ 下列例句，雖然很短，卻是兩個完整的句子，現在試著用 because 將兩個具有因果關係的句子併成一句。

(a) Little Tom did it.

(b) His mother told him to do it.

(c) (a＋b) Little Tom did it because his mother told him to.

➤ 接下來看看引言原來的樣子，這次利用 and 合併相似句意，再用 because 表是因果關係：

(a) Heathcliff was fine to be treated in a less respected way at first.

(b) Catherine taught him what she learnt.

(b) Catherine worked or played with him in the fields.

■ 首先，使用 and，連接兩個動詞片語。

　◇ (b＋c) Catherine taught him what she learnt, and worked or played with him in the fields.

■ 再來，用 because，將表示結果的（a），跟表示原因的（b＋c）合併。

　◇（a＋b＋c）Heathcliff was fine to be treated in a less respected way at first because Catherine taught him what she learnt, and worked or played with him in the fields.

➤ 了解連接詞後，可以試著用具有表因果關係的連接詞 for、cause*去變化句型：

1. The boy didn't go to school for he was ill.

　那個男孩沒有去學校因為他生病了。

PART 1 歐洲篇　PART 2 美洲篇　PART 3 亞洲篇

2. I was late for the doctor's appointment cause I was stuck in traffic.

我看醫生遲到是因為塞車了。

*註：cause 為較不正式的用法，常見於口語表達中。

 文學經典重現 Track13

Heathcliff bore his degradation pretty well at first, because Cathy taught him what she learnt, and worked or played with him in the fields. They both promised fair to grow up as rude as savages; the young master being entirely negligent how they behaved, and what they did, so they kept clear of him. He would not even have seen after their going to church on Sundays, only Joseph and the curate reprimanded his carelessness when they absented themselves; and that reminded him to order Heathcliff a flogging, and Catherine a fast from dinner or supper. But it was one of their chief amusements to run away to the moors in the morning and remain there all day, and the after punishment grew a mere thing to laugh at.

遭受到如此不受尊重的對待，希斯克利夫起先還能接受，那是因為有凱西把她會的都教給他，也和他一起在田裡工作或玩耍。他們答應對方要像野人一樣長大。新主人根本無視於他們的行為舉止，又做了什麼，於是他們也不讓他知道，他甚至沒監督他們星期天有沒有去教堂，只有在約瑟夫和牧師斥責他對於孩子們缺席粗心時，他才會想起給希斯克利夫打一頓，並禁凱薩琳晚餐和宵夜。但他們主要的娛樂之一就是早上溜到荒野去，然後一整天都待在那裡，之後的處罰也不過是一笑置之的事罷了。

單字小解

1. degradation *n.* 降級
2. negligent *adj* 疏忽的
3. curate *n.* 牧師
4. flogging *n.* 鞭打
5. fast *n.* 禁食

來到北約克國家公園必看必去

　　約克（York）與曼徹斯特（Manchester）中間夾著里茲市（Leeds），所以就以里茲為中心，往北可以到蘇格蘭愛丁堡（Edinburgh），往南則可以到倫敦（London），里茲附近的小鎮風光迷人，想要遊覽約克夏郡的優美景色，從里茲出發搭火車就很方便，而北約克夏荒原國家公園（the North York Moors）就是途經的景點之一。若想要在這裡欣賞滿山遍野的水仙花（wild daffodils），每年的三月正是時候，詳細的參觀資訊，可至以下的連結：http://www.northyorkmoors.org.uk/

PART 1 歐洲篇

PART 2 美洲篇

PART 3 亞洲篇

Unit 08
愛爾蘭都柏林
Dublin, Ireland

喬伊斯《都柏林人》 *Dubliners* Track14

66 *North Richmond Street, being blind, was a quiet street except at the hour when the Christian Brothers' School set the boys free. An uninhabited house of two storeys stood at the blind end, detached from its neighbours in a square ground. The other houses of the street, conscious of decent lives within them, gazed at one another with brown imperturbable faces.* 99

—— James Joyce, *Dubliners*

Modern text (Abridged) :

North Richmond Street, the dead end of it, was a quiet street. There at the end of the street stood a two-stored empty house without residents, isolated in the neighborhood. The other houses of the street, aware of respectful lives within them, gazed at one another with brown calm faces.

．．．．．．．．．．．．．．．．．．．．．．．．．．．．．

　　理查蒙北街的尾端總是寂靜，除了基督教兄弟學校的男孩們放學的時候。在街道的盡頭有幢屋子空蕩蕩的，沒住人，孤伶伶地佇立在那街區裡。街上的其他屋子倒是意識到屋內人們，頂著咖啡色的門戶冷冷地互相對望。

——喬伊斯《都柏林人》

文學景點巧巧說

　　《都柏林人》是部短篇小說集，可說是愛爾蘭的代表作品，由喬依斯投注畢生心力完成，書中描述該市居民的性格與城中所發生的事，而《阿拉比市集》（Araby）就是其中的一部短篇故事。從日常的街道名開始，讀者好像也看到了，大多時候都悄然無聲的街尾，還有街尾那棟屋子好像有生命一樣，仿若與世隔絕，但也是那世界似乎太過冷漠，只顧自家事。這裡的褐色更添加了不同的想像和詮釋，可能是引喻冷漠、也可能是指氣候。接著，讀者突然成了一個男孩，由男孩的角度觀看身邊的人事物，這才感受一種男孩的渺小，還有對男孩來說，無以名狀的情感阿。都柏林是愛爾蘭的首都，有豐富多元的文化活動可探究，還有許多博物館和畫廊，也順道去拜訪喬伊斯博物館吧，然後學著說：「那棟屋子仿若有生命一般，孤零零地站在那。」（There stood an isolated/ detached house, gazing at other houses.）形容街區的景色，應該也頗有興味的吧。本引言與稍後的文學經典重現（英文部分）取自 Wadsworth 所出版之 *Portable Literature: Reading, Reacting, Writing*，第五版。

 揭開序幕小對話

　　Leaf Coffee is a coffee shop that is rarely known to people. But once you become a regular customer, you just can't resist its charm. Fiona is one of the loyal customers. In fact, it is an ordinary coffee shop that serves hot and cold beverages, and some pastries. At the same time, it is unusual to find that every customer here is so amiable, even taking this shop as their home. And this is where Fiona became friends with Carlos.

　　知道葉子咖啡廳的人很少，但只要成了它們老主顧後，你就是無法抵抗它的魅力。費歐娜就是忠實的顧客之一。其實這就是間一般的咖啡廳，有供應冷、熱飲和一些糕點。不過這間店的每位顧客各個和善，還把咖啡廳當家，對咖啡廳來說是很少見的。費歐娜也是在這和卡洛斯成為朋友。

(Fiona is writing her blog; every Tuesday she has to post one special report featuring a city and write a lot about the cultures and areas people living in. Now, she is on a phone with Ashley.)

Fiona: Ashley, I can't meet the deadline for tomorrow's special report about Ireland. I am now looking at the screen on my laptop with no ideas at all.

Ashley: You should check some travel pictorial reference books. That might help.

(Meanwhile, Carlos has spent his whole day reading *Dubliners* in the *Leaf Coffee* as usual. Then, he heard that Fiona needs to know more about Ireland. As a warmhearted person, Carlos walks toward Fiona with his book *Dubliners* in his hand.)

Carlos: Hi, I am Carlos. You may like to read *Dubliner*, a collection of short stories by James Joyce. The stories sketch the homes and thoughts of people whose lives are connected through the shared city, Dublin.

（費歐娜正在寫部落格，每個星期四她都要刊登一篇城市報導，要寫很多城市的文化和人們居住的地區。她現在正在與艾希莉通電話中。）

費歐娜：艾希莉，我趕不上明天愛爾蘭特別報導的截稿時間了。我現在盯著我的筆電螢幕，一點想法都沒有。

艾希莉：妳應該去翻翻旅遊書，可能會有幫助喔。

（此時，卡洛斯和平時一樣，在葉子咖啡廳花了一整天看《都柏林人》。他聽到費歐娜需要多了解一些愛爾蘭。卡洛斯一直是個熱心友善的人，於是便拿著《都柏林人》走向費歐娜。）

卡洛斯：嗨，我是卡洛斯。你或許想要看看喬依斯短篇故事合集《都柏林人》，裡面的故事描繪人們的家和想法，故事人物的生命也因為共同的城市：都柏林而連結在一起。

Fiona: Oh, hi, I am Fiona. How do you know I am trying to find information about some cities in Ireland?

費歐娜：噢，嗨。我是費歐娜。你是怎麼知道我在找愛爾蘭城市的資料呢？

Carlos: Do offense. I overheard it when you were on the phone.

卡洛斯：我並無冒犯之意，我剛好聽到妳講電話。

Fiona: That's ok. I would like to learn more about the city.

費歐娜：沒關係。我是很想多了解這個城市。

Carlos: There is a story about a boy going to a bazaar.

卡洛斯：這裡有個男孩去市集的故事。

(Carlos begins to read one of the short stories, *Araby*, aloud.)

（卡洛斯開始大聲念其中一個短篇故事《阿拉比》。）

Carlos: North Richmond Street, being blind, was a quiet street except at the hour when the Christian Brothers' School set the boys free. An uninhabited house of two storeys stood at the blind end, detached from its neighbours in a square ground. The other houses of the street, conscious of decent lives within them, gazed at one another with brown imperturbable faces.

卡洛斯：理查蒙北街的尾端總是寂靜，除了基督教兄弟學校的男孩們放學的時候。在街道的盡頭有幢屋子空蕩蕩的，沒住人，孤伶伶地佇立在那街區裡。街上的其他屋子倒是意識到屋內人們，頂著咖啡色的門戶冷冷地互相對望。

Fiona: I feel I can see the street and buildings personally.

費歐娜：我感覺我好像親自看到了那條街和建築物。

Carlos: Actually, I feel the same way.

卡洛斯：事實上，我也有同感。

(They keep on talking about *Dubliners* in the rest of afternoon.)

（接下來的下午，他們繼續談論《都柏林人》這部作品。）

 好好用單字、片語

1. rarely *adv.* 很少
2. loyal customer *n.* 忠實顧客
3. feature *v.* 以…為特色
4. culture *n.* 文化
5. sketch *v.* 概略地敘述
6. connect *v.* 連結
7. information *n.* 資訊
8. offend *v.* 冒犯
9. become friends *with phr.* 成為朋友
   例 ❶ They finally become friends after the orientation.
   新生訓練後，他們終於成了朋友。
   ❷ Toward the end of Carlos's college life, he became friends with his teacher.
   卡洛斯的大學生活走入尾聲之際，他和他的老師成為朋友。
10. meet the deadline *phr.* 按時完成
    例 ❶ By the end of this year, and election officials are scrambling to meet the deadline.
    年底，選舉的官員們倉促的趕進度。

❷ The engineers couldn't meet the deadline, so the project was just stopped.

工程師們無法按時完成，因此計畫案就此暫停了。

 文學佳句怎麼用

North Richmond Street, the dead end of it, was a quiet street. There at the end of the street stood a two-stored empty house without residents, isolated in the neighborhood. The other houses of the street, aware of respectful lives within them, gazed at one another with brown calm faces.

理查蒙北街的尾端總是寂靜，那有幢屋子空蕩蕩的，沒住人，孤伶伶地佇立在那街區裡。街上的其他屋子倒是意識到屋內人們，頂著咖啡色的門戶冷冷地互相對望。

倒裝句的用法

➤ 一般句子的結構為：

(a) 主詞＋動詞＋補語

Mary is adorable. 瑪莉很可愛。

(b) 主詞＋動詞（不及物動詞）

Renee dances. 芮妮跳起舞。

(c) 主詞＋動詞（及物動詞）＋受詞。

Tom cares about Mary. 湯姆很在乎瑪莉。

以上句型，都是以主詞＋動詞的字序排列，但是倒裝句的結構，不再以主詞為首，而變成（d）副詞片語＋動詞＋名詞→ There at the end of the street stood a two-stored empty house without residents. 街尾佇立一幢兩層樓的空屋。

PART 1 歐洲篇

PART 2 美洲篇

PART 3 亞洲篇

佳句還原

A two-stored empty house without residents stood at the end of the street.

        主詞   動詞   補語

  文學經典重現　　Track15

North Richmond Street, being blind, was a quiet street except at the hour when the Christian Brothers' School set the boys free. An uninhabited house of two storeys stood at the blind end, detached from its neighbours in a square ground. The other houses of the street, conscious of decent lives within them, gazed at one another with brown imperturbable faces.

The former tenant of our house, a priest, had died in the back drawing-room. Air, musty from having been long enclosed, hung in all the rooms, and the waste room behind the kitchen was littered with old useless papers. Among these I found a few paper-covered books, the pages of which were curled and damp: *The Abbot,* by Walter Scott, *The Devout Communicant,* and *The Memoirs of Vidocq.* I liked the last best because its leaves were yellow.

理查蒙北街的尾端總是寂靜，除了基督教兄弟學校的男孩們放學的時候。在街道的盡頭有幢屋子空蕩蕩的，沒住人，孤伶伶地佇立在那街區裡。街上的其他屋子倒是意識到屋內人們，頂著咖啡色的門戶冷冷地互相對望。

我們家的前任房客是位牧師，死在屋子後面的起居室裡，所有房間因封閉太久，空氣散發一股潮濕的氣味。廚房後面廢棄的房間亂糟糟的，到處都是無用的廢紙。我在裡面找到了幾本平裝書，有沃爾特‧史卡特的《修道院院長》、《虔誠的教友》，還有《維多克回憶錄》，書頁都捲曲潮濕了。我最喜歡最後一本，因為它書頁是黃色的。

單字小解

1. uninhabited *adj.* 無人居住的

2. storeys *n.* 【英】樓層

3. detached *adj.* 分離的

4. musty *adj.* 發霉的

5. be littered with *phr.* 佈滿了…而凌亂

到愛爾蘭首都都柏林必看必去

　　喬依斯博物館內有許多大作家喬依斯生前的物品，還有《尤利西斯》的手稿，另外還設立喬依斯生前的起居廳，細節如實呈現在遊客面前，是喜愛喬依斯的讀者不能錯過的去處。到了愛爾蘭還能來場《都柏林人》（*Dubliners*）之旅，跟著導遊一起到訪《都柏林人》出現過的地方，深入了解喬依斯在都柏林的生活，以及他筆下都柏林這個城市。

俄羅斯聖彼得堡
Saint Petersburg, Russia

 Track16

杜斯妥也夫斯基《罪與罰》 *Crime and Punishment*

When he was in the street he cried out, 'Oh, God, how loathsome it all is! and can I, can I possibly.... No, it's nonsense, it's rubbish!' he added resolutely. 'And how could such an atrocious thing come into my head? What filthy things my heart is capable of.'

—— Fyodor Dostoyevsky, *Crime and Punishment*

　　他走在街上，不禁出聲喊道：「天啊，這真是令人憎惡，我怎麼能…不，這真是荒謬！」「太荒謬了！」他又說了一次。「我怎麼能有這麼邪惡的念頭？我的心地怎麼會這麼污穢呢…」

——杜斯妥也夫斯基《罪與罰》

文學景點巧巧說

　　走在四周盡是人潮、熱鬧不已的街道上，拉斯柯尼科夫內心掙扎，明明就已經打定主意，明明這就就是萬無一失的計畫，明明這麼做是為了伸張正義啊，但謀害的還是一條人命，就算對方是放高利貸的老太婆。《罪與罰》男主角就是抱著這樣搖擺不定的心情，一早就心事重重，一邊為了繳不出房租、生計而煩惱；一邊帶著凌駕世俗標準的心理，想著如何才配當一個偉人，那麼一條人命又如何，更何況是個視錢財如命的老太婆。帶著這樣的心情，我們好像也身在陌居裡，和男主角一樣坐在床邊掙扎，並跟著他走在街上；這段路程：從他的租屋處（Raskolnikov's Apartment）、人來人往的木匠街（Carpenters' Lane）等等，也成了每個朝聖《罪與罰》的讀者必經、必訪的，而且還要吶喊「天啊，這樣真的對了嗎？我怎能有這樣邪惡的念頭啊…」（God, is it right? How could I have such evil thought?）本引言取自 Cricket House Books LLC, 2010 所出版之 *Crime and Punishment*。英文版譯者為 Constance Garnett。

揭開序幕小對話

　　Last year, Alisa had a trip to St. Petersburg, Russia alone. Although she wore no fancy clothes and bags, she got robbed. Thus, she had a bad impression of Russians and labeled them as uncivilized and even barbaric. Now she is in the Leaf coffee shop with Fiona, talking about their ideas about traveling around the world.

　　愛麗莎去年一個人去了一趟俄羅斯的聖彼得堡旅行，雖然她並身上的衣服並不昂貴，也沒有配戴高級的包包，她還是被搶了，也就是那時候，她就對俄羅斯人有很差的印象，還把他們當作野蠻的人。現在她和費歐娜在葉子咖啡廳，聊聊環遊世界的想法。

Fiona: Alisa, I am sorry for what you went through in Russia. But St. Petersburg is a dynamic city; it's rich in histories of religion, art, and literature. You know how much I admire Dostoyevsky's works. Visiting his home, his favorite places, and the sites of famous scenes from *Prime and Punishment* can make me occupied for days.

Alisa: All right, but just be careful and keep a low profile. In fact, my story in Russia is way more terrifying than what I told you last time.

Fiona: What do you mean?

Alisa: Actually, I was seeing a Russian guy then. We were walking on Nevsky Prospect to a bar. I didn't notice that we were being tracked, and suddenly my purse was grabbed. I cried out "Go to the hell." furiously.

Fiona: That's terrible. Were you guys ok?

費歐娜：愛麗莎，聽到妳在俄羅斯發生的事真覺得難過，但話說回來，聖彼得堡確實是座充滿活力的城市，它在宗教、歷史和文學上的歷史豐富。妳也知道我很崇拜杜斯妥也夫斯基的作品，拜訪他的家、他喜歡的地方還有《罪與罰》裡面有名的場景肯定會讓我忙個好幾天，心思全都在這些地方上。

愛麗莎：好吧，只是妳要小心點，保持低調，而且我在俄羅斯發生的事可比上次跟妳說的還要可怕。

費歐娜：妳是指？

愛麗莎：其實我之前和一個俄羅斯人交往，那時我和他正要去酒吧，並走在涅瓦大街上，我沒有發現我們被跟蹤了，然後我的皮夾突然被奪走。我那時生氣地大喊：「下地獄吧！」

費歐娜：真是可怕，你們還好嗎？

Alisa: I don't know how to tell you about this. I felt complicated then. Oh, God, how loathsome it was! and can I, can I possibly ···. No, it's ridiculous, it's rubbish!

Fiona: Calm down, Alisa. What happened that day?

Alisa: My boyfriend suddenly went crazy. The pickpocket ran away. How could such an evil idea come into my head? How filthy my heart is.

Fiona: Oh, Alisa, you should rest for while.

愛麗莎：我不知道該怎麼跟妳說，這感覺很複雜，天啊，這件事真討厭，而且我怎麼能…，不，這真是太荒謬了，垃圾！

費歐娜：冷靜一點，愛麗莎，那天到底發生了什麼事？

愛麗莎：我的男朋友突然抓狂，扒手也跑走了。我也不知道我為什麼會有這麼可怕的念頭，我的心地怎麼能這麼壞。

費歐娜：噢，妳應該休息一下。

 ## 好好用單字、片語

1. fancy *adj.* 別緻的
2. rob *v.* 搶劫
3. uncivilized *adj.* 野蠻的
4. dynamic *adj.* 有活力的
5. occupy *v.* 占用（時間或空間）
6. track *v.* 跟蹤
7. furiously *adv.* 狂怒地
8. go through *phr.* 經歷，英文意思為 to experience or suffer something，也就是體會或經歷（困難）。

例 ❶ Pakistan has gone through too many wars.

巴基斯坦經歷了太多戰爭了。

9. keep a low profile *phr.*保持低調，英文意思為 not to attract attention from the public，也就是不要吸引民眾的注意。低調為 a low profile, 高調為 a high profile.

例 ❶ The government attempts to keep a low profile on the controversial issue.

政府試著對這個爭議性的議題保持低調的態度。

 文學佳句怎麼用

When walking in the street, he cried out, "Oh, God, how loathsome it is! and can I, can I possibly ⋯. No, it's ridiculous, it's rubbish!" he said resolutely. How could such an evil idea come into my head? How filthy my heart is.

他走在街上，不禁出聲喊道：「天啊，這真是令人憎惡，我怎麼能⋯不，這真是荒謬！」「太荒謬了！」他又說了一次。「我怎麼能有這麼邪惡的念頭？我的心地怎麼會這麼污穢呢⋯」

字詞解析

➢ loathsome *adj.* 令人厭惡的

➢ ridiculous *adj.* 荒謬的

➢ evil *adj.* 邪惡的

➢ filthy *adj.* 骯髒的

本篇的佳句大量使用形容詞，你是否感受到說話者內心強烈的負面情緒了呢？這就是形容詞的魅力。

形容詞

形容詞，adjective，文法中縮寫為 adj.，英文意思為 a word that describes a person or thing，也就是用來形容人或事物。常見的形容詞用法如下：

(1) 放在 be 動詞後面做補語，也就是主詞＋be 動詞＋補語的句型。

> I think your idea is awesome, but his idea is ridiculous.
  我認為你的想法很棒，但是他的想法就太荒謬了。

(2) 放在名詞前面做前位修飾，形成一個名詞片語。

> The evil idea comes to his mind.
  他起了邪惡的念頭。

形容詞的強調用法

請比較下列兩句，（a）句的語氣較為平緩，而（b）句的語氣強調 loathsome 的語氣更為強烈。

(a) It is loathsome.

(b) How loathsome it is!

形容詞強調語氣的句型為：How＋adj.＋主詞＋動詞。

> How filthy my heart is.
  我的想法好邪惡。

> How beautiful the woman is.
  好漂亮的女人。

📷 來到俄羅斯聖彼得堡必看必去

跟著《罪與罰》男主角拉斯柯尼科夫的腳步，拜訪他的租屋處（Raskolnikov's Apartment）、還有人潮川流不息的木匠街（Carpenters' Lane），還有男主角心神不寧的地方：The Kokushkin Bridge…；若想轉換一下沉重的心情，聖彼得堡有俄羅斯博物館、自來水博物館還有埃爾米塔日博物館（Hermitage Museum）等等，其中埃爾米塔日博物館的規模最大，前身為皇家宮殿，藝術藏品豐富，來此地可感受宮殿建築自然散發的磅礴氣勢。

PART 1 歐洲篇

PART 2 美洲篇

PART 3 亞洲篇

海明威《流動的饗宴》 *A Moveable Feast* Track 17

But Paris was a very old city and we were young and nothing was simple there, not even poverty, nor sudden money, nor the moonlight, nor right and wrong nor the breathing of someone who lay beside you in the moonlight.

—— Ernest Miller Hemingway, *A Moveable Feast*

　　然而，巴黎是座古老的城市，當時我們都還年輕，在那沒有一件事是容易的，貧困不容易、突來的一筆錢也不容易、月光不容易、是非對錯都不簡單，還有月光下、身旁睡著的人的氣息也是，都不那麼容易啊。

—— 海明威《流動的饗宴》

🌐 文學景點巧巧說

巴黎那麼美，看羅浮宮、巴黎鐵塔、凱旋門⋯巴黎，好不浪漫，如果能在街邊喝露天咖啡，邊看人來人往，好不愜意；巴黎也是文人雅士的集散地，是海明威、費茲傑羅（F. Scott Fitzgerald's）等文壇巨擘來場文人交流的地方；《流動的饗宴》，透過文字，將動人的巴黎、海明威的最愛，流傳下去。海明威曾在巴黎住過一段時間，並在這段時間和格楚特斯坦（Stein）互為好友，海明威在她的影響下參加了「巴黎現代主義運動」（*Parisian Modern Movement*），期間寫下了《太陽照常升起》和《流動的饗宴》，成了美國「迷失一代」（Lost Generation）一詞的來由。寫作時，海明威特別喜歡坐在咖啡廳裡，是丁香園咖啡廳（Café Closerie des Lilas）的常客，這到了冬天溫馨舒適，讓海明威讚譽有加，咖啡廳外的庭院春天則有綠蔭圍繞，成了本店的特色，數十年來如一日。本引言取自 New York: Scribner Classics, 1996. Scribner Classics, 1996 所出版之 *A moveable feast*。

 揭開序幕小對話

Austin is a European exchange student in Taiwan. He spent his child-hood in Paris. When he turned eighteen, he decided to travel around the world. Finally, he fell in love with a Taiwanese girl named Fiona, and started to run his own business, the *Leaf* coffee shop. The couple is so close with each other that they like to share their feelings and thoughts anywhere, anytime, especially before the opening time of the shop.

奧斯丁是歐洲交換生，目前在台灣唸書。他小時候在巴黎生活，18 歲的時候決定環遊世界。最後，他愛上一位叫費歐娜的台灣女孩，並開始經營他的事業，也就是葉子咖啡廳。這對情侶關係親密，經常隨時隨地互相分享自己的感受和想法，尤其是咖啡廳準備開門前的那段時間。

PART 1 歐洲篇

PART 2 美洲篇

PART 3 亞洲篇

Fiona: It has been seven years since you left Paris. When do you plan to go home and see your parents?

Austin: Oh, Paris. There are lots of historic buildings and monuments. My parents and I had a great time visiting Louvre museum, the gothic Cathedral, and the Eiffel Tower. The memories were too good to forget. Even now, I still can dream of my home.

Fiona: We can go there anytime you want.

Austin: Going back to my hometown is a good idea. I miss my family and old friends. In *A Moveable Feast*, Hemingway used to say: "**Paris was a very old city and we were young and nothing was simple there, not even poverty, nor sudden money, nor the moonlight, nor right and wrong nor the breathing of someone who lay beside you in the moonlight.**" It's from Hemingway I learned to cherish friendship. I do miss those good old times.

費歐娜：你離開巴黎已經七年了，你什麼時候計畫回家，看看你父母呢？

奧斯丁：噢巴黎呀。那有許多具有歷史性的建築和紀念碑，我常和父母一起去羅浮宮、歌德式風格的教堂，還有艾菲爾鐵塔呢，我們一起度過了美好的時光，回憶太美好了，到現在還是記憶猶新，就算是現在，我還是會夢到我的家呢。

費歐娜：如果你想，我們隨時都可以出發去那喔。

奧斯丁：我想回家是個很好的提議，我很想念我的家人和朋友。海明威曾在《流動的饗宴》這麼說：「然而，巴黎是座古老的城市，當時我們都還年輕，在那沒有一件事是容易的，貧困不容易、突來的一筆錢也不容易、月光不容易、是非對錯都不簡單，還有月光下、身旁睡著的人的氣息也是，都不那麼容易啊。」海明威教我珍惜友誼。我真的很想念那些往日時光啊。

Fiona: I wish I was there with you. Also, I can't wait to visit the famous scenes from *A Moveable Feast,* one of the classic works of Ernest Hemingway.

費歐娜：我真希望那時候我也在你身邊。而且我等不及去拜訪《流動的饗宴》裡出現的場景了，這可是海明威經典的作品之一啊。

 好好用單字、片語

1. exchange student *n.* 交換學生
2. decide *v.* 決定
3. close *adj.* 親密的
4. parents *n.* 雙親
5. historic *adj.* 歷史的
6. monument *n.* 歷史遺跡
7. cathedral *n.* 大教堂
8. classic *adj.* 有長遠歷史或文學意義的
9. fall in love with someone *phr.* 愛上某人

    例 ❶ Hayley and Isaac met at school and fell in love with each other at the first sight.
    海莉與伊薩克在學校認識並且第一眼就愛上彼此。

    ❷ I fell in love with the red dress when I saw it and bought it at once.
    我看到這件紅色小洋裝就愛上了，並且立刻買下它。

10. too... to *phr.* 太…以至於不能

    例 ❶ The girl is still too young to go to school.
    這個小女孩年紀太小了還不能去上學。

    ❷ Molly is too short to be a flight attendant.
    茉莉身高太矮了沒辦法當空服員。

文學佳句怎麼用

But Paris was a very old city and we were young and nothing was simple there, not even poverty, sudden money, nor the moonlight, nor right and wrong nor the breathing of someone who lay beside you in the moonlight.

然而，巴黎是座古老的城市，當時我們都還年輕，在那沒有一件事是容易的，貧困不容易、突來的一筆錢也不容易、月光不容易、是非對錯都不簡單，還有月光下、身旁睡著的人的氣息也是，都不那麼容易啊。

字詞解析

➤ nor *conj.* 也不，英文意思為 and not。Nor 為具有否定意思的連接詞，通常會與 not, no, never 連用，例如：I do not like you, nor you family

我不喜歡你，我也不喜歡你的家人。

例 ❶ Percy became seriously ill. He won't know the day, nor the hour, nor the minute.

波西生了重病。他將不再知道每日的推移，甚至是每小時或是每分鐘。

❷ A gentle man would not covet their neighbors' houses, nor their furniture, nor their smart phones.

一位紳士是不會覬覦鄰居的房子、家具、甚至是智慧型手機。

佳句活用

➤ 引言中，作者使用了四次 nor＋名詞，來表示年輕時每件事的不容易，這樣排比的呈現，讓作者想表達「沒有一件事情是容易的」意象更有深度。

■ Paris was a very old city and we were young and nothing was simple there, not even poverty, nor sudden money, nor the moonlight, nor right and wrong nor the breathing of someone who lay beside you in the moonlight.

➤ 例如，你想感嘆目前 21 世紀原創不斷被抄襲的現象，並希望用豐富的例子來支持你的想法，可以這麼用：

■ In the 21 century, your original work can never be protected from plagiarism, not even your ideas, nor the writings, nor the paintings. 在 21 世紀，你的原創作品很難免於於剽竊，不管是你的想法、著作、甚至是你的畫作都無法避免。

來到巴黎必看必去

艾菲爾鐵塔（La tour Eiffel），又稱為巴黎鐵塔肯定是必看的景點。巴黎鐵塔興建過程困難重重，最初巴黎市民很不能接受這樣破壞市容的建設，一直到後來才慢慢接受，並成為世界知名的地標（landmark）之一。若以凱旋門為中心，附近的街道是以放射狀呈現，附近有知名的香榭麗舍大道和蒙馬特山丘（Montmartre），是到巴黎不能錯過的幾個重要景點。蒙馬特山丘也素有藝術村之稱，20 世紀初期許多如畢卡索（Pablo Picasso）、雷諾瓦（Auguste Renori）等的畫家曾在此出沒，因此這裡總是洋溢著藝術的氛圍，來到這可看到許多街頭畫家以及典雅的特色商店。

法國巴黎聖母院
Notre-Dame Cathedral, Paris, France

Track18

維克多雨果《鐘樓怪人》　*The Hunchback of Notre Dame*

" *Suddenly, Dom Claude sprang up, seized a compass and engraved in silence upon the wall in capital letters, this Greek word: ANATKH.* "

—— Victor-Marie Hugo, *The Hunchback of Notre Dame*

　　就在那，查漢看到克勞德站了起來，手裡拿起一對指南針，默默地將希臘文 ANATKH 刻印在牆上。

—— 維克多雨果《鐘樓怪人》

文學景點巧巧說

　　巴黎聖母院（Cathédrale Notre-Dame de Paris）位於法國巴黎市中心，這座天主教教堂矗立在西堤島（Île de la Cité）（塞納河（Seine）中的兩座島之一）上，宏偉壯觀，是大文豪雨果所寫《鐘樓怪人》巨作中的主要建築物，也是外貌奇醜驚人的主角加西莫多（Quasimodo）從小長大的家，將加西莫多收養，並將之扶養長大的克羅德神父（Archdeacon Claude Frollo）也經常站在聖母院的塔頂，觀察底下來往的人潮與狀況，可想而知那樣的景觀在當時必是雄偉盛大的吧。這次的引言寫到神父將「ΑΝΑΓΚΗ」像是咒語般的文字刻寫在牆上，其實「ΑΝΑΓΚΗ」（希臘文，意指命運）是有玄機的，據說雨果創作《鐘樓怪人》的靈感就是來自聖母院，有次他參觀聖母院時，發現某個角落上寫著「ΑΝΑΓΚΗ」，（希臘文，意指命運），於是便決定探究人類的命運。而這個「命運」的概念也用在《鐘樓怪人》裡，還成了神父的座右銘。這股冥冥之中的力量，將故事人物牽連一起，美麗的吉普賽女孩、神父和加西莫多，似乎無法擺脫，最終引領故事走向讓人哀嘆的結局，命運啊（Is it all about fate?）！本引言與稍後的文學經典重現（英文部分）取自e-artnow, 2012所出版之 *The Hunchback of Notre Dame (Hapgood Translation, Unabridged)*。

 揭開序幕小對話

　　Carlos and Alisa didn't decide the destinations for their trip. Finally, both of them agreed that France would be the most optimal place for them. They are taking a boat tour in Paris now. While their boat is lazily drifting down the Seine River, they got a glimpse of the world's most famous gothic architecture, Notre Dame Cathedral.

　　卡洛斯和愛麗莎遲遲無法決定他們旅行要去的地方，最後決定法國是最適合的去處。現在他們正搭船環遊巴黎，就在他們的船慵懶地流經塞納河時，他們瞥見世界最著名的歌德式建築，巴黎聖母院。

Alisa: I love Paris for it houses many spiritual relics. The cathedral was completed in the fourteenth century. Can you imagine that the building has been standing there watching us creating our cultures for hundreds of years?

愛麗莎：我愛巴黎，這裡處處是宗教上的遺跡。聖母院於 14 世紀完工，你能想像那棟建築數百年來就聳立在那，看著我們創造我們的文化嗎？

Carlos: Yes, I can. How amazing it is. The cathedral became even more famous when a 19th-century writer, Victor Hugo took it as the main stage of his work, *the Hunchback of Notre Dame*.

卡洛斯：我想我可以想像，這真的很驚人，19 世紀，維克多將這裡當作《鐘樓怪人》的主要舞台，讓這座教堂的聲名更加遠播。

(After the boat tour, they wandered around the street and walked into the cathedral.)

（下船後，他們兩人一起在街上漫步，並走進教堂裡。）

Carlos: Alisa, I want to be a great man like Victor Hugo.

卡洛斯：愛麗莎，我想要成為和維克多雨果一樣的偉人。

(Then, Carlos stopped in front of the wall with the carving of the Greek word 'ANATKH.')

（卡洛斯於是停在刻有希臘字 ANATKH 的牆面前。）

Carlos: It's incredible to think that someone stood there and carved the Greek word quietly on the wall: ANATKH, centuries ago. And the sign inspired the

卡洛斯：一想到有人站在那靜靜地在牆上刻下希臘文 ANATKH，就覺得不可思議，而這個符號給了年輕的雨果靈感，促

young Victor Hugo to search about its origin and then produced the great work.

Alisa: No worries. Always being such a sophisticated and affectionate person, your work is undoubtedly very engaging. I will always be your fan.

Carlos: Thanks for being so supportive. Let's take a picture in front of this amazing place.

使他尋找其源頭,並寫下曠世鉅作。

愛麗莎:別擔心,你一直都是心思細膩、感情豐富的人,你的作品當然也一樣深得人心,我永遠都是你的粉絲。

卡洛斯:謝謝妳這麼支持我,讓我們在這個地方一起合影留念吧。

 好好用單字、片語

1. optimal *adj.* 最理想的
2. architecture *n.* 建築物
3. spiritual *adj.* 心靈上的、宗教的
4. relic *n.* 遺跡
5. hunchback *n.* 駝背者
6. wander *v.* 閒逛
7. carved *n.* 雕刻
8. sophisticated *adj.* 心思縝密的
9. drift down *phr.* 往下漂流,drift *v.* 漂流,英文意思為 move along smoothly and slowly in water or air,在水中或空氣中緩慢地漂流,drift 後可加上表方向的介系詞,例如:drift across the sky(在天空中飄散開來),或是 drift out to the sea(飄向海洋)。

　　例 ❶ The snow slowly drifted down onto the ground.
　　　　雪漸漸地降落到地上。

❷ The fog was beginning to drift down into the open cave.

霧氣開始緩緩地向洞穴擴散進去。

10. get a glimpse of *phr.* 瞥見，英文意思為 a look at somebody or something for a very short time，將目光停留在某人或某物上一段時間，也可以指對某個領域初步的了解。

例 ❶ He twisted his head around and tried to get a glimpse of the man in colorful dress.

他轉頭，試著瞥一眼那個穿著彩色洋裝的男子。

❷ In order to get a glimpse of what's happening inside the business world, they have to learn to speak the language of Wall Street.

為了要了解商場的運作，他們必須要學習華爾街的語言。

文學佳句怎麼用

All at once Dom Claude rose, took up a pair of compasses, and engraved in silence on the wall in capital letters, the Greek word 'ANATKH.

接著查漢看到克勞德站了起來，手裡拿起一對指南針，默默地將希臘文 ANATKH 刻印在牆上。

中文與英文的時態差異

1. 我昨天去購物。 2. 我喜歡購物。	A. I went shopping yesterday. B. I like to go shopping.

過去式

用來表達過去時間，動作發在現在之前。在中文，若要表達過去做了某事，你只需要加上過去的時間，如例句 1 的昨天，在中文動詞上無需變動，但在英文

中，要表達過去的時間，除了加上過去時間如例句 A 的 yesterday，還必須將動詞變形為過去式的動詞。

過去式與現在簡單式的差異

現在簡單式，如例句 B，在描述一個人的習慣，或是一件事情以前如此、現在如此，以後也可能會如此時也適用現在簡單式，如喜歡購物，這個時候動詞使用原形動詞即可。

過去式的動詞變化

不規則變化

- see; saw *v.* 看見
- stand; stood *v.* 站
- take; took *v.* 拿

規則變化：於動詞字尾＋ed，若字尾為 e 時，只須加上 d。

- work; worked *v.* 工作
- open-opened *v.* 開
- carve-carved *v.* 刻劃

與過去式連用的過去時間副詞

1. This morning 今天早上
2. Three months ago 三個月前（數字＋表時間的名詞＋ago）
3. Last year 去年（last＋表時間的名詞）

註：英文中表示過去時間的特徵有兩個，一為動詞變成過去式，二為搭配過去時間。但是當你不清楚過去時間到底是什麼時候，或是你不想強調那個時間點的時候，只要使用動詞過去式即可表達過去時間。

➤ 下列例句雖然沒有使用過去時間，卻因為動詞的時態轉變，明確地表達事件發生在過去，現在已經不是這麼回事了。

例：I fell in love with an American, but the interracial relationship didn't last for long.
我以前曾愛上一個美國人，但是這段異國戀並沒有持久。

 文學經典重現 Track19

"And he flung away the hammer in a rage. Then he sank down so deeply on the arm-chair and the table, that Jehan lost him from view behind the great pile of manuscripts. For the space of several minutes, all that he saw was his fist convulsively clenched on a book. **Suddenly, Dom Claude sprang up, seized a compass and engraved in silence upon the wall in capital letters, this Greek word: ANATKH.**"

他憤怒地甩下槌子，並重重陷在桌邊的扶手椅上，讓查漢看不到巨大椅背後的他。有幾分鐘的時間，他只看到他的手緊抓著一本書。接著查漢看到克勞德站了起來，手裡拿起一對指南針，默默地將希臘文 ANATKH 刻印在牆上。

單字小解

1. flung v. fling 的過去形，甩
2. sank v. sink 的過去形，陷入
3. engrave v. 刻

來到巴黎聖母院必看必去

你知道石像鬼（Gargoyle）嗎？仔細往聖母院的外觀瞧一瞧，就會發現外面好像站了幾個面貌兇惡、讓人過目不忘的怪物，這些怪物除了充分展現聖母院歌德式（gothic）的建築風格外，它真正的作用其實是排水。另外聖母院的建築物本身就是一個發掘不完的大型藝術品，從大門上繁複的人物雕刻，到精巧的拼貼窗框等都是；走入內部空間開闊的教堂，內心的崇敬感油然而生，心情也忍不住平靜了起來。是來到法國巴黎絕對不能錯過的景點。

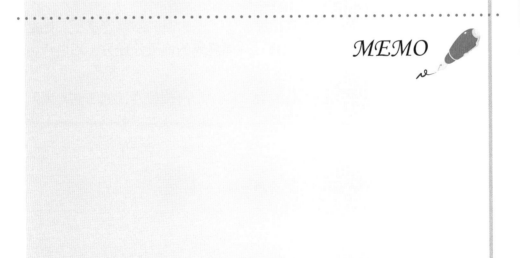

PART 1 歐洲篇

PART 2 美洲篇

PART 3 亞洲篇

法國諾曼第的盧昂、聖米歇爾山
Rouen and Mont-Saint-Michel of Normandie, France

 Track20

福樓拜《包法利夫人》 *Madame Bovary*

66 *At the bottom of her heart, however, she was waiting for something to happen. Like shipwrecked sailors, she turned despairing eyes upon the loneliness of her life, seeking some white sailboats far away in the mists veiling the horizon.* 99

—— Gustave Flaubert, *Madame Bovary*

　　然而，在她內心深處在等著什麼發生，就像遇上船難的水手，她絕望地看著她孤獨的生命，尋找籠罩在迷濛霧氣的地平線遠方，那白色帆船。

——福樓拜《包法利夫人》

文學景點巧巧說

　　寫出《包法利夫人》（*Madame Bovary*）的作家福婁拜（Gustave Flaubert）生於法國西北部諾曼第地區的盧昂，盧昂的藝術氣息濃厚，這裡還有聖米歇爾山（Mont-Saint-Michel）和盧昂並列旅遊勝地，來到諾曼地絕不能錯過。書中的包法利夫人來自鄉村，個性天真浪漫，後來因父親腿骨折受傷而認識平凡的小鎮醫生包法利，最後成了包法利夫人，但平淡的婚姻生活和想像不同，包法利轉而過著不切實際的虛幻美夢中，成天夢想追求轟轟烈烈的愛情，先後和不同的男子展開婚外情，雖曾一度痛地思痛，決心痛前非，但又再次陷入同樣的境地，最後遭殘酷的現實所吞沒。包法利夫人一生追求愛戀，讓人不禁反思現實和理想的界線（How to deal with the desire? To find a way out of the solitude of life; or to face the reality that such solitude can never be exterminated.）。本引言與稍後的文學經典重現（英文部分）取自 New York: Barnes & Noble, 2003 所出版的 *Madame Bovary / Gustave Flaubert*，英文版譯者為 Eleanor Marx-Aveling。

揭開序幕小對話

　　Alisa and Carlos are heading toward Rouen, Normandy. It's a northern city of France and the hometown of Gustave Flaubert, the author of *Madame Bovary*. Alisa is super excited to be in the city in person because she has longed for to visit Rouen, a place where the masterpiece is born.

　　愛麗莎和卡洛斯正前往位於諾曼第的盧昂。盧昂是座位於法國北部的城市，

Alisa: Look! The timber framed houses, the narrow streets, and the old coffee shops. I like Rouen. I feel like I can meet Madame Bovary somewhere.

愛麗莎：看哪！木造的房屋、狹小的街道，加上古老的咖啡廳，我愛盧昂，而且好像可以在這遇到包法利夫人呢。

Carlos: Wow-wow, somebody is so into literature.

卡洛斯：哇，有人完全沉浸在文學中呢。

Alisa: Hey, the coffee shop across the street looks nice. How about having coffee, there?

愛麗莎：嘿，對街那間咖啡廳看起來很不錯，要不要喝個咖啡？

Carlos: I prefer to go to Mont-Saint-Michel for today is our last day in Rouen.

卡洛斯：我比較想去聖米歇爾山，因為今天是我們在盧昂的最後一天。

Alisa: Fine. I may just stay here and meet up with you later today.

愛麗莎：好吧，那我就在這邊等你，晚點再和你碰面吧。

(Sitting in the coffee shop on her own, Alisa feels bored. She is using her smart phone and chatting with Fiona on Facebook now.)

（一個人坐在咖啡廳的愛麗莎覺得無聊，於是就用她的手機和費歐納在臉書上聊天。）

Fiona: Hey, bestie, how is everything in France?

費歐納：小愛，你在法國好嗎？

Alisa: I am all alone. What do you think? Fiona, I told myself that being a friend with him is fine. At the bottom of my heart, however, I was waiting for something to happen.

愛麗莎：你說呢？我現在一個人在這，費歐納，我告訴我自己和他當朋友沒關係，但在我內心深處，我又期待會有什麼發生。

(Like shipwrecked sailors, Alisa turns despairing eyes upon the loneliness of her life, seeking some white sailboats far away in the mists veiling the horizon.)

（就像是碰上船難的水手，愛麗莎絕望地看著她孤獨的生命，尋找籠罩在迷濛霧氣的地平線遠方，那白色帆船。）

(Suddenly, Carlos comes back, walking toward Ailsa.)

（突然間，卡洛斯回來了，他正走向愛麗莎。）

Carlos: Hey, I think I may just stay here and keep you company. We can go check the attraction later together.

卡洛斯：我想我還是回來陪在你身邊好了，我們可以等等再一起去看看景點。

同時也是《包法利夫人》作者福樓拜的家鄉。能親自造訪盧昂的愛麗莎感到非常興奮，因為她嚮往來這很久了，這裡正是大師級著作誕生的地方。

 ## 好好用單字、片語

1. in person *phr.* 親自
2. long for phr *v.* 渴望
3. masterpiece *n.* 名作
4. narrow *adj.* 窄的
5. meet *v.* 遇見
6. for *conj.* 因為
7. on one's own *phr.* 獨自
8. company *n.* 陪伴
9. into + someone/something *idm.* 對…極有興趣、入迷。英文意思為 to be interested in something in an active way。

例 ❶ The guy you met in the bar is not that into you.

你在酒吧認識的男生並沒有那麼喜歡你。

❷ Lily is deeply into sewing and cooking.

莉莉對於縫紉及烹飪非常著迷。

10. have coffee *phr.* 喝咖啡。have *v.* 吃、喝，英文意思為 to eat or drink something，句型通常為 have ＋食物或是 have＋早餐、中餐、晚餐。

例 ❶ I am having dinner with my parents.

我正在跟我的父母吃晚餐。

❷ I had a sandwich for breakfast this morning.

我今天早上吃三明治當早餐。

文學佳句怎麼用

At the bottom of her heart, however, she was waiting for something to happen. Like shipwrecked sailors, she turned despairing eyes upon the loneliness of her life, seeking some white sailboats far away in the mists veiling the horizon.

然而，她內心深處正等待什麼發生，像是碰上船難的水手，絕望地看著她孤獨的生命，在霧氣迷濛、看不清的水平線上找尋遠方的船隻。

進行式的用法

➢ 現在進行式

使用時機：表示現在正在發生的動作，或是目前持續發生的事情。英文表示事件發生的時間先後順序時，需要在動詞做變化，若想要表示動作現在正在進行，則需套用 Be 動詞（is, am, are）＋動詞 Ving 的公式。

例 ❶ She is writing an essay.

她正在寫一份報告。

❷ They are playing chess.

他們正在下西洋棋。

➤ 過去進行式

使用時機：表示過去某個時段正在進行的事情，表示過去持續的動作。表示動作過去正在進行，一樣需使用 Be 動詞（was, were）＋動詞 Ving 的公式，但是要注意，be 動詞的部分要改成過去式的 was 或 were。

例 ❶ She was dancing with her friends yesterday.

她昨天在跟她的朋友跳舞。

❷ We were discussing the issue last night with Mr. Chen. Don't you remember?

我們昨晚在跟陳先生討論這個議題，難道你（現在）忘了嗎？

➤ 比較：也許你以前在為了考試學英文時，會覺得前面的句子如果是過去式，後面也必須是過去式。但是當你在自然的情境與人對話時，英語的時態其實很重要，沒分辨好，可是會造成誤會的。

例 ❶ I was having breakfast with my family this morning. I am reading a novel now.

我今天早上在跟我的家人吃早餐（過去），現在我在看小說。

❷ I was dating an engineer last year, but I am not dating with him anymore. I am single now.

我去年跟一位工程師在一起，但是現在沒有了。現在是單身。

 文學經典重現 Track21

At the bottom of her heart, however, she was waiting for something to happen. Like shipwrecked sailors, she turned despairing eyes upon the solitude of her life, seeking afar off some white sail in the mists of the horizon. She did not know what this chance would be, what wind would bring it her, towards what shore it would drive her, if it would be a shallop or a three-decker, laden with anguish or full of bliss to the portholes. But each morning, as she awoke, she hoped it would come that day; she listened to every sound, sprang up with a start, wondered that it did not come; then at sunset, always more saddened, she longed for the morrow.

然而，在她內心深處在等著什麼發生，就像遇上船難的水手，她絕望地看著她孤獨的生命，尋找籠罩在迷濛霧氣的地平線遠方，那白色帆船。她不知道她會遇上什麼機會，風又會將她帶向何方、駛去什麼樣的岸邊，不曉得來得會是三層甲板的大船，船上裝滿至舷窗的，又會是苦惱還是幸福。但每天一早她一醒來，就希望機會當天就會來；她聽著每個聲音，想著機會沒來，覺得納悶，然後等到日落時分，情緒更加悲傷，她只希望明天快來。

單字小解

1. shipwrecked *adj.* 船難的
2. afar *adv.* 遙遠地
3. shallop [ˈʃæləp] *n.* 淺水敞艙艇
4. be laden with *phr.* 負重
5. anguish [ˈæŋgwɪʃ] *n.* 痛苦

來到諾曼第的盧昂、聖米歇爾山必看必去

　　盧昂是歷史、藝術匯聚的地點，這裡的博物館密度高，內藏有諾曼第珍貴稀有的展品，這裡也是印象派運動（The Impressionism）的發源地，諾曼第還會定期舉行藝術家莫內、高更的展覽和活動；講到諾曼第，當然不能忘記它在二次世界大戰的地位（別忘了諾曼第大登陸）。所以來到盧昂，不妨搭乘觀光馬車、遊船或是小火車，來趟歷史、藝術之旅，遊遍市區及港口吧。另外，聖米歇爾山也是法國奇特的景觀之一，這裡與法國陸地隔絕，也是世界文化遺產地，由於其為天主教的聖地之一，因此有不少教徒來此朝聖。

MEMO

Unit 13

法國馬賽、伊夫島

Marseille and the Island of If, France

 Track22

大仲馬《基督山恩仇記》 *The Count of Monte Cristo*

> *Moral wounds possess this peculiarity—they may be hidden, but they never healed and always painful, always ready to bleed when touched, they remain fresh and open in the heart.*

—— Alexander Dumas, *The Count of Monte Cristo*

這是道德傷口特有的，傷口或許可以遮掩，卻永遠不會癒合，且永遠感到疼痛，一碰就流血，血肉淋漓地留在心上。

——大仲馬《基督山恩仇記》

文學景點巧巧說

《基督山恩仇記》（*Le Comte de Monte-Cristo*）描述馬賽水手年紀輕輕便當上船長後，遭同船夥伴誣陷坐黑牢，其後逃獄、變換身分並展開復仇的故事。作者大仲馬（Alexander Dumas）透過文學作品將他滿腔的正義感展露無遺；書中主角改頭換面，化身為神祕的基督山伯爵（The Count of Monte Cristo），施展一連串的復仇行動，其中高潮迭起，讀來一氣呵成，大快人心。馬賽（Marseille）是法國最大的港口，有地中海最繁忙的商業活動，還有美麗的沙灘、歷史和建築，這裡文化興盛，是法國旅遊勝地之一，也是南法的娛樂重地，處處可見博物館、電影院、酒館、餐廳、精品店和藝廊等。另外，來到馬賽還要去看看伊夫島（the Island of If），囚禁主角 14 年來的監獄（伊夫堡 the Château d'If）就在這座島上，想像主角困坐四周環海監獄、那無助悲憤的心情可想而知。最終他終於得以逃離孤島，完成復仇；故事傳達貶惡揚善的中心思想，別想要做壞事，就算逃的了一時，也逃不了自己的良心啊（moral wounds always remain painful and fresh in the heart.）本引言出自Project Gutenburg，為網路資源。

 揭開序幕小對話

Austin and Fiona are in France on vacation, and they planned to visit Austin's family in Marseille. Fiona is excited about meeting her husband's family, and she is also looking forward to having a sunbath under the Mediterranean sun at Marseille, the largest port in French. However, Austin is acting nervously when they arrived at the city.

奧斯丁和費歐納在法國度假，他們還計畫去拜訪奧斯丁在馬賽的家人。費歐納很期待見到她先生的家人，也很期待能在法國最大的港口馬賽港，來個地中海日光浴。不過，奧斯丁卻顯得非常緊張。

Fiona: Honey, is anything ok with you ? You sweat so much, and you look pale.

Austin: From the moment my feet touched Marseille, a mixture of complicated feeling came to me. I feel like I made a mistake as the villain in *The Count of Monte Cristo* written by Alexander Dumas, feeling so guilty when the wrongdoing is exposed: I have lost contact with some of my friends here.

Fiona: You are such a drama king.

Austin: Just kidding. I was just thinking of the story of *The Count of Monte Cristo* since we are at the author's hometown right now. I haven't read it for a long time; however, some quotes still remain fresh to me. *The Count of Monte Cristo* is a story where the justice would finally find its way out because **"Moral wounds possess this peculiarity—they may be hidden, but they never healed and always painful, always ready to bleed when touched, they remain fresh and open in the heart."**

費歐納：親愛的，你還好嗎？你汗好多，臉色慘白。

奧斯丁：當我踏上馬賽的那刻起，內心是五味雜陳。就像《基督山恩仇記》中的犯錯的人那樣，不法行為昭然若揭：我好久沒有和我的朋友連絡了啊，內心充滿罪惡感。

費歐納：你還真是有夠誇張。

奧斯丁：開玩笑的啦，我只是正好想到《基督山恩仇記》的故事，畢竟我們現在就在作者的家鄉啊。我很久沒讀這本書了，但很多句子對我來說仍然印象深刻。《基督山恩仇記》是個正義終將得以伸張的故事，「這是道德傷口特有的，傷口或許可以遮掩，卻永遠不會癒合，且永遠感到疼痛，一碰就流血，血肉淋漓地留在心上。」。

Fiona: Sounds very philosophical and still workable in the modern society as well.

費歐納：聽起來非常有哲理，而且就算套在現在的社會也行得通呢。

 好好用單字、片語

1. have a sunbath *v.* 曬日光浴

2. port *n.* 海港

3. sweat *v.* 流汗

4. pale *adj.* 蒼白的

5. mixture *n.* 混合物

6. villain *n.* 壞人

7. guilty *adj.* 罪惡感

8. fresh *adj.* 新鮮的

9. make a mistake *phr.* 犯錯。mistake *n.* 失誤，英文意思為 error。

   例 ❶ What happens if the president made a mistake? How does he rebuild his reputation?
   如果總統犯錯怎麼辦？他會怎麼重建他的名聲呢？

   ❷ How hard is it for you to admit that you made a mistake?
   對你來說承認錯誤是有多難?

10. lose contact with somebody *phr.* 與…失聯。contact *n.* 聯繫，英文意思為 a touching or meeting of two things or people，人或事物間的接觸之意。

    例 ❶ Lily doesn't want to lose contact with her old friends so soon after the graduation ceremony .
    莉莉不希望在畢業典禮後那麼快就跟老朋友失去聯繫。

    ❷ People who focus more than they should on their own problems are likely to lose contact with the rest of the world.
    過度專注於自身問題的人很容易與世界失去連結。

 文學佳句怎麼用

Moral wounds possess this peculiarity－they may be hidden, but they never healed and always painful, always ready to bleed when touched, they remain fresh and open in the heart.

這是道德傷口特有的，傷口或許可以遮掩，卻永遠不會癒合，且永遠感到疼痛，一碰就流血，血肉淋漓地留在心上。

副詞

➢ 副詞基本上的功能是去修飾動詞，也就是說明這個動作是如何進行。由於句子中的核心為主詞與動詞，而副詞的角色是可有可無的，因此在位置上，有較多變化。請比較下列例句，副詞讓一個句子提供的訊息更多、更完整。

例 **❶** Tony and his classmates play the commuter game.
　　　　　主詞　　　　　　　　　　動詞

　❷ Tony and his classmates play the commuter game happily.
　　　　　主詞　　　　　　　　　　動詞　　　　　副詞

　❸ Tony and his classmates always play the commuter game happily.
　　　　　主詞　　　　　頻率副詞　　　　動詞　　　　　副詞

104

頻率副詞

➤ 頻率副詞是用來表達動作發生的頻率。

➤ 頻率副詞通常放在在一般動詞之前，句型為主詞＋頻率副詞＋動詞。

例

■ Coco seldom takes a walk after dinner.

可可很少在飯後去散步。

➤ 頻率副詞通常放在 be 動詞之後，緊連在形容詞之前，句型為主詞＋be＋頻率副詞。

例

■ It is always painful to think of her ex boyfriend.

對她來說，想起前男友很痛苦。

➤ 常見頻率副詞列表

頻率高	always
	usually
	often
	sometimes
	occasionally
	seldom
	hardly ever
頻率低	never

➢ 引言中大量使用頻率副詞去強調道德所造成的心靈傷口呈現的狀態，以 are never healed，以及 are always painful，強調永遠不癒合以及不間斷的疼痛感。

■ Moral wounds are never healed and are always painful, always ready to bleed when touched.

■ 你也可以試試看在句子中加入頻率副詞，如：

Tony always goes to school by bus, but he is never late for school.

東尼總是搭公車去學校，但是他從來沒有遲到過。

來到馬賽、伊夫島必看必去

伊夫島雖然在《基督山恩仇記》中瀰漫沉重的氛圍，但親自拜訪後，才發現其實這裡因為靠海，所以天氣好的時候去，可以看到心曠神怡風景，不過這裡畢竟是和故事有關，這裡就提一下引言的背景吧，或許能讓您到此處時有不同的感受：本引言描述馬爾賽夫面臨審判的心情，在愛德蒙・鄧蒂斯（Edmond Dantès，也就是後來的基督山伯爵 the Count of Monte Cristo）一步步的安排之下，馬爾賽夫踏上公審之路，一聽到亞尼納（Yanina，也就是希臘王）和弗爾南多上校（Colonel Fernand）也就是他成為馬瑟夫伯爵（the Count de Morcerf）前的名字時，臉色蒼白，得知過去出賣希臘之王且將其女兒（Haydée）賣給土耳其王做奴隸一事終究得受法律與良心的制裁。良心的制裁就像產生裂痕的道德，不管如何掩蓋傷口，終究還是得面對它帶來的責罰，像是永遠不會癒合的疤，永遠疼痛流血不已。

Unit 14

法國南部 地中海沿岸城市土倫
Toulon, the Southern France

維克多雨果《悲慘世界》 *Les Misérables* Track23

" *See here. My name is Jean Valjean. I am a convict from the galleys. I have passed nineteen years in the galleys. I was liberated four days ago, and am on my way to Pontarlier, which is my destination. I have been walking for four days since I left Toulon.* "

—— Victor Hugo, *Les Misérables*

Modern text :

Listen and look here. My name is Jean Valijean. I am a convict from the prisons. I have spent nineteen years inside the galleys. I was freed four days ago and am on my way to the destination, Pontarlier. I have been walking for four days since I left Toulon.

請聽我說，我叫尚萬強，是個逃獄的罪犯，已經坐了十九年的牢。我在四天前被放出，正要前去蓬塔利耶（Pontarlier），那是我的目的地。從土倫監獄出來後，我已經走了整整四天。

——維克多雨果《悲慘世界》

文學景點巧巧說

人性的光輝總蘊藏在最不起眼的角落裡，觀察底層人民的生活，就能看得到一個國家、文化最真實的一面。雨果的《悲慘世界》多次改編為電影，百老匯的舞台劇更是到紐約或倫敦不能錯過的好戲，而舞台劇裡，最令人印象深刻的畫面，就是學生們一起高聲合唱：「你可聽見人民在歌唱？（Do You Hear the People Sing?）」，表達對君主制的不滿，史稱 1832 年巴黎共和黨人起義，又稱六月暴動。而原著中令人印象深刻的，則是對人性的刻畫，像是引言中的主角尚萬強，多次靠偷竊維生，卻屢次獲得主教的包容與機會；小罪小惡實不可取，主教或許看出尚萬強本性並不壞，心胸寬大讓人感動，也感化了尚萬強，讓他下定決心改過自新。而引言中的土倫是指土倫監獄（Bagne of Toulon），靠近土倫海港（the Bay of Toulon），來到這可參觀國家海軍博物館（The National Naval Museum），來趟如舞台劇大合唱的撼動人心之旅，細細品味人性的善與惡，成長與反省。本引言與稍後的文學經典重現（英文部分）取自 Collins, 1955 所出版之 *Les Misérables*，英文版譯者為 Isabel Florence Hapgood。

 揭開序幕小對話

The Bay of Toulon is Austina's[1] next destination after Marseille. While they are traveling south, Austin was feeling upbeat. He is now in the mood to enjoy the vacation as if he has got over the gloomy aura of *The Count of Monte-Cristo*. They both think it's great fun to just wander around the street. Now, they stopped in a crowed plaza, with many people watching a group of buskers performing the play, *Les Misérables*.

土倫港是奧斯丁納（見註 1）緊接在馬賽的下一站。他倆一起往南走去，奧斯丁的心情非常好，好像一掃《基督山恩仇記》的愁雲慘霧，現在終於有心情享受假期了。他倆覺得在街上閒逛很有趣，此刻，他們停在人潮擁擠的廣場上，那兒有許多人駐足在那看街頭藝人表演《悲慘世界》。

註 1：美國人有時候會將情侶的名字合在一起，當作情侶間專屬的暱稱，這裡的 Austina 是 Autin 和 Fiona 的合體。

Actor: See here. My name is Jean Valijean. I am a convict from the prisons. I have spent nineteen years inside the galleys. I was freed four days ago and am on my way to the destination, Pontarlier. I have been walking for four days since I left Toulon.

(Austin and Fiona watched the show for a while.)

Austin: Fee, shall we go and take a boat tour around the bay of Toulon?

Fiona: Can I just stay here a little bit longer? Watching the performance here is like immersing myself into the play. Also, if the show is performed in the theater, the admission fee might cost astronomically!

Austin: All right, you persuaded me.

Fiona: Deal! Don't worry. I know how much you are fascinated with the military heritages and the historical naval base here. We'll go to the National Naval Museum right after the show. I promise.

演員：請聽我説，我叫尚萬強，是個逃獄的罪犯，已經坐了十九年的牢。我在四天前被放出，正要前去蓬塔利耶，那是我的目的地。從土倫監獄出來後，我已經走了整整四天。

（奧斯丁和費歐納看了一會戲。）

奧斯丁：費兒，我們要不要搭船瀏覽一下土倫港呀？

費歐納：我能在這待久一些嗎？在這看戲，感覺就好像沉浸在裡面一樣，而且若表演搬到劇場，入場費可是天價啊！

奧斯丁：好吧，你説服我了。

費歐納：那麼就這麼説定了，別擔心，我知道你很喜歡這裡留下來的軍事遺跡和富有歷史傳統的海軍基地。看完戲後，我們等下就會去國家海軍博物館，我説話算話。

好好用單字、片語

1. upbeat *adj.* 開心的
2. temporally *adv* 短暫地
3. crowed *adj.* 擁擠的
4. busker *n.* 街頭藝人
5. perform *v.* 表演
6. convict *n.* 囚犯
7. persuade *v.* 說服
8. naval *adj.* 海軍的
9. in the mood *phr.* 有興致。mood *n.*心情，英文意思為 a conscious state of mind，一種心情狀態之意，片語中用 the mood，表示說話者在某種心情下，有興致從事某事之意。

   例 ❶ Isaac: Let's go grocery shopping. Hayley: Sorry, I am not in the mood.

   伊撒克：我們去買日用品吧。海莉：抱歉，我現在沒心情。

   ❷ Don't go to the blind date if you are not in the mood to meet a new friend.

   如果你沒有意願認識新朋友，就不要去相親。

10. for a while *adv.* 一陣子，屬於時間副詞片語，常放在句子的尾端。while *n.*一段時間，英文意思為 a period of time。

    例 ❶ Austin felt upset and stood on the street for a while, letting the snow fall down upon him

    奧斯丁覺得煩悶，站在街道上好一陣子，任由雪花落在他身上。

    ❷ After sobbing quietly for a while, the little kid fell asleep.

    一陣低聲的啜泣後，這個小孩睡著了。

PART 1 歐洲篇

PART 2 美洲篇

PART 3 亞洲篇

📖 文學佳句怎麼用

"See here. My name is Jean Valjean. I am a convict from the galleys. I have passed nineteen years in the galleys. I was liberated four days ago, and am on my way to Pontarlier, which is my destination. I have been walking for four days since I left Toulon."

聽著看好了，我叫尚萬強，是個逃獄的罪犯，已經坐了 19 年的牢。我在四天前被放出，正要前去蓬塔利耶（Pontarlier）。從土倫監獄出來後，我已經走了整整四天。

自我介紹怎麼說

➤ 本篇佳句為一個囚犯的自我介紹，包含他的名字、身份、以及你做的事情。當然一般人的身分應該不像尚萬強那麼特別，接下來將分解以上的句型，讓你也能在一分鐘內完整的介紹自己，底線部分可以替換成其他資訊：

a 介紹名字：My name is Leo. 我的名字是李奧。

b 介紹身分：I am a scientist from northern Taiwan. 我是來自北台灣的科學家。

c 你做的事情：

● I have spent ten years researching about the Universe.（花了多少時間做某事）我花了十年的時間研究宇宙。

● I just presented my latest paper, *the Big Bang Theory Revisited*, at an international conference last month. 我上個月在一個國際會議上發表我最新的論文，題目是《再訪大爆炸理論》。

➤ 常見職業及工作內容，你也試著填看看吧：

Name	Job	What's done	Duration	What's happening now
Carlos	Writer	Collect information about British literature	Three months	Try to find inspirations by traveling
Hayley	Travel enthusiastic	Take a flight to Peru	Ten hours	Arrive at the airport
Austin	Owner of a coffee shop	Invent a new recipe of lemon pie	Three days	Taste the new pastry
You				

➢ 以 Hayley 為例，可以這樣說：

My name is Hayley. I am a travel enthusiast from the U.S.. I had spent ten hours taking a flight to Peru. I just arrived at the Peru International Airport an hour ago. 我叫海莉，來自美國，非常愛好旅遊，我花了十個小時搭機飛往秘魯。我一小時前才抵達秘魯國際機場。

PART 1 歐洲篇

PART 2 美洲篇

PART 3 亞洲篇

 文學經典重現 Track24

See here. My name is Jean Valjean. I am a convict from the galleys. I have passed nineteen years in the galleys. I was liberated four days ago, and am on my way to Pontarlier, which is my destination. I have been walking for four days since I left Toulon. I have travelled a dozen leagues to-day on foot. This evening, when I arrived in these parts, I went to an inn, and they turned me out, because of my yellow passport, which I had shown at the town-hall. I had to do it. I went to an inn. They said to me, 'Be off,' at both places. No one would take me. I went to the prison; the jailer would not admit me. I went into a dog's kennel; the dog bit me and chased me off, as though he had been a man. One would have said that he knew who I was. I went into the fields, intending to sleep in the open air, beneath the stars. There were no stars. I thought it was going to rain, and I re-entered the town, to seek the recess of a doorway.

請聽我說，我叫尚萬強，是個逃獄的罪犯，已經坐了十九年的牢。我在四天前被放出，正要前去蓬塔利耶(Pontarlier)，那是我的目的地。從土倫監獄出來後，我已經走了整整四天。離開土倫後，我已經走了四天，今天一天就走了12哩。晚上我抵達此處，去了一間客棧，因為我的黃護照，他們把我趕了出來，可是我又不能不拿出來給他們檢驗。我又去了另一家客棧，他們對我說：『滾吧！』這兩家都把我趕了出去。我又走到了監獄，獄卒也不肯開門；我走到狗窩，連狗也咬我、追趕我，好像他是個人一樣，好像看了我也知道我是誰一樣。然後我就跑到田裡去，打算在星光下餐風露宿，可是天空沒有興，我想天要下雨了，於是又回到城裡，打算找個門簷。

單字小解

1. league *n.* 聯盟，這裡指距離單位理格

2. kennel [ˈkɛnḷ] *n.* 狗舍

3. recess *n.* 凹陷處

 來到法國南部地中海沿岸城市土倫必看必去

　　土倫（Toulon）是法國南部地中海海岸城市，有地中海特有的藍天。土倫也是法國海軍基地的所在地，來到這可以看看這裡的自由廣場（Place de la liberté）、老城區內的土倫大教堂（Cathédrale de Toulon）；還可以到史特拉斯堡大道（Boulevard de Strasbourg）上的土倫劇院（Opéra de Toulon）前方喝杯咖啡喔。關於引言之背景介紹：本引言描述尚萬強和米里艾主教（Bishop Myriel）碰面的情形，尚萬強介紹他的來歷，以及出獄後長途跋涉下，急需借宿一宿的心情。這裡提到的土倫（Toulon）是指土倫監獄，靠近土倫海港（the Bay of Toulon）。

MEMO

法國小鎮維勒布勒萬
Villeblevin, France

 Track25

卡繆《異鄉人》 *The Stranger*

66 *He seemed so sure about everything, didn't he? And yet none of his certainties was as sure as a lock of woman's hair. He couldn't even be so assured that he was alive because he was like a corpse. I might seem to have nothing at all holding in my hands. But I was certain of myself and of everything.* 99

—— Albert Camus, *The Stranger*

他到是很確定，但他的信念還不如女人的一綹頭髮，他就像死屍般，甚至無法肯定他還活著。我可能看來一無所有，可我至少對自己和其他一切有把握。

——卡謬《異鄉人》

文學景點巧巧說

「這就是為什麼我會覺得格格不入，就像個局外人。」（This was how I felt out of place when I saw such a particular situation. I felt I was like an intruder.）這是《異鄉人》（*The Outsider*）內，以第一人稱自白的主角心聲，當時的他因誤殺一條人命，正等著接受審判；他看著庭上的人們，包括記者熱絡地互相招呼、聊天時，內心不禁這麼想。而局外人正好也呼應本書的主題，當整個社會的價值觀似乎和自己行走在平行的兩條線時，看來相安無事，可當有天兩條線相交時，無論是哪一方，都像是誤闖入異地的來客，怎麼看怎麼怪；作者卡謬（Albert Camus）透過《異鄉人》這部作品，讓讀者看到主角的被動（不主動爭取）、法律審判的不公（只因在母親的葬禮漠然，就被控訴人性泯滅）和價值觀的殘暴性質（只要和大多數人不同，就是異類；宗教只有上帝這個選項，沒有其他…）；讀者邊看時，也邊思考並反省生命的意義和本質，這就是這部作品的精神，也證明了文學對生命思考的重要價值。卡謬死於一場車禍，地點在法國的維勒布勒萬（Villeblevin）小鎮，為了紀念這位偉大的作家，後人在這裡建了一座卡謬紀念碑（the monument to Camus），附近的銅牌上則寫著：「約那省部總理事會在此向作家阿伯特卡謬致敬，自 1960 年 1 月 5 日那晚起，他便長眠於維勒布勒萬小鎮。」（"From the General Council of the Yonne Department, in homage to the writer Albert Camus whose remains lay in vigil at the Villeblevin town hall on the night of 4 to 5 January 1960."）（本引言取自 Penguin Books, 2000 所出版的 *The Outsider*。）。

 ### 揭開序幕小對話

Austin and Fiona are now in the central part of France, Villeblevin, a small town next to Paris. Fiona has always aspired to take a look of the monument of the French writer Albert Camus ever since she read his famous novel: *The Stranger*.

奧斯丁和費歐娜正在法國南部，一個在巴黎旁，叫做維勒布勒萬的小鎮。費歐娜自從讀了卡謬著名的《異鄉人》後，就一直想來看看他的紀念碑。

Fiona: Look! It's a bronze plaque in memory of Camus who was killed in a car crash half century ago. This town seems to be a friendly place in a quiet peace. It's so nice to be here where the great writer once existed.

費歐娜：這是紀念卡謬在半世紀前因車禍過世的銅製牌匾。這裡看起來是一座安祥友善的小鎮，這裡曾是偉大作家生活過的地方，能到此一遊還不錯。

Austin: In *The Stranger*, I think Meursault's ideas about morally right and wrong are controversial. Many readers believe that he detached himself from the society and didn't care much; while others think it's just a matter of people having different opinions on the same thing.

奧斯丁：在《異鄉人》中，我認為莫梭在道德是非上的想法是非常有爭議性的。很多讀者相信主角已脫離社會，什麼都不在乎；但也有其他人認為，這不過是在同一件事上，持不同的看法罷了。

Fiona: Although he showed indifference to the world, he actually was being himself. He criticized the world's hypocrisy with such a provocative question: **"He seemed so sure about everything, didn't he? And yet none of his certainties was as sure as a lock of woman's hair. He couldn't even be so assured that he was alive because he was like a corpse."** The attitude and behavior of Meursault reflected the author's idea of the humanity as well.

費歐娜：雖然他對這世界的態度冷漠，但事實上他只是做他自己。他用挑釁的方式批評世界的虛偽，並問：「他到是很確定，但他的信念還不如女人的一綹頭髮，他就像死屍般，甚至無法肯定他還活著。」莫梭的態度和行為也反映了作者對於人性的看法。

Austin: Yeah, that reminds me of my high school teacher's comment about the book. It's all about absurdity, indicating the illogical and irrational nature of human beings.

Fiona: I don't agree with Camus's point of view about humanity. But his ideas about certainty have made me think about it once again.

Austin: Honey, you don't have to be that serious. But I do love it when we are sharing different ideas with each other.

奧斯丁：是啊，這讓我想到我高中老師對這本書的評論。這一切都和人類本質毫無道理、常理與荒誕有關。

費歐娜：我不同意卡謬對於人性的看法，但他關於「確定」的想法，讓我開始思考「確定」的意義。

奧斯丁：親愛的，別這麼認真，但我倒是很喜歡我們互相交換意見。

 好好用單字、片語

1. aspire *v.* 渴望
2. monument *n.* 紀念碑
3. stranger *n.* 陌生人
4. plaque *n.* 牌匾
5. crash *n.* 撞擊
6. indifference *n.* 冷漠
7. reflect *v.* 反射、表現出
8. absurd *adj.* 不合理的
9. in memory of *phr.* 紀念，memory *n.*記憶，英文意思為 recalling of mental impression，也是內心對某事某物的印象。

PART 1 歐洲篇

PART 2 美洲篇

PART 3 亞洲篇

例 ❶ The monument was built in memory of all soldiers died in the World War II.

這座紀念碑是建造來紀念第二次世界大戰死去的士兵。

❷ A business man donated funds for the rose garden in memory of his wife.

這位商人把錢捐給玫瑰花園以紀念他死去的太太。

10. detach oneself from *phr.* 使分離、與世隔絕，detach *v.* 分開，英文意思為 to become separated from something，也就是從某個環境中分離開來之意。

例 ❶ I am very relaxed playing in the cornfields with the farm cats. It is when I can detach myself from the intensity of the work and everything

在玉米田裡跟貓咪玩讓我很放鬆，終於可以遠離工作跟生活的壓力了。

❷ The crazy murder does not have any feelings. In fact, he has detached himself from feeling anything.

這位瘋狂的殺人犯沒有任何感情，應該是說他已經沒有感受的能力了。

文學佳句怎麼用

He seemed so sure about everything, didn't he? And yet none of his certainties was as sure as a lock of woman's hair. He couldn't even be so assured that he was alive because he was like a corpse. I might seem to have nothing at all holding in my hands. But I was certain of myself and of everything.

他到是很確定，但他的信念還不如女人的一綹頭髮，他就像死屍般，甚至無法肯定他還活著。我可能看來一無所有，可我至少對自己和其他一切有把握。

代名詞

代名詞的概念，即是替代前面出現的動詞。

➤ 最常見的為人稱代名詞，請見下列例句：

■ <u>Mary</u> is just a teenager. <u>She</u> is not able to afford the tuition fee by <u>herself</u>.
　1.　　　　　　　　　　1.　　　　　　　　　　　　　　　　　　2.

■ Mary's mother pays for <u>her</u>.
　　　　　　　　　　　3.

➤ 解析：

1. 人稱代名詞-主詞前面出現過的 Mary，由 she（人稱代名詞）代替，並注意 Mary 跟 she 都在主詞的位置。

2. 反身代名詞

　a. 同一個句子中，同一個名詞出現第二次時，便需要使用反身代名詞來表示前面提到的名詞，例如 she 第二次出現時，使用 herself 代替。

　b. 反身代名詞於人稱代名詞（受格）之後加上字尾 self 或是 selves 字尾。

例

1. Hayley considers herself luckier than others.

海莉認為自己比別人還幸運。（herself 代替前面提到的 Hayley）

2. **Cuts and scrapes often heal** themselves.

刀傷跟擦傷會自己癒合。

3. 人稱代名詞-受詞當人稱代名詞出現在受詞的位置時，必須使用代名詞的受格。

注意：在使用代名詞時，不宜於文章的一開頭或對話的一開始就使用，這樣別人會不理解那個 he/she 到底是哪位先生或女士。

4. 人稱代名詞（主詞、受詞）與反身代名詞（受詞）的整理表格

	人稱代名詞（主詞）	人稱代名詞（受詞）	反身代名詞（受詞）
你	you	you	yourself
我	I	me	myself
我們	we	us	ourselves
他	he	him	himself
她	she	her	herself
他們	they	them	themselves

來到維勒布勒萬必看必去

維勒布勒萬（Villeblevin）是法國勃艮第（Bourgogne）大區的一個市鎮，所以先把沉重的荒謬主義（absurdism）放一邊，來世界有名的葡萄酒產區勃艮第，參觀這裡的「葡萄酒之路」吧，法國最有名的兩種酒：夏布利（Chablis）和薄酒萊（Beaujolais）就是在這條路上的酒廠產出。美食配美酒，大概就是來到法國勃艮第必須做的事吧。

MEMO

Unit 16 義大利佛羅倫斯
Florence, Italy

 Track26

但丁《神曲－地獄篇》 *Divine Comedy-Inferno*

" *The soles of all were on fire and because of their joints so strongly twitched, they would have snapped green twigs and cords of grass.* "

—— Dante Alighieri, *Divine Comedy-Inferno*

他們的腳跟燃著火焰，關節扭曲地嚴重，足以扭斷最堅韌的樹枝和草繩。

——但丁《神曲－地獄篇》

文學景點巧巧說

　　《神曲》（*Divine Comedy*）創於西元 14 世紀，由但丁（Dante Alighieri）所寫，經過七百多年的歷史淬煉下，已然成為義大利的代表作品，人文主義（humanism）時代也因這部作品而揭開。這部史詩般的巨作共有 14, 233 行，旨在探討人類的「罪」與「贖」，並詳細描述但丁在維吉爾（Vigil）的帶領下，深入地底，行經地獄層（The Inferno）、煉獄層（The Purgatory），最後到天堂（The Paradise）的過程。在地獄篇出現前，中古世紀對刑罰的概念從未如此具體且鮮明；而《神曲》在發行後，則啟發了許許多多的藝術創作，有波提切利（Botticelli）、杜雷（Gustave Doré）和威廉布萊克（William Blake）的畫作，近期更成了丹布朗長篇小說《地獄》的故事主軸。本篇的引言取自原文地獄篇內的第八圈，這一圈的人犯下了買賣聖職的罪，並以頭下腳上的姿勢塞在洞口裡，僅露出雙腿，且兩隻腳掌都燃著火焰。但丁是義大利佛羅倫斯人，曾歷經政治上的動盪並遭放逐，直到死前都無法回到家鄉；丹布朗的小說《地獄》巧妙地將但丁的地獄篇和佛羅倫斯作結合，帶著讀者來了一趟佛羅倫斯深度之旅：到聖瑪加利大教堂（Chiesa di Santa Margherita）看看但丁與貝德麗采（Beatrice）邂逅的地方，在這裡還留有一處紀念碑，許多因愛所困的人們會到這裡，祈求貝德麗采保佑他們的愛情；或到舊宮（Palazzo Vecchio）瞻仰但丁的面容（The Death Mask of Dante），死亡面具是以石膏或蠟製成，為了紀念死者而作。本引言與稍後的文學經典重現（英文部分）取自 New York: P. F. Collier, 1937 出版的 *The Divine comedy of Dante Alighieri*，英文版譯者為 Henry F. Cary。

 揭開序幕小對話

　　Carlos found himself in a dark, old, bare little church. The wall of the church wrote Chiesa Santa Margherita dei Cerchi. He was frightened and confused because he should be sitting in the *Leaf* coffee shop. A fierce pain suddenly struck him. **The soles of his feet were on fire and because of**

125

their joints so strongly twitched, they would have snapped green twigs and cords of grass. Carlos couldn't help but screaming loudly.

卡洛斯發現自己身在又黑且破舊，空無一物的教堂中。教堂上的牆上寫著聖瑪加利大教堂（*Chiesa Santa Margherita dei Cerchi*）。他又是害怕又是困惑，因為他應該坐在葉子咖啡廳才對。突然一陣劇痛襲來，他的腳跟燃著火焰，關節扭曲地嚴重，足以扭斷最堅韌的樹枝和草繩。卡洛斯忍不住尖叫起來。

Carlos: Where am I?

卡洛斯：我人在哪？

Men: You are in your dream.

男人：你在夢裡。

Carlos: Can you stop the fire burning? It hurts so much.

卡洛斯：你可以別讓火繼續燒嗎？我腳很痛。

Men: I will stop the fire once you ac-knowledged what you have done that led others into tragedy.

男人：只要你承認你所做的事讓他人陷入悲劇，我就不讓火繼續燒。

Carlos: I was just sitting in the coffee shop. Before that, I met a little boy on my way to the coffee shop. He asked me for help, but I wasn't able to give him a hand. I didn't hurt anybody, not even an ant.

卡洛斯：我只是坐在咖啡廳裡欸。不過之前到咖啡廳的路上有碰上一個小男孩，他向我尋求協助，可是我沒辦法。可是我沒有傷害任何人，連一隻螞蟻都沒有。

Men: In addition to your burning legs, don't you feel like something heavy is on your shoulders the whole time?

男人：你的雙腳燃燒著，但你沒發現你的肩膀上也很沉嗎？

Carlos: Why should I suffer in this church? And who are you?

Men: It doesn't matter who I am. What matters is that your indifference to the young boy has caused him into trouble.

(Suddenly, Carlos woke up from his wired dream. He is still holding the book in his arms, *Divine Comedy.* Carlos soon realized that he was actually in the Church of Dante, where Dante fell in love with his muse Beatrice. Carlos is murmuring:)

Carlos: The man I met in my dream must be Dante, and he was reminding me of the karma. Maybe I should be nice to people and even strangers, so something good might happen to me.

卡洛斯：我為什麼會在教堂裡受苦？你到底是誰？

男人：我是誰不重要，重要的是你對男孩冷漠的態度，已造成他的麻煩了。

（卡洛斯突然從詭異的夢中清醒。他的手臂下還夾著書《但丁神曲》，卡洛斯這才了解他剛是在但丁的教堂，也就是但丁愛上靈感女神貝德麗采的地方啊。卡洛斯喃喃自語：）

卡洛斯：出現在我夢中的男人一定就是但丁了，他提醒我因果輪迴關係，我下次可能要對陌生人好一點了，這樣才會有好事發生啊。

 好好用單字、片語

1. bare *adj.* 無擺設的
2. frightened *adj.* 感到害怕的
3. fierce *adj.* 強烈的
4. tragedy *n.* 悲劇
5. heavy *adj.* 沉重的

6. indifference *n.* 冷漠

7. realize *v.* 了解

8. muse *n.* 提供你靈感的人事物

註：muse 源自於希臘神話中的 Muse 女神繆思，掌管文藝、音樂、美術。

9. on somebody's way to *phr.* 我在去⋯的路上，way *n.*方法、道路，在本句是
道路的意思（a route or road）。I am on my way（我在路上了）也就等於英文的
I am coming（我要到了）。

例 ❶ Fiona picked up the phone and explained that she was on her
way while she was putting on makeup at home.
當費歐娜在家裡化妝時，她接起電話並解釋說她在路上了。

❷ Austin is never late. He must be on his way to the meeting.
奧斯丁是個準時的人，他一定在來開會的路上了。

10. give somebody a hand *phr.* 幫助某某人。英文意思為 help a person。

例 ❶ The boy is in trouble; he asks everyone who passes by to give
him a hand.
小男孩遇到麻煩了，他向每位經過的人尋求幫助。

❷ Isaac passed by and was going to give the boy a hand but he de-
clined.
伊薩克路過正要出手協助，卻被他拒絕了。

 文學佳句怎麼用

The soles of his legs were on fire and because of their joints so
strongly twitched, they would have snapped green twigs and cords of
grass.
他們的腳跟燃著火焰，關節扭曲地嚴重，足以扭斷最堅韌的樹枝和草繩。

字詞解析

1. sole *n.* 腳底、鞋底，英文意思為 the bottom of the food，本字的重點是 bottom（底部）。

2. cord *n.* 繩索。英文意思為 *thick* string or thin rope，細繩或是粗線。

   介係詞的用法 of of (prep.) 屬於…的，由…做成的。

➤ 介系詞在英文中數量很少，但是扮演很重要的角色，介系詞後面通常接名詞，可以修飾名詞扮演形容詞的功能，也可以修飾動作扮演副詞的功能。

➤ 本單元介紹〔名詞＋介系詞＋名詞〕形成的名詞片語。

解析 1

■ Cords of grass *phr.* 草繩，文法上屬於名詞片語。

   ● of grass 介係詞＋名詞，扮演形容詞功能，修飾 cord，用草做成的繩子。

   ● of 英文意思為 something is consist of，由…製成或組成之意。

例

   1. a crowd of people 人群（由人組成的群組）

   2. a house of bricks 磚房（由磚頭做成的房子）

解析 2

■ The sole of his feet *phr.* 他的腳底，文法上屬於名詞片語。

   ● of his feet 介係詞＋名詞，扮演形容詞功能，修飾 his feet。

   ● of 英文意思為 belonging to something，（屬於）…的之意。

例

   1. the courage of the little girl 小女孩的勇氣（屬於小女孩的勇氣）

   2. a friend of mine 我的朋友（屬於我的朋友）

名詞片語怎麼活用

(1) 放在 be 動詞後，當補語：Your mother is a women of power. 妳的媽媽是個女強人。

(2) 放在句首，當主詞：The plays *of* William Shakespeare are interesting. 莎士比亞的戲劇很有趣。

(3) 放在一般動詞後，當受詞：I like the lecture of Dr. Yeh. 我喜歡葉教授的課。

 文學經典重現 Track27

Out of the mouth of each a sinner's feet protruded, and, as far as to the calf, his legs; the rest of him remained within. **The soles of all were, both of them, on fire; because of which their joints so strongly twitched, they would have snapped green twigs and cords of grass.** And as a flame on oily things is wont to move along the outer surface only; so likewise was it there from heels to toes.

罪人的雙腳、雙腿露出洞口，其他則塞在洞裡。兩隻腳掌都燃著火焰，關節扭曲地嚴重，足以扭斷最堅韌的樹枝和草繩。洞口上浮著一層油，上面燃燒著火焰，腳跟和腳趾也都有火燒著。

單字小解

1. sole *n.* 腳跟
2. twig *n.* 樹枝
3. wont *adj.* 慣於……

📷 來到義大利佛羅倫斯必看必去

　　來到義大利佛羅倫斯（Florence），除了要拜訪剛剛說的聖瑪加利大教堂（Chiesa di Santa Margherita）、舊宮（Palazzo Vecchio），其實還可以照著丹布朗小說《地獄》內提及的地點，一一造訪，從碧迪宮（Pitti Palace）、碧迪宮內的波波里庭園（Boboli Gardens），接著穿越維奇歐橋（The Ponte Vecchio; "Old Bridge"）上的瓦沙利走廊（Vasari's Corridor），進入維奇歐宮（Palazzo Vecchio），最後以主教大教堂（百花聖母院）（Santa Maria de Fiore; The Duomo）畫下句點。碧迪宮內的波波里庭園造景壯觀，內有露天劇場，還有噴泉、矮叢、石像等；維奇歐橋上的瓦沙利走廊是一條空中走廊，這條走廊將維奇歐宮、烏菲茲、碧迪宮串連起來，最早是柯西莫一世用來避開佛羅倫斯的街道；而主教大教堂的洗禮堂銅門上有許多方格，刻有一系列浮雕描述舊約的故事，人物生動細膩。

PART 1　歐洲篇

PART 2　美洲篇

PART 3　亞洲篇

德國萊茵河畔
The Rhine, Germany

《浮士德》 *Faustus* Track28

> *And then I've neither goods nor gold,*
> *No worldly honour, or splendour hold:*
> *Not even a dog would play this part!*
> *So I've given myself to Magic art,*
> *To see if, through Spirit powers and lips,*
> *I might have all secrets at my fingertips.*

—— Johann Wolfgang von Goethe, *Faustus*

我沒有財產也無金錢，
也沒有世俗的名譽和奢華；
就是狗也不願意如此，
所以我才獻身魔法，
才能了解是否能透過神力與神口，
從指尖將神秘看透。

——歌德《浮士德》

文學景點巧巧說

　　歌德（Johann Wolfgang von Goethe）出身萊茵河畔，《浮士德》便是由他所寫的劇本，全書分為兩個部分，將魔鬼梅菲斯（Mephistophles）和上帝打賭、到主人翁浮士德（Dr. Faustus）答應和魔鬼交易，與交易後的故事娓娓道來。藉由魔鬼的幫助，浮士德無所不能，一吐之前遭大地之靈所嘲弄的恥辱（disgrace），他不再是卑微的人類了。浮士德甚至得到了青春、愛情，也得到了名聲，但他卻發現他失去了自己，也了解自己不過是任梅菲斯擺佈的棋子，甚至害了無辜的生命，他知道他無法扭轉與惡魔的交易，但還是向上帝祈禱，請求讓他的故事流傳世間，讓後人得以引以為戒，最終，浮士德捨己救人的精神感動了上天，靈魂得以進入天堂，留下憤怒不已的梅菲斯。《浮士德》一作不僅要人們懂得謙遜，也讚揚人類懂得反省改過的行為。摘取的引言描述仍然自視甚高的浮士德，深夜在桌前感嘆自身的無能，並解釋鑽研魔法的原因。既然來到了歌德出生的萊茵河畔，就要來看看歌德曾經到訪過的高貴巖（Stolznfels）城堡，感受氣派建築和周圍美麗風光。本引言出自網站 Poetry in Translation，為網路資源，由 A.S.KLINE 所翻。

 揭開序幕小對話

　　Carlos makes a living by writing novels, and he is good at creating impressive characters. The key is simple. He talks to his characters in his mind every day. As usual, Carlos is having a coffee date with one of his characters, Mr. Fortner.

　　卡洛斯以寫小說為生，他很擅長創造令人印象深刻的角色，秘訣很簡單，他每天都在腦袋裡和他的角色說話。一如往常，卡洛斯和他的一個角色，福特納先生約在咖啡廳。

Carlos: Could you please introduce yourself?

卡洛斯：你可以介紹一下你自己嗎？

Mr. Fortner: I am a normal Germen guy who lives by the riverside of Rhine, a vital waterway that flows through several countries.

福特納先生：我是一個住在萊茵河畔的德國人，萊茵河是一條流經許多國家的重要河流。

Carlos: I see. You and Goethe, the author of *Faustus,* come from the same place. I like Germany, go on please.

卡洛斯：我懂，你和歌德，也就是《浮士德》的作者都來自同一個地方，我愛德國，請繼續說。

Mr. Fortner: I've neither goods nor gold. No worldly honour, or **splendour** hold. I am poor, and I believe your readers will feel compassion for me.

福特納先生：我沒有財產也無金錢，也沒有世俗的名譽和奢華；我是個窮小子，我相信你的讀者會同情我。

Carlos: Poverty can't make an impressive story for people to remember.

卡洛斯：窮困好像沒辦法讓人為故事留下深刻的印象，看了就忘了。

Mr. Fortner: I also aggressively tries to change the miserable situation. As Goethe said in *Faustus*, "**Not even a dog would play this part! So I've given myself to Magic art, To see if, through Spirit powers and lips, I might have all se-**

福特納先生：我很積極的想要改變這樣的情況，就像歌德在《浮士德》所說：「就是狗也不願意如此，所以我才獻身魔法，才能了解是否能透過神力與神口，從指尖將神秘看

crets at my fingertips." Poverty drives me crazy.

透。」貧窮讓人抓狂。

Carlos: I like it. Then I think my latest story would be about magic, courage, and love. It will definitely be a page-turner.

卡洛斯：我喜歡，那麼我想我最新的故事要和魔法、勇氣和愛有關，這一定會成為暢銷書的。

Mr. Fortner: Then in your story, make me to show my power to the world at the hill of Castle Stolzenfels because the place means a lot to me. It was built in mid-13th century.

福特納先生：那麼讓我在你的小説中站在高貴巖城堡上，向世界展現我的力量吧，因為這個建於 13 世紀前期的地方，對我的意義很大。

 好好用單字、片語

1. impressive *adj.* 令人印象深刻的
2. character *n.* 角色
3. introduce *v.* 介紹
4. riverside *n.* 河畔
5. vital *adj.* 重要的
6. splendor *n.* 顯赫、傑出
7. aggressively *adv.* 有進取精神地、積極地
8. page-turner *n.* 暢銷書
9. show/have compassion for *phr.* 對⋯表示同情，英文意思為 a strong feeling of sympathy for someone who is suffering，也就是對於遭受苦難的人表示同情。

例 ❶ The promotion of energy efficiency and conservation is a way for us to show compassion for our children and grandchildren.

能源有效利用及能源節約的推動，是我們對未來子孫表示同情的方法之一。

❷ For those gays and lesbian, we should be open-minded and have profound compassion for those who are dealing with sexual identity disorders.

我們應該以開闊的心胸對待同性戀者，特別是那些對於自我性別認同混亂者，更該給予深深的同情。

10. make a fortune *phr.* 賺大錢，英文意思為 make a large amount of money。

例 ❶ Many people successfully made a fortune in the real estate market.

很多人成功地在房地產業中致富。

❷ Carlos believes that he could write a best-selling book and make a fortune.

卡洛斯相信自己可以寫出暢銷書並且賺大錢。

文學佳句怎麼用

And then I've neither goods nor gold,

No worldly honour, or splendour hold:

Not even a dog would play this part!

So I've given myself to Magic art,

To see if, through Spirit powers and lips,

I might have all secrets at my fingertips.

我沒有財產也無金錢，

也沒有世俗的名譽和奢華；

就是狗也不願意如此，

所以我才獻身魔法，

才能了解是否能透過神力與神口，

從指尖將神秘看透。

助動詞 助動詞通常放在動詞之前，功能為輔助表達動詞之意，本單元學到的 would 表示說話者做某動作的意願，might 則表達動作的可能性。

■ 助動詞的特性：助動詞後面需加原形動詞。

■ 句型為：主詞＋助動詞＋ (not) ＋動詞。

句型 1

➤ would *aux.* 願意、想要，英文意思為 to express intention, willingness, preference，用來表達説話者做某事時心中的意志。

　例 ❶ Max said he would not stop doing exercise.

　　　麥斯説他不會停止運動。

　　❷ We would like to acknowledge all the engineers who contributed to the design of the Apps.

　　　我們誠摯的感謝那些為手機軟體貢獻的工程師們。

句型 2

➤ might *aux.* 可能，英文意思為 to express possibility，用來表達某事的可能性。

　例 ❶ The flight might not arrive on time.

　　　這班飛機可能無法準時抵達。

　　❷ The system might be temporarily unavailable.

　　　這個系統可能暫時無法使用。

來到德國萊茵河畔必看必去

　　萊茵河連綿上千公里，搭上船後，就能來一趟萊茵河之旅，並拜訪德國西北方的第一大城：科隆。科隆是座古老的城市，位於市中心的科隆大教堂興建於十三世紀，直到十九世紀才完工，當高聳入雲的哥德式尖塔映入眼簾時，心中不禁興起讚嘆，也難怪這裡是科隆最顯著的地標。沿著萊茵河畔的大小城市裡有數十座不同類型的博物館，其中較為重要的大多位於科隆內，如科隆的羅馬日耳曼博物館（Roman-Germanic Museum）和華爾拉夫·利歇茲博物館（Wallraf Richartz），還有巧克力博物館，來這裡不但可以認識巧克力的製造流程，當然還有香氣四溢的巧克力可以試吃囉。

MEMO

希臘希俄斯、土耳其特洛瓦
Chios, Greece and Truva, Turkey

《伊里亞德》 *The Iliad* 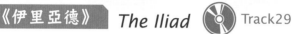 Track29

❝*He showed us favourable signs by flashing his lightning on our right hands; therefore let none make haste to go till he has first lain with the wife of some Trojan, and avenged the toil and sorrow that he has suffered for the sake of Helen.*❞

—— Homer, *The Iliad*

他把閃電打在我們的右手邊，閃光中閃著祥兆，所以，在和特洛伊人的妻子行房之前，也就是作為我們因海倫所遭受的磨難和報復，我們都不要急著起程回返。

——荷馬《伊里亞德》

文學景點巧巧說

你可能沒聽過荷馬（Homer）或《伊里亞德》（The Iliad），但一定聽過木馬屠城記，也就是著名的特洛伊之戰（The Trojan War），可能還看過布萊德彼特演的阿基里斯（Achilles）。荷馬的《伊里亞德》（是兩部偉大史詩的其中一部，另外一部則為《奧德賽》）描述阿迦曼儂王（Agamemnon）率領希臘軍隊進攻特洛伊城的故事，而引起兩城邦間的導火線，則是美麗的海倫（Helen）。這段引言則描述阿迦曼儂的夢境，夢境裡顯現宙斯的閃電、像是預告著這次征戰的勝利，堅定了阿迦曼儂出征的決定，堅持非要讓特洛伊的男人也嚐到妻子遭奪取的痛苦，體會他的妻子海倫（Helen）遭帕里斯王子（Paris）奪取後，他所遭受到的磨難那樣，才能罷休。關於荷馬，據說他出身希俄斯（Chios），這裡是希臘的第五大島嶼，位於愛琴海東部，與土耳其隔海相望，這裡的氣候宜人，海天連成美麗的藍，動人心弦。從這搭船就能抵達土耳其大陸，往上沿著沿岸走，就可到達名為特洛瓦的小鎮（small township of Truva），一窺木馬屠城記中的木馬模型呢。本引言與稍後的文學經典重現（英文部分）取自 Wlidside Press LLC, 2007 所出版之 The Iliad，英文版譯者為 Samuel Butler。

 揭開序幕小對話

While Hayley and Isaac are enjoying making dumpling in the kitchen, the telephone rings. It's a call from Hayley's older sister, Mimi, who married to a Greek guy, Adam, and settled down in Chios after the marriage. She calls to invite Hayley to her house for the coming vacation.

當海莉和伊薩克在廚房包水餃，這時候電話響了。是海莉大姐咪咪的來電，她嫁給希臘人亞當，婚後定居在希俄斯。她打來邀請海莉趁著假期到希臘拜訪她們。

Mimi: Hello my dear, it's me, Mimi. How's everything in Taiwan?

咪咪：嗨親愛的，是我咪咪，妳在台灣好嗎？

Hayley: Mimi, I miss you so much. Everything is going well in Taiwan. How are you and Adam?

海莉：咪咪，我好想妳，台灣一切都好，妳和亞當呢？

Mimi: Fantastic. I want to invite you and Isaac to visit us in Athens for the new year vacation. We can take you to Chios. It's a beautiful small town by the sea, and you can walk on the beach of endless white sand.

咪咪：我們很好，只是想要邀你和依薩克來雅典過新年，我們會帶你去看看美麗的海港小鎮希俄斯，你們可以走在綿延無盡白色沙灘上。

Hayley: Sounds good. I also want to walk on the white beach.

海莉：聽起來很不錯耶，我自己也想要走在白色沙灘上。

Mimi: That won't be a problem once you are here. And don't worry about Isaac. Chios is known as the birthplace of Homer. We can go to Truva to get a glimpse of Trojan horse. My husband can tell you more about Greek mythologies.

咪咪：那當然也是沒有問題，而且不用擔心伊薩克，希俄斯是荷馬的出生地，我們可以去特洛瓦看一看木馬，我的老公也會跟你們多聊聊希臘神話的。

Hayley: I believe he will have a great conversation with Isaac.

海莉：我相信他和伊薩克會聊得很開心。

Mimi: I will never doubt it.

咪咪：那是肯定的。

Hayley: I can't wait! They can watch the Trojan horse with their imagination actively turned on. Imagine, it is when Zeus showed Agamemnon and his army **favorable signs by flashing his lightning on their right hands; therefore, let none make haste to go till he has first lain with the wife of some Trojan, and avenged the toil and sorrow that he has suffered for their sake of Helen.**

Mimi: Hayley! Stop! You are talking like Isaac.

海莉：我等不及了，而且他們看到木馬後，想像力也會變得非常活躍。想像吧，宙斯在亞佳曼儂前現身，他把閃電打在我們的右手邊，閃光中閃著祥兆，所以，在和特洛伊人的妻子行房之前，也就是作為我們因海倫所遭受的磨難和報復，我們都不要急著起程回返。

咪咪：海莉，夠了，你這樣好像伊薩克。

 ## 好好用單字、片語

1. marriage *n.* 婚姻

2. fantastic *adj.* 極好的（口語）

3. endless *adj.* 無盡的

4. birthplace *n.* 出生地

5. mythology *n.*神話

6. doubt *v.* 懷疑

7. imagination *n.* 想像力

8. avenge *v.* 報仇

9. settle down *phr.* 安頓下來，英文意思 to become established in some routine，也就是在某種日常規律中安頓下來。

例 ❶ The young, rich, and beautiful college teacher finally wants to get married and settle down.

那位年輕、富有又美麗的大學教授終於想要結婚並且安頓下來了。

❷ With darkness approaching, all the students are ready to settle down in the camping tent.

黑夜降臨，所有學生都準備好在帳篷內安頓下來。

10. turn on *phr.* 打開。英文意思為 put into operation，啟動之意。一般我們學到的意思為打開電器產品，例如：turn on the light （打開電燈），但這邊指的是啟動某一種思維或特質。

例 ❶ In my class, you will be engaged in a variety of tasks that turn on your imagination and turn off your boredom.

上我的課，你會參與一系列的任務，想像力因此飛揚，終結無聊。

❷ If you want to find a girlfriend before this Christmas, you will have to turn on your charm.

如果你想要在聖誕節前交到一個女朋友，你必須要魅力全開。

文學佳句怎麼用

He showed us favourable signs by flashing his lightning on our right hands; therefore, let none make haste to go till he has first lain with the wife of some Trojan, and avenged the toil and sorrow that he has suffered for the sake of Helen.

他把閃電打在我們的右手邊，閃光中閃著祥兆，所以，在和特洛伊人的妻子行房之前，也就是作為我們因海倫所遭受的磨難和報復，我們都不要急著起程回返。

授與動詞

➤ 所謂授與動詞，即是給「某人」「某某東西」，某人即受惠者，為間接受詞，

某某東西則為直接受詞。

➤ 句型為：主詞＋授與動詞＋某人（間接受詞）＋某物（直接受詞）

例

1. Peter give his girlfriend a Valentine's Day gift.

　　　　　　　　間接受詞　　　　直接受詞

彼得給他的女朋友一份情人節禮物。

2. I show the staff of the train station my ticket.

　　　　　　　　　間接受詞　　　　直接受詞

我給鐵路的站務員看我的票。

➤ 常見的授與動詞：

> give (v.) 給
>
> send (v.) 寄
>
> show (v.) 展示
>
> teach (v.) 教
>
> tell (v.) 告訴
>
> buy (v.) 買

till 的用法

➤ till (conj.) 直到，同意字: until，英文意思為 to the time that or when。

➤ till 在本單元中為連接詞，連接兩個句子，表示句子間的時間關係

例 ❶ A host should never shut a party down till the last person is ready to leave.

　　　　　　　　句子 1　　　　　　　　　　　　句子 2

主人應該等最後一個客人離開時才能結束宴會。

❷ Wait till I tell you to move.

句子 1 (註)　　句子 2

等一下，等我叫你做再做。

註：祈使句：使用動詞表示說話者希望對方做的事。文法上，只需要一個動詞，即能形成句子。

145

文學經典重現　🎵 Track30

　　Stand, therefore, son of Atreus, by your own steadfast purpose; lead the Argives on to battle, and leave this handful of men to rot, who scheme, and scheme in vain, to get back to Argos ere they have learned whether Jove be true or a liar. For the mighty son of Saturn surely promised that we should succeed, when we Argives set sail to bring death and destruction upon the Trojans. **He showed us favourable signs by flashing his lightning on our right hands; therefore let none make haste to go till he has first lain with the wife of some Trojan, and avenged the toil and sorrow that he has suffered for the sake of Helen.**

　　阿特柔斯之子，不要動搖，而是要貫徹最初的計劃，率領阿爾吉維的將士們奔向戰場！就讓那些逃兵自身自滅吧，他們將空手回到阿爾戈斯，最後才了解宙斯的能耐抑或是騙子。冥王之子允諾我們的成功，阿爾戈斯則會為特洛伊人帶來死亡和毀滅；他把閃電打在我們的右手邊，閃光中閃著祥兆，所以，在和特洛伊人的妻子行房之前，也就是作為我們因海倫所遭受的磨難和報復，我們都不要急著起程回返。

單字小解

1. steadfast *adj.* 堅定的
2. battle *n.* 戰爭
3. toil *n.* 辛勞

 來到希臘希俄斯、土耳其特洛瓦必看必去

　　希臘是歐洲古文明的源頭，到希臘旅遊，除了要走訪雅典之外，愛琴海地區

的克里特聖托里尼（Santorini）、米克諾斯（Mykonos）和羅德（Rhodes）島更是不能錯過的度假島嶼，尤其是聖托里尼，在這裡看得到沿著山丘一棟倚著一棟的白色小屋，看來十分迷人，也很有悠閒的氣息。

MEMO

Part 02

美洲篇

美國華盛頓紀念碑、國家廣場
The Washington Monument and National Mall, the United States

喬治華盛頓《1789 年就職演說》

Washington's Inaugural Address of 1789　　Track31

"*All I dare hope, is, that, if in executing this task I have been too much swayed by a grateful remembrance of former instances, or by an affectionate sensibility; and have thence too little consulted my incapacity; my error will be palliated by the motives which misled me, and its consequences be judged by my Country, with some share of the partiality in which they originated.*"

—— George Washington, *Washington's Inaugural Address of 1789*

　　我能期望的就是，若我在執行任務時，因過於受往事或各位的情感所影響，並忽視了自己的無能，我的錯誤將會因動機正當而減輕，而大家在評判後果時，也會寬恕容忍這些因此動機而造成的失誤。

—— 喬治華盛頓《1789 年就職演說》

🌏 文學景點巧巧說

這次的引言取自喬治華盛頓（George Washington）於 1789 年成為美國第一任總統時，所發表的就職演說（inaugural speech）。1787 年，於華盛頓所主持的憲政會議上，誕生了現在的美國憲法，進而將華盛頓推向成為美國第一任總統之路。擔任總統後，他表示未來的總統不會變成獨裁的君主，國家也不會有無政府的狀態；他在演說中表達對上帝的崇敬，而國家與人民對上帝堅定的信仰，也正如同人民於追求目標與理想時，並不會輕易動搖的態度。任何地方上的偏見、意見上或黨派間的分歧，他說，都不能忽視全盤公正的觀點，要異中求同，盡力維護全體人民的權利與福祉。在這段摘錄引言中，華盛頓動之以情，展現謙虛的態度，誠實坦承第一次擔任總統的不足之處，但他也希望人民相信，這些錯誤都是出自於他對受命擔任總統的責任與使命感，盼望人民的體諒，並相信他的領導能力。

說到盛頓的就職演說，就要看看位於國家廣場（National Mall）的華盛頓紀念碑（The Washington Monument），這塊長條形一飛衝天的紀念碑經常出現在電影裡，最經典的，應該是《阿甘正傳》（Forest Gump）裡的一幕，當時二戰還未結束，民主運動盛行，人民穿著嬉皮的服裝，鼓吹世界和平，站在人群中的阿甘，因身穿軍服而意外受邀上台演說，講台位於林肯紀念堂（the Lincoln Memorial），前方隔著美麗的映像池（reflecting pool）正對著華盛頓紀念碑，是一個可以感受民主改革與宏偉歷史時代的地方。本引言與稍後的文學經典重現(英文部分)取自National Archives and Records Administration，為網路資源。

 揭開序幕小對話

Austin is thinking about opening a branch of *Leaf* coffee shop. However, the lack of funding is the biggest problem to execute the plan. He went to seek help from Fiona's uncle, Ron, an entrepreneur in the real estate industry. But, Ron is a stingy person who only offers the help to the plan which is profitable for him. Persuading him is the most difficult part.

PART 1 歐洲篇

PART 2 美洲篇

PART 3 亞洲篇

This is the reason why Austin and Fiona are trying to figure out how to be persuasive.

　　奧斯丁考慮開幫葉子咖啡廳開分店，但是目前最大的問題就是資金不足。他跑去向費歐納的榮恩叔叔求助，榮恩叔叔在做房地產，是一位企業家。但榮恩叔叔很吝嗇，只願幫助對他有益處的計劃。說服他是最困難的部分。這也是為什麼奧斯丁和費歐納正在想辦法說服榮恩叔叔。

Fiona: You know, I am always so touched by Washington's Inaugural Address. When my high school teacher introduced him and his speech, I finally believed how people at that time trusted in themselves and successfully achieved democracy in 1790s. Anyway, I think we can learn some persuasion skills from him.

費歐納：我老是深受華盛頓的就職演說感動，我的高中老師介紹他和他的演說時，我終於了解那時的人們相信自己，並順利在 18 世紀末達成民主。總而言之，我想我們可以跟他學學演說的技巧。

Austin: Really? How? Doing business is very different from being a president.

奧斯丁：真的嗎？怎麼做？做生意和當總統是兩回事耶。

Fiona: Yes, they are different, and yet, they share one characteristic- knowing people's need and try to satisfy it.

費歐納：對，是不一樣，但他們有一個共通的特色—了解人們的需求，並滿足它。

(**Fiona** is looking up on the Internet to find the speech.)

（費歐納上網找了一下演講詞。）

(After reading several paragraphs of the speech...)

（看了演講詞的一些段落後…）

Austin: I still don't see the connection between them.

Fiona: Listen, Washington as a great man at that time showed humbleness by admitting his limited ability. Also, he unreservedly expressed his gratitude for all the trust given by the people. That's one reason to show his greatness. Don't you see the point now?

Austin: I see. You are a genius. I will just follow this principle and talk to your uncle.

奧斯丁：我不知道他們之間的關聯耶。

費歐納：聽著，華盛頓在當時已是偉大的人物，但他還是承認他的能力有限，展現他謙虛的態度。而且對於人民的信任，他毫無保留地表達她的感謝。這是他為什麼偉大的原因，你現在了解了嗎？

奧斯丁：我懂了，你真是天才，我現在就照著這樣的原則，然後和你的叔叔談談。

 好好用單字、片語

1. branch *n.* 分店
2. funding *n.* 資金
3. entrepreneur *n.* 企業家
4. stingy *adj* 吝嗇的
5. persuade *v.* 說服
6. inaugural address *n.* 就職演說
7. democracy *n.* 民主
8. humbleness *n.* 謙虛
9. figure out *phr.* 想出。figure *v.*思考，英文意思為 think、decide。figure out 的英文意思為 think about something until you understand it，也就是將某一件事情想到透徹理解為止.。

例 **1** Max can't figure out how to do solve the problem.

麥斯不知如何解決這個問題。

2 It's *hard* for most of us to figure out how the homicide can treat another human being like this.

大部分的人很難理解那個殺人犯這樣對待他同類的方式。

10. look up *phr.* 查詢。英文意思為 look for information，也就是查詢資訊，來源可以是字典（dictionary）、各類參考書（reference book）、或是網路（internet）。

例 **1** Learning to cook is easy now, and we can always look up recipes online.

學習做菜不難，網站上隨時都有食譜可供查詢。

2 As a novice in the company, you should look up the correct procedure in the manual.

身為公司的新人，你最好先查查公司的程序手冊。

 文學佳句怎麼用

All I dare hope, is, that, if in executing this task I have been too much swayed by a grateful remembrance of former instances, or by an affectionate sensibility; and have thence too little consulted my incapacity; my error will be palliated by the motives which misled me, and its consequences be judged by my Country, with some share of the partiality in which they originated.

我能期望的就是，若我在執行任務時，因過於受往事或各位的情感所影響，並忽視了自己的無能，我的錯誤將會因動機正當而減輕，而大家在評判後果時，也會寬恕容忍這些因此動機而造成的失誤。

說話之道

➤ 華盛頓總統的就職演說之所以動人，因為他身為一國總統，是一個大人物，而當一位大人物在眾人面前透露出他的人性時，產生一種「我也是人」我也有情感、弱點，順利地把自己跟民眾拉在同一條船上了，因此他在前幾句用大量關於情感及失誤的字詞鋪成（見語用分析 a、b），就是為了要帶出人民對他的體諒及偏愛（見語用分析 c）。

字詞解析

1. execute *v.* 執行
2. sway *v.* 動搖
3. consult *v.* 考慮
4. palliate *v.* 緩和
5. judge *v.* 評論

語用分析

華盛頓對自己的觀點		華盛頓期望人民對他產生的觀點
(a) 情感面的字詞	(b) 關於失誤的字詞	(c) 人民對他的體諒及偏愛
➤ a grateful remembrance of former instances（沉溺於往事） ➤ an affectionate sensibility（情感上的動容）	➤ my incapacity（我的能力不足） ➤ my error（我的失誤）	➤ partiality（偏愛）

語用練習

➤ 一段有說服力的文字，與其開門見山的說：「請你體諒我」，反而是先鋪陳，把對方拉到與自己同一條線上，這是利用人類的同理心（empathy）一種方法。我

PART 1 歐洲篇　PART 2 美洲篇　PART 3 亞洲篇

們來看看 Austin 怎麼說服 Fiona's uncle.

➤ If I have been too much swayed by my ambition when planning the opening of a branch; and have thence too little consulted my incapacity. I hope for your understanding. I was just attempting to improve the quality life of me and Fiona. 我知道我開分店的野心太大，而忽略了我能力上的不足。但我希望您的理解，我只是希望能改善我和費歐納的生活品質。

 文學經典重現 Track32

In this conflict of emotions, all I dare aver, is, that it has been my faithful study to collect my duty from a just appreciation of every circumstance, by which it might be affected. **All I dare hope, is, that, if in executing this task I have been too much swayed by a grateful remembrance of former instances, or by an affectionate sensibility to this transcendent proof, of the confidence of my fellow-citizens; and have thence too little consulted my incapacity as well as disinclination for the weighty and untried cares before me; my error will be palliated by the motives which misled me, and its consequences be judged by my Country, with some share of the partiality in which they originated.**

懷著複雜的情緒，我敢斷言的是，克盡職責考量所有情況所受到的影響，是我的信念。我能期望的就是，若我在執行任務時，因過於受往事或各位的情感所影響，並忽視了自己的無能，我的錯誤將會因動機正當而減輕，而大家在評判後果時，也會寬恕容忍這些因此動機而造成的失誤。

單字小解

1. sway *v.* 撕開
2. affectionate *adj.* 情感深厚的
3. consult *v.* 諮詢
4. incapacity *n.* 無能
5. palliate *v.* 減輕
6. partiality *n.* 偏頗

來到華盛頓紀念碑、國家廣場必看必去

　　來到華盛頓特區（Washington-Columbia Of United States of America United Government Direct control Capital District），除了能去看看國家藝廊（National Gallery of Art）、林肯紀念堂（Lincoln Memorial）、美國國會圖書館（Library of Congress）、國家航空和航天博物館（National Air and Space Museum）外，還能走一趟喬治城（Georgetown），親自來場吸血鬼與鬼怪之旅（Washington DC Ghost Tours），順便跟著導覽增長歷史和政治知識囉。

Unit 20

美國紐約市
New York City, the United States

 Track33

法蘭克辛納奇《紐約、紐約》 *New York, New York*

❝ *Start spreading the news, I'm leaving today.*
I want to be a part of it, New York, New York.
These vagabond shoes, are longing to stray
Right through the very heart of it, New York, New
York. ❞

—— *New York, New York* sang by *Frank Sinatra*

開始放出風聲，我今天就要離開，

想要成為它的一份子，紐約啊，就是紐約啊。

這雙漂泊的鞋，渴望去流浪，

走進它的核心地帶，我是說紐約，紐約啊。

——法蘭克辛納奇《紐約、紐約》

文學景點巧巧說

　　紐約紐約（*New York New York*）這首歌就算不會唱，但那四個字 New York, New York 總會在想起這首歌時，耳中響起熟悉的歌手法蘭克辛納奇（Frank Sinatra）唱這四字的特殊語調；這首歌也幾乎和紐約這個地方密不可分了（inseparable）。另外，這首歌也叫紐約紐約的主題歌（*Theme from New York, New York*），原來是馬丁史柯西斯（Martin Scorsese）所導電影《紐約、紐約》的主題曲，由約翰坎德（John Kander)作曲、弗萊德埃布（Fred Ebb）填詞，電影主題曲演唱人則為麗莎明妮莉（Liza Minnelli），但真正唱紅這首歌的其實是法蘭克，最後則變成是最能代表紐約市(New York City)的名曲。紐約這區的許多體育隊伍都會在球場上撥放這首歌，最著名的球隊例子就是紐約洋基隊（New York Yankees）。講到音樂，紐約市的音樂文化豐富多元，想來趟紐約音樂之旅，就要去林肯中心（Lincoln Center）看看藝文表演，或是前進中央公園（Central Park）的草莓園(Strawberry Fields）看看拼貼有 Imagine 字的地磚，向偉大的音樂人與和平者（peace activist）致敬。中央公園也經常出現在電影或影集的場景裡，所以來到紐約市，絕對不能錯過中央公園。本引言取自Lyrics Freak，為網路資源。

 揭開序幕小對話

　　Lucas was once a popular vocalist of a rock band in New York University (NYU). He was also the people of the year in the *Rolling Stone Magazine* when he made his debut performance on the stage of Lincoln Center. Being an Ex, Hayley recalled the conversation between her and Lucas.

　　盧卡斯曾經是紐約大學搖滾樂團的主唱，在林肯中心舞台首次亮相表演後，就當上滾石雜誌的年度人物。身為他的前任女友，海莉回想起她和盧卡斯間的對話。

Lucas: Babe, shall we take a walk in Central Park after I finished the band practice.

盧卡斯：寶貝，等我團練完後，我們一起到中央公園散步吧。

Hayley: Sure. Can we have a ride on the horse-drawn carriage? Although we are not tourists, I still find it romantic. Shall we?

海莉：好啊，我們可以坐馬車嗎？雖然我們不是觀光客，但我覺得坐馬車好浪漫喔，可以嗎？

Lucas: We can do that if you want to. And I have something to tell you.

盧卡斯：你想做就做吧，然後我有些話想要跟你說。

Hayley: So, I will meet you at the Strawberry Fields where the memorial ground for John Lennon is.

海莉：那我跟你約在草莓園碰面吧，就是約翰藍儂的紀念地那。

Lucas: Ok, see you later.

盧卡斯：好的，那就等下見。

(Hayley stood in front of the memorial mosaic while Lucas was walking toward her. As usual, Hayley always arrived earlier than Lucas, and he always had excuses.)

（盧卡斯走向海莉時，她正站在磚塊拼貼的紀念地前，一如往常，海莉總是比盧卡斯早到，而他總是有一堆藉口。）

Lucas: Sorry, I am late. Hey, there is an outdoor Jazz concert at Great Lawn.

盧卡斯：抱歉，晚到了，對了，大草原那邊有戶外爵士音樂會耶。

Hayley: Ok, we can go there.

Lucas: Babe, we can take the horse-drawn carriage next time. Central Park is just a ten-minute drive from our dormitory.

Hayley: Let's go.

Singer: Start spreading the news, I'm leaving today. I want to be a part of it, New York, New York. These vagabond shoes, are longing to stray. Right through the very heart of it, New York, New York….

Lucas: The lyric of the song is so touching. It's like we are also a part of New York although we come from different places. Babe, my application to the Juilliard School is accepted. I am planning to go there next semester.

(Hayley became wordless; she knew long distance love would no doubt be a killer for their relationship.)

海莉：好啊，我們可以去那。

盧卡斯：寶貝，我們下次再去坐馬車吧，從我們的宿舍開車到中央公園只需要 10 分鐘。

海莉：走吧。

歌手：開始放出風聲，我今天就要離開，想要成為它的一份子，紐約啊，就是紐約啊。這雙漂泊的鞋，渴望去流浪，走進它的核心地帶，我是說紐約，紐約啊…

盧卡斯：這歌詞好動人，雖然我們來自不同的地方，但感覺我們都是紐約的一份子。還有，茱莉亞學院接受我的申請了，下個月就要去那邊。

（海莉沉默不語，她知道遠距離戀愛無疑是感情的殺手啊。）

好好用單字、片語

1. appear *v.* 露面、演出

2. recall *v.* 回想

3. carriage *n.* 四輪馬車

4. concert *n.* 音樂會

5. no doubt *phr.* 毫無疑問地，用來加強説話者確定的語氣。doubt *n.* 疑問，英文意思為 be uncertain about，不確定的意思。若加上 no doubt，就是 very certain about，非常確定的意思。

   例 ❶ Ang Lee is a great film director. There is no doubt about it.

   毫無疑問地，李安是位偉大的導演。

6. ten-minute drive *phr.* 十分鐘的車程。minute *n.*分鐘，時間量詞；drive *n.* 開車的車程。

   ■ ten-minute 為〔數字+量詞〕形成的〔形容詞〕，中文翻譯為〔十分鐘的〕。

   例 ❶ They are going for a three-**week** holiday.

   他們要去度假三個星期。

文學佳句怎麼用

Start spreading the news, I'm leaving today. I want to be a part of it, New York, New York. These vagabond shoes, are longing to stray. Right through the very heart of it, New York, New York.

開始放出風聲，我今天就要離開，想要成為它的一份子，紐約啊，就是紐約啊。這雙漂泊的鞋，渴望去流浪，走進它的核心地帶，我是説紐約，紐約啊。

未來式

➤ 使用〔be+ Ving〕表示未來即將要發生的事情粗體，這件事情已經是計畫好的，可能在幾小時或是幾分鐘內就要發生。

例 ❶ I am meeting Tom this afternoon.

我下午就會見到湯姆了。（說話時還沒見到湯姆，但是馬上就會見到了。）

❷ The journalist is interviewing the mayor tonight.

這位記著今晚要採訪市長。（說話時市長還沒有被採訪，但是馬上就要開始了。）

➤ 比較未來式也可以用 will 或是 be going to 來呈現，表示動作將在未來發生，但是在意思上有些許的差異。

例 ❶ I will buy a big house when I grow up.

等我長大我要買大房子。〔動作即將在未來發生，雖然尚未有詳細的計畫，但說話者確定自己會這麼做。〕

❷ I am going to take a day off next Monday.

下週一我要休假一天。〔動作即將在未來發生，已經規劃好將要發生的時間點，已經有初步的計畫了。〕

❸ I am leaving Paris soon.〔動作即將在未來發生，這個未來已經馬上就要發生了。在時間上會比例句(b)更快發生。〕

生活應用

➤ 使用〔be+Ving〕來表達未來的用法最常使用在日常對話中，例如當 Hayley 在路上遇到 Lucas，隨口約他看電影，但是 Lucas 表示晚上跟姊姊有飯局無法去看電影時，就是使用 be+Ving，來說明當天晚上即將要發生的事情。

例

Hayley: Hi, What's up? How about go to a movie tonight?

Lucas: Sorry, I can't. I am having dinner with my sister in town.

海莉：嗨，你好嗎，晚上要不要去看個電影？

盧卡斯：抱歉，今天沒辦法，我要和我姊在市區吃晚餐。

Unit 21

美國紐約廣場飯店
Plaza Hotel, New York, the United States

費茲傑羅《大亨小傳》 *The Great Gatsby* Track34

❝ *There was music from my neighbor's house through the summer nights. In his blue gardens men and girls came and went like moths among the whisperings and the champagne and the stars.* ❞

—— Francis Scott Key Fitzgerald, *The Great Gatsby*

整個夏天，鄰居夜夜笙歌。星空下，男男女女在主人的花園內來來去去，穿梭在香檳中。

——費茲傑羅《大亨小傳》

PART 1 歐洲篇

PART 2 美洲篇

PART 3 亞洲篇

 文學景點巧巧說

　　本次引言摘錄自《大亨小傳》（*The Great Gatsby*），貼切寫下蓋茲比夜夜笙歌的生活。本書的寫作背景為美國 20 世紀初所經歷的「咆嘯的年代」（the Roaring Twenties），當時美國的經濟蓬勃發展，前所未有（unprecedented economic prosperity）。作者費茲傑羅（Francis Scott Key Fitzgerald）將 1920~30 年代的社會發展，如奢華生活等的細節放入小說，描述透過犯罪文化（crime culture）而致富的年代，深具批判意涵，並成為費茲傑羅最廣為人知的作品之一。2013 年，《大亨小傳》的同名改編電影上映，如實將小說與當時特殊的時代背景呈現在大銀幕上，服裝與場景都特別講究，讓人印象深刻。欣賞作品與電影的同時，也要來看看紐約的地標之一，廣場飯店（Plaza Hotel），這座位在曼哈頓的飯店歷史悠久，也是電影曾出現的實景。當時蓋茲比、男主角尼克(Nick)、黛西（Daisy）與她的丈夫，和黛西友人一同齊聚在飯店裡，最後還爆發蓋茲比與黛西丈夫之間的衝突（conflict），戲劇張力十足。本引言與稍後的文學經典重現（英文部分）取自 Scribner, 2004 出版的 *The great Gatsby*。

 揭開序幕小對話

　　Hayley used to hang out with Rita during her years in the U.S.A. as an undergraduate student. They liked to explore every corner of New York city after school. One night, they went to the movie theater for the latest movie, *The Great Gatsby*.

　　當海莉在美國念大學時，她跟瑞塔兩人常常聚在一起，他們放學後喜歡到紐約的各個角落去探險，有晚他們去電影院看最新上映的《大亨小傳》。

Rita: I did find that busy, sparkling and dazzling nights in this movie have impressed me a lot.

Hayley: It is just like a sleepless city. Rolls-Royce among the traffic, carrying people in and out to join endless parties here and in Gatsby's mansion.

Rita: Now, I just can imagine how tiring it must be for servants working in the Gatsby's, to fix and clean the mess after parties.

Hayley: See who's talking. No more literature classes. Let's get inside the Plaza Hotel now.

(In front of the Plaza Hotel.)

Rita: We are at the Plaza Hotel, finally. Can't wait to have a fancy meal inside.

Hayley: Hold on, be patient. Remember we are here for feeling some literature aura?

瑞塔：我真的覺得電影裡金光閃閃夜晚，人們忙進忙出的畫面很讓我印象深刻。

海莉：那就像是不夜城，勞斯萊斯排在車陣中，載著人們進出蓋茲比開個沒完的豪宅派對。

瑞塔：我現在可以想像替蓋茲比工作的僕人有多忙了，他們還得收拾派對留下來的混亂。

海莉：這真不像妳說的話，文學課就到這了，我們趕快進去廣場飯店吧。

（在廣場飯店前。）

瑞塔：終於到廣場飯店了，等不及進去享用豪華大餐囉。

海莉：等等，別急。還記得我們是來享受文學氣氛的嗎？

Rita: Right, what can we learn from the Plaza Hotel?

Hayley: As a big fan of Leonardo DiCaprio, you definitely wouldn't miss the movie "*The Great Gatsby,*" would you?

Rita: I knew this movie and I knew it is adapted from the novel under the same name and its author is F. Scott Fitzgerald.

Hayley: You always amaze me, Rita. Exactly. The Plaza Hotel is a very important setting both in the novel and the movie. Whenever I come here, **I would be reminded of Gatsby's luxurious mansion and his park always packed with men and girls, drinking champagne under stars**.

Rita: I'm wondering where the great mansion is in the movie.

Hayley: Ha, to tell you the truth. There is no such "real" mansion in the movie. The mansion and the park we saw in the movie are actually settings. But the Great Plaza we are at now is real and made as the

瑞塔：好吧，那廣場飯店有什麼特別之處呢？

海莉：你這個李奧納多的大粉絲，一定不會錯過電影《大亨小傳》的吧？

瑞塔：我知道這個電影，也知道它從同名小說改編而來，作者是費茲傑羅。

海莉：妳真是太神了，瑞塔，妳說的沒錯。而廣場飯店在小說和電影裡都是非常重要的場景，每次來到這裡，我都會想起蓋茲比的豪宅，還有他那座總是塞滿男男女女賓客的花園，人人在星光下享受香檳的畫面。

瑞塔：不知道電影內的那棟豪宅在哪。

海莉：哈，老實說，電影內的那棟豪宅根本不是真的，包括豪宅和花園都是搭出來的景，但是我們所在的廣場飯店就是真的啦，這裡也是蓋茲比和湯

setting when Gatsby confronts Tom, Daisy's husband in one boiling hot day.

姆面對面爆發衝突的地方，黛西也在場，那天還是個炎炎夏日。

 好好用單字、片語

1. fancy *adj.* 豪華的，頂級的

2. aura *n.* 氣氛，氛圍

3. amaze *v.* 驚奇

4. setting *n.* 佈景

5. luxurious *adj.* 奢華的

6. champagne *n.* 香檳酒

7. confront *v.* 對立

8. boiling hot *adj.* 炎熱，炙熱

9. be adapted from *phr.* 某物改編自某物，adapt *v.*改編，英文意思為 to change something for other uses，若將介系詞 from 改成 into，「adapt ... into ...」則可以表示「將某物改編為某物」的意思，如例 2。

   例 ❶ *Harry Potter* films series are adapted from the best-selling fiction series under the same name.

   《哈利波特》系列電影改編自暢銷同名系列小說。

   ❷ *Universal Studio* decided to adapt *Harry Potter* fiction series into film series.

   環球電影決定將《哈利波特》系列小說改編為系列電影。

10. impress somebody *phr.* 使某人印象深刻。impress *v.*讓某人對你留下深刻的印象，英文意思為 having people admire you by something you have said or done。

    例 ❶ The manager says "Let's impress our customers with our attentive service."

    經理說：「讓我們用熱忱的服務感動我們的顧客吧」。

❷ In a job interview, you have to try your best to impress your future boss who might offer you a position and give you money.

在求職面試中，你必須盡你最大的努力讓你未來的老闆，那個可能給你一份工作給你薪水的老闆對你印象深刻。

 文學佳句怎麼用

I would be reminded of Gatsby's luxurious mansion and his park always packed with men and girls, drinking champagne under stars.

從廣場飯店到《大亨小傳》的電影場景，聯想到書中夜夜笙歌的華麗場景，短短一句話深刻描繪出蓋茲比豪宅的畫面，男男女女手中拿著香檳，穿梭在星空下。

引言解析

句型 1 be reminded of something *phr.* 思想起過去的某事，必須用在回憶過去的情況下：

例 Every time rereading this book, I would be reminded of those good days.

每回重讀這本書，就會讓我想起過去那段美好時光。

■ 也可以這樣用：remind sb of sth，表示「使某人想起某事」之意：

例 Those pictures remind him of his first love. 這些照片挑起他對初戀的回憶。

句型 2 be packed with *phr.* 充滿⋯，本片與表示空間中滿滿都是人，而不只是擁擠（crowded）的意思。

例 ❶ During the peak season of tourism, famous attractions are always packed with tourists.

旅遊旺季期間，著名的旅遊景點總是擠滿了遊客。

❷ This detective novel is packed with suspense and surprises.

這本推理小説瀰漫懸疑氣氛，情節常出人意表。

*註：packed (adj.) 擠滿人的，語意不只是人潮擁擠，也有事物匯聚的意思

■ 另外 packed 當作形容詞，能單獨使用，後接名詞。

例：The orchestra gave a great performance for the packed audience.

交響樂團為滿場觀眾盛大演出。

句型 3 分詞構句的活用 每回都用關係代名詞膩了嗎？善用分詞可以讓文句更優美喔，引言中...drinking 在這裡是 who drank 的變形，更多分詞構句的解説請見。★I've never talked to the man who is standing there. 此句可省略 who is（關係代名詞），改為 I've never talked to the man standing there. 我從來沒跟站在那裡的男人説過話。

 文學經典重現 Track35

There was music from my neighbor's house through the summer nights. In his blue gardens men and girls came and went like moths among the whisperings and the champagne and the stars. At high tide in the afternoon I watched his guests diving from the tower of his raft, or taking the sun on the hot sand of his beach while his two motor-boats slit the waters of the Sound, drawing aquaplanes over cataracts of foam. On week-ends his Rolls-Royce became an omnibus, bearing parties to and from the city between nine in the morning and long past midnight, while his station wagon scampered like a brisk yellow bug to meet all trains. And on Mondays eight servants, including an extra gardener, toiled all day with mops and scrubbing-brushes and hammers and garden-shears, repairing the ravages of the night before.

　　整個夏天，鄰居夜夜笙歌。星空下，男男女女在主人的花園內來來去去，穿梭在香檳中。在海潮高漲的午後，我看見他的賓客從他的浮臺塔一躍而下，或是在他的沙灘上做日光浴，還聽到他的兩艘汽艇劃過水面的聲響，船後拖曳的滑水板掀起大片海花。到了週末，他的勞斯萊斯成了接駁車，一早九點就帶著賓客進出城鎮，川流不息直到午夜過後，就像隻黃色甲蟲般急著替賓客趕上火車。然後一到星期一，豪宅內的八位侍從，外加一位園丁整天清掃善後凌亂的豪宅，整理前夜留下來的一片狼籍。

單字小解

1. slit *v.* 撕開
2. aquaplane [ˈækwəˌplen] *n.* 滑水板
3. cataract [ˈkætəˌrækt] *n.* 瀑布
4. foam *n.* 泡沫
5. scamper *v.* 疾走
6. ravage *n.* 蹂躪

來到諾丁漢必看必去

　　廣場飯店特別設有《大亨小傳》的套房，房中設計宛如回到電影場景，復古奢華感一百分，當然住宿費也不便宜，所以不妨到廣場飯店門口坐坐，還是能享受到悠閒自在的午後囉。

美國 馬里蘭州巴爾地摩
Baltimore, Maryland, the United States

愛倫坡《告密的心》 *The Tell-Tale Heart* Track36

> *Oh God! what could I do? I foamed –I raved –I swore! I swung the chair upon which I had been sitting, and grated it upon the boards, but the noise arose over all and continually increased. It grew louder --louder -- louder! And still the men chatted pleasantly, and smiled.*

—— Edgar Allan Poe, The *Tell-Tale Heart*

老天，我該怎麼做？我胡言亂語、咆哮咒罵，拿著剛坐著的椅子亂揮，敲打著地板，但吵雜只是更大聲了，越來越大，越來越大，而那些人卻聊的更開心，還面帶微笑。

—— 愛倫坡《告密的心》

文學景點巧巧說

　　一邊看《告密的心》（*The Tell-Tale Heart*），彷彿也在看一種歇斯底的自白文（hysteric confession），讀者的情緒也在自白的過程中被騷動、挑起，自我似乎也一分為二，既成了替自己辯護的自白者，也深怕自己成為那樣的瘋子（mad-man），犯下滔天大罪。整篇故事的氣氛詭異且瘋狂，節奏緊湊一氣呵成，是愛倫坡（Edgar Allan Poe）特有的寫作風格，他一生寫了六七十篇的短篇小說，也寫過四五篇精彩的推理小說，如《莫爾格街兇殺案》（*The Murders in the Rue Morgue*）和《失竊的信》（*The Purloined Letter*）。愛倫坡曾和他的阿姨瑪麗亞（Maria Clemm）和家人在巴爾地摩（Baltimore）住過三年，在這裡編輯《南方文學信使》（*the Southern Literary Messenger*）、也進行寫詩、文學評論和短篇小說的創作，並稱這裡為家。若你是愛倫坡的忠實讀者，來到馬里蘭州就不能錯過愛倫坡之家和博物館（The Edgar Allan Poe House and Museum），親眼看看愛倫坡創作的地方，另外也不能錯過普瑞特圖書館（Enoch Pratt Free Library），這裡特別設有愛倫坡室（the Edgar Allan Poe Room），收藏有愛倫坡珍貴的手稿、信件，甚至還有他的頭髮與一部分的棺木，真的是連藏品都很有一種愛倫坡的風格阿。本引言與稍後的文學經典重現(英文部分)取自http://xroads.virginia.edu/~hyper/POE/telltale.html，為網路資源。

 揭開序幕小對話

　　Before Isaac goes to bed, he usually reads some bedtime stories. On the sofa, he is reading *The Tell-Tale Heart* by Edgar Allen Poe, and Hayley is watching the midnight news.

　　伊撒克常常會在睡前看一些睡前讀物，在沙發上，他正在看愛倫坡《告密的心》，此時海莉正在看夜間新聞。

Isaac: Oh God! what could I do? I foamed — I raved — I swore! I swung the chair upon which I had been sitting, and grated it upon the boards, but the noise arose over all and continually increased.

伊撒克：老天，我該怎麼做？我胡言亂語、咆哮咒罵，拿著剛坐著的椅子亂揮，，敲打著地板，但吵雜只是更大聲了

Hayley: Don't be so emotional. What the hell is wrong with you?

海莉：不要這麼情緒化好嗎？你到底怎麼了？

Isaac: It grew louder — louder — louder! And still the men chatted pleasantly, and smiled.

伊撒克：聲音越來越大，越來越大，而那些人卻聊的更開心，還面帶微笑。

Hayley: Honey, there is only two of us, and there isn't any noise either.

海莉：親愛的，這裡只有我們兩個，而且這裡沒有任何聲音啊。

Isaac: I was just trying to figure out the real emotion state of the character in the story.

伊撒克：我只是想要揣摩故事中主角的真實情緒而已。

Hayley: You scared me.

海莉：你嚇到我了。

Isaac: I am sorry. I just can't help mimicing the character. Poe is such a great writer that his words intrigue all my imagination. No wonder people called him

伊薩克：我很抱歉，我情不自禁就模仿起那個角色的，愛倫坡真的事一位很棒的作家，他的文字激發你所有的想像力，

"America's Shakespeare."

難怪人們說他是美國的莎士比亞。

Hayley: Don't tell me how extraordinary the writer is. I wouldn't want a husband as morbid as the bizarre character.

海莉：不要跟我說這個作家有多超凡優秀，我可不想我的老公跟那個奇怪的角色一樣病態。

Isaac: I won't. No worries. But I do want to spend my next vacation touring around the Enoch Pratt Free Library in Baltimore where he lived, wrote, and had family. The library not only collects the manuscripts of Poe's but also the parts from his coffin and locks of hair.

伊撒克：我不會的，別擔心。不過我確實想要去巴爾地摩的愛倫坡之家和博物館，那是他之前居住、寫作、跟家人一起生活的地方那裡不僅收藏有愛倫坡珍貴的手稿、部分棺木，甚至還有他的頭髮。

 好好用單字、片語

1. scare *v.* 使恐懼
2. mimic *v.* 模仿
3. intrigue *v.* 激起…的好奇心
4. extraordinary *adj.* 非凡的
5. morbid *adj.* 病態的
6. bizarre *adj.* 奇異的
7. collect *v.* 收集
8. manuscript *n.* 手寫稿
9. no wonder that *phr.* 難怪、不足為奇。wonder *v.* 感到驚奇，英文意思為 to feel

surprise。No wonder 即對驚奇事物感到不以為然。No wonder (that) 後面可以直接加句子，that 通常會省略。

例 ❶ No wonder Isaac is so artistic. Look at his father who is doing Chinese calligraphy.

難怪伊撒克那麼有文藝氣息。你看他爸爸，那位在寫毛筆字的。

❷ Men and women are so different. Men usually think less and talk fast. No wonder men were so good at lying.

男女大不同。男生通常說話很快不經思考，難怪男生很擅長說謊。

10. **can't help doing something** *phr.* 無法控制。英文意思為 not able to control，沒辦法控制或阻止某件事的發生。can't help 後面通常會直接接代名詞 it，來代替前面說過的無法控制的事情；也可以接動作，接動作時需使用動詞 ing。

例 ❶ If you want to stare your audience confidently, you have to practice in front of the mirror. Standing in front of the mirror, Mary laughs all the time. She just can't help it.

如果你希望能夠在自信的注視著觀眾，你必須在鏡子前練習。鏡子前的瑪莉，卻總是無法控制的爆笑出聲。

❷ The divorced woman can't help telling herself: maybe someday I'll find someone who loves me unconditionally.

那位離婚婦女不同的告訴自己，也許某一天會遇到無私愛著自己的人。

文學佳句怎麼用

Oh God! what could I do? I foamed –I raved –I swore! I swung the chair upon which I had been sitting, and grated it upon the boards, but the noise arose over all and continually increased. It grew louder –louder – louder! And still the men chatted pleasantly, and smiled.

老天，我該怎麼做？我胡言亂語、咆哮咒罵，拿著剛坐著的椅子亂揮，敲打

著地板，但吵雜只是更大聲了，越來越大，越來越大，而那些人卻聊的更開心，還面帶微笑。

了解形容詞子句

➤ 首先要瞭解「形容詞修飾名詞」的原則，而形容詞子句就是「用一整句話來解釋前面出現的名詞」。

例 ❶ Anya envies <u>the girl</u> <u>who won the lottery.</u>

　　　　　　　名詞　　+　　形容詞子句

安亞羨慕那個中樂透的女孩。

❷ I swung the <u>chair</u> upon <u>which I had been sitting.</u>

　　　　　　　名詞　　+　　形容詞子句

我拿著剛坐著的椅子亂揮。

➤ 第二，要瞭解句子與句子的關係，在英文中一個句子一定要有「主詞與動詞」才能稱之為句子，而句子與句子若連結起來，不是像中文一樣打個逗號就可以了，「必須加上連接詞」，形成形容詞子句的「連接詞」(註)，又稱「關係代名詞」。

➤ 關係代名詞，簡稱關代，顧名思義就是「代替前面出現過的名詞」，而他的功能是「連接兩個句子」，當代替「人」時使用 who 或 that，代替「物」時使用 which 或 that。

關係代名詞實戰演練：關代的學習，一般要先從兩個句子的合併練習開始。

例 1：

步驟1 2	Anya envies <u>the girl</u>.（主要句子） The girl won the lottery.（形容詞子句）
步驟3	Anya envies the girl. The girl won the lottery.
步驟4	Anya envies <u>the girl</u> who won the lottery.

(1) 判斷誰是主要句子，誰是形容詞子句，也就是誰形容誰的關係。可以借助中文的思考邏輯，例如：安亞羨慕「那個中樂透的女孩」，「那個中樂透的」就屬於形容詞功能，因此為形容詞子句。

(2) 判斷關係代名詞要用誰，根據例句所示，「女孩」就是那個重複出現的名詞，女孩屬於「人」，使用 who。

(3) 合併句子時，先將主要子句抄下來，再將形容詞子句抄在後面。

(4) 將重複的名詞（The girl）以 who 代替。

例 2：

步驟1 2	I swung the chair.（主要句子） I had been sitting upon **the chair.**（形容詞子句）
步驟3	I swung the chair. I had been sitting **upon** **the chair**.
步驟4	I swung the chair **upon which** I had been sitting.

(1) 判斷誰是主要句子，誰是形容詞子句，也就是誰形容誰的關係。可以借助中文的思考邏輯，例如：我拿著「剛坐著的椅子」亂揮，「剛坐著的椅子」就是形容詞功能，因此為形容詞子句。

(2) 判斷關係代名詞要用誰，根據例句所示，「椅子」就是那個重複出現的名詞，椅子屬於「物」，使用 which。

(3) 合併句子時，先將主要子句抄下來，再將形容詞子句抄在後面。

(4) 由於重複的名詞（The chair）位在受詞的位置，合併句子時需將 which 提前，緊連著要代替的 which，另外 sit upon（坐上…之上）中的「介係詞」upon，須放在關代之前。

註：連接詞的種類、位置、是否要搭配逗號都要看連接詞的特性決定，本單元僅介紹的關係代名詞的用法。

文學經典重現  Track37

Oh God! what could I do? I foamed –I raved –I swore! I swung the chair upon which I had been sitting, and grated it upon the boards, but the noise arose over all and continually increased. It grew louder – louder –louder! And still the men chatted pleasantly, and smiled. Was it possible they heard not? Almighty God! –no, no! They heard! –they suspected! –they knew! –they were making a mockery of my horror!-this I thought, and this I think.

老天，我該怎麼做？我胡言亂語、咆哮咒罵，拿著剛坐著的椅子亂揮，敲打著地板，但吵雜只是更大聲了，越來越大，越來越大，而那些人卻聊地更開心，還面帶微笑。他們可能會沒聽到嗎？我的老天，不可能，他們聽到了，而且起疑心了，他們知道了，他們現在是在嘲諷我啊，我這麼想，我是這麼想的。

單字小解

1. chat *v.* 閒聊
2. mockery *n.* 嘲弄

 馬里蘭州必看必去

到這除了來看愛倫坡之家暨博物館（The Edgar Allan Poe House and Museum）和普瑞特圖書館（Enoch Pratt Free Library）裡的愛倫坡室(the Edgar Allan Poe Room)以外，也不要錯過看看位於巴爾的摩的巴爾的摩城市生活博物館、馬里蘭歷史協會，以及巴爾的摩美術館等地方，來趟深度馬里蘭文化之旅；這裡的戶外活動也很多元，如划船、健行、野餐、露營和釣魚。

美國 波士頓女巫博物館
Witch Museums, Boston, the United States

霍桑《紅字》 *The Scarlet Letter* Track38

Such helpfulness was found in her—so much power to do, and power to sympathise—that many people refused to interpret the scarlet A by its original signification. They said that it meant Able, so strong was Hester Prynne, with a woman's strength.

—— Nathaniel Hawthorne, *The Scarlet Letter*

　　紅字不再帶有原來的意義，而是成為她行動的力量，同情的力量。她終於得以發揮她助人的長處，她是那麼有力量，同情的力量，於是人們不願意把紅字A當成原來的意思。他們說那是指行動的力量，也說是海斯特具有女性特有的堅強。

—— 霍桑《紅字》

PART 1 歐洲篇
PART 2 美洲篇
PART 3 亞洲篇

文學景點巧巧說

《紅字》（*The Scarlet Letter*）和巫術(witchcraft)、巫女(witch)有很深的淵源，據說本書作者霍桑的祖先威廉霍桑（William Hathorne）【註：霍桑(Hawthorne)多了 w。】曾判一名貴格會（Quaker）的女性徒遊街鞭打的刑罰；而威廉霍桑的兒子則曾在賽勒姆（Salem）主持巫女的審判大會，其中遭他判死刑的女子甚至向霍桑的家族下詛咒（curse）。姑且不論這詛咒是真是假，但這倒是成了霍桑筆下的故事。賽勒姆位於美國麻薩諸塞州東北部，由於 1692 年的巫女審判大會（trials），這地方成了有名的巫女城（Witch City）。賽勒姆在 18 與 19 世紀時是座有名的海港，如今則為世界公認深具美國歷史文化的地方。每年約有百萬名遊客造訪此地，逛逛這裡的博物館、歷史遺跡和景點，其中還包括霍桑的出生地、他曾工作的地方：賽勒姆海關大樓（the Salem Customhouse），還有女巫博物館（witch museums）呢。《紅字》一書探討身為人都會碰到的情感、罪惡、責罰、復仇等的考驗，書中的女主角海斯特白蘭雖然遭世人（當時的清教徒）指責犯下通姦罪（adultery），胸口被迫繡上代表通姦的大寫 A 字母，甚至過著與世隔絕的生活，她卻依然堅強地活著，勇敢面對自己的罪，且隨著時間過去，人們也感受到她善良的本性，甚至 A 的意涵也成了 Able，或許從這裡看得到人性並非全然邪惡，時間會帶來改變。本引言與稍後的文學經典重現（英文部分）取自 Lovell brothers & Company, 1851 出版的 *The Scarlet Letter*。

揭開序幕小對話

One of Hayley and Isaac's leisure activities is to watch Travel and Living Channel together. They share their opinions about culture, food, and people. This afternoon, they are immersed themselves into the fascinating history of witch and witchcraft in Salem, Boston. With a strong obsession with magic, Issac is all eyes and ears.

　　空閒時，海莉跟伊薩克喜歡的休閒活動之一是看旅遊生活頻道，他們會互相分享文化、食物、風土民情，今天下午他們沉浸在波士頓，賽勒姆的的女巫歷史故事中，著迷魔法的伊撒克全神貫注的看著。

Hayley: Look at the Salem Witch Museum. The tourism industry in Boston is thriving.

海莉：你看賽勒姆的女巫城，波士頓的旅遊產業正在蓬勃的發展呢。

Isaac: That's true. People are always fascinated with the supernatural power. For witches, we not only fear them but are also enchanted by them.

伊撒克：真的，大家都被超自然的能力所吸引，以女巫來說好了，我們儘管怕她們，但同時也對她們感到著迷。

Hayley: Hey, we have never been to Boston before. That could be our next vacation spot.

海莉：嘿，我們從來沒有去過波士頓，下次去旅行的景點就是它了。

Isaac: Let's do it then. I have always wanted to pay a visit to the hometown of Hawthorne.

伊撒克：就這麼定了，我一直都想去霍桑的家鄉走走看看。

Hayley: The writer of *The Scarlet Letter?* The story impressed me a lot.

海莉：是《紅字》的作者嗎？那個故事讓我很難忘。

Isaac: You are right. The story is about a woman, named Hester, with a scarlet letter A on her breast.

伊撒克：沒錯，故事是關於一位名叫海斯特的女子，她的胸口有一個紅字 A。

Hayley: Letter A stands for adultery. It's her punishment. Even so, she accepted the sin, helping others who were in need. The humility she showed turned the meaning of scarlet letter A for herself. **The scarlet A became her power to do and to sympathize, replacing its original meaning** Finally, the letter A changed it meaning from adultery to able, indicating a woman who possessed female strength. This is my favorite part.

Isaac: People forgaves her. Anyway, it's easier to love than to hate.

海莉：字母 A 代表通姦，這是她受到的處罰。儘管如此，她接受自己的罪過，並且開始從事慈善事業，她謙遜的態度改變了世人對紅字 A 的觀感，紅字不再帶有原來的意義，而是成為她行動的力量，同情的力量。最後字母 A 的意義從通姦變成力量，代表女性的力量，這是我最喜歡的部分。

伊撒克：眾人原諒她了，不管怎樣，比起恨，愛其實更容易。

 好好用單字、片語

1. witchcraft *n.* 巫術
2. obsession *n.* 著迷
3. develop *v.* 發展
4. supernatural *adj* 超自然的
5. enchant *v.* 使…入迷
6. adultery *n.* 通姦
7. sin *n.* 罪、過錯
8. in need 需要幫助的
9. be fascinated with *phr.* 對…著迷。英文意思為 to be attracted by someone or something with special quality，受到神祕的力量、人物魅力等等而著迷之意。

例 ❶ I think it's human nature to be fascinated with whatever they don't have.

我覺得人就是會對得不到的東西著迷。

❷ How can I not be fascinated with and attracted to my boss, a man who is charming and looks like the movie star, Chris Evans.

跟一個有魅力又長得像演員克里斯·埃文斯的老闆共事，怎麼能不受吸引跟為之著迷呢。

10. all eyes and ears *phr.* 全神貫注。英文意思為 to listen and watch eagerly and carefully。可以搭配 be 動詞，例如: I am all eyes and ears。或是如同下列例句，放在句中當作副詞。

例 ❶ The detector, all eyes and ears, is watching, trying to find clues to the murderer's identity.

那位偵探全神貫注的看著，試著找出能診斷出兇手身分的線索。

❷ The audience watches the magic show with all eyes and ears.

觀眾全神貫注的看著魔術秀。

文學佳句怎麼用

The scarlet A became her power to do and to sympathize, replacing its original meaning.

紅字不再帶有原來的意義，而是成為她行動的力量，同情的力量。

become 的用法

➤ become *v.* 變得、成為。文法上 become 屬於連綴動詞（ linking verb ）。

➤ 最常見的連綴動詞即為 be 動詞，後面需接補語，補與可以以名詞或是形容詞的的方式呈現。

句型 1 ：主詞+become+名詞

例 ❶ The scarlet A became her power.
紅字 A 成為她的力量。

❷ Mandy is learning to become a lawyer.
曼蒂在學習成為一位律師。

句型 2 ：主詞+become+形容詞

例 ❶ Lisa became tired.
麗莎累了。

❷ It is becoming harder and harder to live on a waiter's salary.
要靠服務生的薪水越來越難過生活了。

不定詞的用法

不定詞就是〔to＋動詞〕，這個 to 會夾在兩個動詞之間當做橋樑，形成〔動詞＋to＋動詞〕的句型，但是不要以為出現 to 就代表不定詞，to 這個字有很多功能，其中一個為不動詞：

例 ❶：He travels to Taiwan to see his parents.

　　　　動詞　　　　　+不定詞

　　　　(1)　　　　　　(2)

(1) travel 本身為動詞，to 為表示方向的介系詞，後面直接接地點 Taiwan。
Travel to Taiwan 可是為一個動詞片語，本質上即為動詞。

(2) to 夾在兩個動詞中間時，即扮演不定詞的角色，英文意思為 in order to，
表是目的之意，中文要翻譯成「為了要」。

例 ❷：The scarlet A became her power to do and to sympathize.

　　　　動詞　　　　　　　　+不定詞 1　　　　+不定詞 2

　　　　(1)　　　　　　　　　　　　(2)

(1) became 在此為連綴動詞的用法，後需接補語，才算完整呈現語意，became
her power 在此視為一個動詞片語。

(2) 不定詞的句型為 to+動詞。to do 以及 to sympathize 使用〔連接詞〕and 連
接後，一同說明前面的 her power。To 在本句中一樣有 in order to，為了要
完成…事件的意思，但是中文翻譯不需要特地翻出來，翻成「行動以及同
情的力量」即可，畢竟這樣的力量就是能讓主角「去行動、去憐憫」，
「為了要」的意思已經涵蓋其中了。

 文學經典重現 Track39

　　In such emergencies Hester's nature showed itself warm and rich –a
well-spring of human tenderness, unfailing to every real demand, and in-
exhaustible by the largest. Her breast, with its badge of shame, was but the
softer pillow for the head that needed one. She was self-ordained a Sister
of Mercy, or, we may rather say, the world's heavy hand had so ordained
her, when neither the world nor she looked forward to this result. The let-

ter was the symbol of her calling. **Such helpfulness was found in her—so much power to do, and power to sympathise—that many people refused to interpret the scarlet A by its original signification. They said that it meant Able, so strong was Hester Prynne, with a woman's strength.**

就是在情急時，海斯特展現了她溫暖的本性和她源源不絕的溫柔，從不吝於回應他人的需求。標上恥辱的胸口，對於那些需要協助的人們來說，有如柔軟的枕頭。她成了慈悲的姊妹，不，我們寧可說是現世賦予她的責任，就算這個現世和她從來沒想過這樣的事會發生。那個字母象徵她的責任，她終於得以發揮她助人的長處，她是那麼有力量，同情的力量，於是人們不願意把紅字**A**當成原來的意思。他們說那是指行動的力量，也說是海斯特具有女性特有的堅強。

單字小解

1. emergencies *n.* 緊急狀況
2. badge *n.* 徽章
3. ordain *v.* 注定

波士頓必看必去

到波士頓就要造訪自由之路（Freedom Trail）、波士頓國家歷史公園(Boston National Historical park)和波士頓美術館等地，尤其是自由之路，因為這裡涵蓋了16 個點，如波士頓公園、麻薩諸塞州議會大廈、老街角書店（Old Corner Bookstore）等地，走完這 16 個景點，就像親自經歷了一場美國獨立的過程。

美國 密蘇里州
Missouri, the United States

 Track40

馬克吐溫《哈克歷險記》 *The Adventures of Huckleberry Finn*

Goodness gracious, is dat you, Huck? En you ain' dead—you ain' drownded—you's back agin? It's too good for true, honey, it's too good for true.

—— Jim in Mark Twain, *The Adventures of Huckleberry Finn*

天啊，哈克，真的是你嗎？你沒死，沒有淹死又回來了啊？真是好到不可思議了，不可思議啊。

——馬克吐溫《哈克歷險記》中的吉姆

文學景點巧巧說

　　馬克吐溫（Mark Twain）本名塞繆克萊門斯（Samuel Clemens），《湯姆歷險記》（*The Adventures of Tom Sawyer*）和《哈克歷險記》（*The Adventures of Huckleberry Finn*）是他最有名的兩部作品，改編後的作品不計其數，在《湯姆歷險記》中，湯姆和其他玩伴間的趣事層出不窮，加上尋寶歷險的元素，激起不少小讀者感動與共鳴。1884 年，《哈克歷險記》出版，延續湯姆與哈克間的尋寶冒險，並生動描述哈克與黑人吉姆（Jim）之間的友誼，兩人各自在逃離的路上碰上彼此，患難見真情，孩童的純真超越當時黑白人種之分，讀者在閱讀同時也不禁聯想起當時特殊的時代背景：盛行於美國南方的奴隸制度（slavery），那時的黑人奴隸經常受到不平等且殘酷的對待，最終觸發為期四年（1861~1865）的南北戰爭（The Civil War）。希望能逃到自由州的黑奴吉姆遇上哈克，兩人便合作一同沿著密西西比河（the Mississippi River）展開驚險重重的逃亡之旅，哈克也在這段過程中，逐漸了解吉姆的真性情。哈克和吉姆間的互動也成了有趣的對比，相較起哈克必須從經驗與學習才懂得達禮，吉姆對待人處事卻一視同仁，渾然天成，這不是人們才該學習的典範嗎？馬克吐溫獨特的口語化風格在本引言中表露無遺，也替他奠定文壇不可取代的地位。馬克吐溫的少年時期在漢尼伯（Hannibal）度過，這裡位於密蘇里州（Missouri）東北部，密蘇里河與密西西比河分別流經該州的西境與東境，來這可以看看馬克吐溫的兒時故居，或是參觀馬克吐溫洞（Mark Twain Cave Complex），來趟歷史之旅，逛逛馬克吐溫小說裡提到的地點；也可以搭乘馬克吐溫號（Mark Twain Riverboat），享受美好的密西西比河風光。本引言與稍後的文學經典重現（英文部分）取自 United Holdings Group, 2010 出版之 *The Adventures of Huckleberry Finn*。

PART 1 歐洲篇

PART 2 美洲篇

PART 3 亞洲篇

 揭開序幕小對話

　　Carlos believes that traveling by walking can be the best way to find the beauty of the place. Alisa can't agree him more; yet, the price Carlos and Alisa have to pay is the sore legs that are killing them.

　　卡洛斯深信以行走的方式去旅行最可以看遍美景，愛麗莎也非常同意他的觀點，但是走路逛景點的代價是痠到快受不了的雙腿。

Alisa: Carlos, I am thinking if we can continue our trip by traveling on a riverboat to explore the Mississippi River.

愛麗莎：卡洛斯，我在想我們能不能以搭船的方式繼續我們的旅程，探訪密西西比河呢？

Carlos: That's what I was planning before you just said it. I am tired of walking.

卡洛斯：在你提議之前我也是這麼想的，真的走太多路了。

Alisa: Then we can drop by Hannibal where we can visit Mark Twain Boyhood Home and Museum.

愛麗莎：搭著船，我們可以在漢尼伯停一下，看看馬克吐溫小時候的家還有博物館。

Carlos: We surely will. How can I miss the chance to follow the literary giant's footsteps and. This could be a trip I will treasure forever.

卡洛斯：我們一定要的，這位大文豪走過的足跡，怎麼能錯過呢，這趟旅程一定讓我終生難忘。

Alisa: Don't exaggerate so much.

愛麗莎：你太誇張了。

Carlos: Sorry. I become too excited when I get tired.

(On a riverboat, while Alisa and Carlos are enjoying the speed of boat ride and the beauty of riverside, a man's screaming drew their attention. The woman held a little boy tightly, and cried.)

Man: Goodness gracious! Is dat you, Huck? And you ain't dead-you are not drowned. You're back? It's too good for true, honey, it's too good for true.

(Alisa and Carlos looked at each other in astonishment. It seems that they were thinking the same thing.)

Carlos: Are they shooting a movie, *The Adventures of Huckleberry Finn?*

Alisa: No way! Wait! I might have seen the little boy in the latest movie. Let's go and see if we could ask the movie stars for autographs.

卡洛斯：抱歉啦，我每次都會累到太興奮。

（在船上，當艾麗莎與卡洛斯正在享受速度與河岸美景時，一陣男人的尖叫聲吸引了他們的注意，那位女子緊抓住一位小男孩哭喊著。）

男人：天啊，哈克，真的是你嗎？你沒死，沒有淹死又回了啊？真是好到不可思議了，不可思議啊。

（愛麗莎與卡洛斯驚訝的看著彼此，兩人似乎在想著同一件事。）

卡洛斯：他們在拍《頑童流浪記》這部電影嗎？

愛麗莎：怎麼可能！等等！我好像在最近的電影中看過那個小男孩，我們過去湊熱鬧看看能不能拿到電影明星的簽名照吧。

好好用單字、片語

1. sore *adj.* 痠痛的

2. continue *v.* 繼續

3. tired *adj.* 疲倦的

4. literary giant *n.* 大文豪

5. treasure *v.* 珍藏

6. exaggerate *v.* 誇張

7. shoot *v.* 拍攝（電影等）

8. autograph *n.* 簽名照

9. pay the price *phr.* 付出代價，英文意思為 accept the bad results of what you have done，也就是承擔自己所造成的苦果，通常在使用 pay the price 時，也會描述到自己曾經做過的怎樣的事，因此導致負面的結果。

   例 ❶ The educator sees that many parents pay the price of over parenting.

   那位教育家看到很多家長為了過度照顧孩子付出代價。

   ❷ The irresponsible father abandoned his children when he was in twenties, and now he gets old and ill. He's paying the price.

   那個不負責任的爸爸在二十幾歲時拋棄自己的孩子，又老又病的他，現在付出代價了。

10. drop by *phr.* 順道拜訪（人或地方）。英文意思為 pay an informal visit to some place or people，拜訪某個地方或親戚朋友等，但是這趟旅程是順道去的，而不是特地去的。

    例 ❶ Why don't you two drop by my house this afternoon and have some home-made cake?

    何不下午時順道來我家並嚐嚐家常蛋糕呢？

    ❷ Linda decided to drop by the city hall to see her old colleagues.

    琳達決定順道去市政府看看她以前的同事們。

文學佳句怎麼用

Goodness gracious! Is dat you, Huck? And you ain't dead-you are not drowned. You're back? It's too good for true, honey, it's too good for true.

天啊，哈克，真的是你嗎？你沒死，沒有淹死又回了啊？真是好到不可思議了，不可思議啊。

口語與書面語之比較**在本質上**，說出去的話就像潑出去的水，覆水難收，而寫下的字詞，卻可以修正修改，如同世界上的各種語言，書面語總比口語較為正式。

書面語文體常見於：學術文章報告或求職信等。

口語文體常見於：網路社群軟體的聊天、電影以及影集或是小說（口語譯成書面語的形式）中的對話、或朋友間的聊天，以上的場合都是在聊天雙方是朋友、或是很熟悉的關係。

在使用上，說話筆寫字快，因此在英語口語中，以「發音快速」為原則，常常會有「簡化發音」的情形，「句子的長度」也會比書面語還要「短」，另外「說話的語氣」也能改變語意。

口語	書面文字	口語特徵解析
Goodness gracious!	-	在英語口語中，表示驚訝時常會使用 " Goodness gracious!" 或是 "Goodness me!"，中文翻譯為「天啊」。
Is dat you?	Is that you?	口語的表達需要快，所以在發音上，常會「跟前面的音節連在一起」，Is 的尾音為有聲子音[z]，而 that 的起頭音為[ð]，在發音上由於舌頭需置於牙齒中間，為求快速，將[ð]簡化為[d]。
And you ain't dead-you are not drowned.	And you are not dead-you are not drowned.	(1)同樣的以「發音快速」為原則，ain't 為 am not; are not; is not 的縮寫。 (2)破折號（——），用來表示說話的間歇（interruption），可以用來連接兩個句子。

PART 1 歐洲篇
PART 2 美洲篇
PART 3 亞洲篇

You're back?	You are back.	(1)通常在書面語中，"You are back." 屬於肯定句，表示說話者對於某事件的肯定。但是在口語中，同樣的 "You are back?" 只需將「語氣上揚」即可以表示說話者的疑問。 (2)快速至上原則，You are 縮寫為 You're。

 文學經典重現 Track41

Goodness gracious, is dat you, Huck? En you ain' dead—you ain' drownded-you's back agin? It's too good for true, honey, it's too good for true. Lemme look at you chile, lemme feel o' you. No, you ain' dead! you's back agin, 'live en soun', jis de same ole Huck—de same ole Huck, thanks to goodness!

天啊，哈克，真的是你嗎？你沒死，沒有淹死又回了啊？真是好到不可思議了，不可思議啊。天啊，哈克，真的是你嗎？你沒死，沒有淹死又回了啊？真是好到不可思議了，不可思議啊。讓我看看你的的樣子，好好看看你，真的，你沒死，還好好地活著，還是那個原來的哈克，感謝老天！

單字小解

1. dat = that
2. ain't = is/ are not
3. chile = child
4. lemme = let me
5. live en soun = alive and sound

來到密蘇里必看必去

　　既然密蘇里州和馬克吐溫有不淺的淵源，來這當然就要來趟馬克吐溫深度之旅，就從搭乘馬可吐溫號、欣賞密西西比河的景色開始吧；或是參觀馬克吐溫洞，想像一趟冒險之旅就要展開。另外還要拜訪聖路易市兒童博物館（City Museum）、聖路易市蝴蝶館（Sophia M Sachs Butterfly House & Educational Center）、密蘇里植物園（The Missouri Botanical Garden）等必去景點，為自己留下美好的回憶。

PART 1 歐洲篇

PART 2 美洲篇

PART 3 亞洲篇

MEMO

美國 麻州新伯福
New Bedford, Massachusetts, the United States

梅爾維爾《白鯨記》 *Moby Dick* Track42

" *Consider the subtleness of the sea; how its most dreaded creatures glide under water, unapparent for the most part, and treacherously hidden beneath the loveliest tints of azure.* "

—— Herman Melville, *Moby Dick*

想想這大海的存在多麼微妙，多少看不見的可怕生物悠游其中，狡猾地藏匿在美麗的深藍色裡。

——梅爾維爾《白鯨記》

文學景點巧巧說

　　看到《白鯨記》這故事名稱會讓你聯想到什麼？一定少不了鯨魚（whale），還有大海吧。《白鯨記》1851 年 10 月首次於英國發行時，書名為 *The Whale*，同年 11 月於美國出版後則改為 Moby Dick；作者赫曼梅爾維爾（Herman Melville）不但是美國知名作家，他還曾經做過水手，當年出海的經驗也成了日後書寫《白鯨記》的靈感。他第一次的捕鯨之行是在新伯福港（New Bedford harbor）出發，新伯福是美國麻薩諸塞州（Massachusetts）南部最大城市，在梅爾維爾那年代，也就是 19 世紀中葉時，捕鯨業（whaling）興盛，這段背景也寫在《白鯨記》裡，書中的主角以實瑪利（Ishmael）紐約出身，就像當時大多的小夥子一樣，對海岸生活不感興趣，而萌生出海探險的念頭，於是跑來新伯福，計畫搭上前往南塔基特島（Nantucket）的捕鯨船，但最先是錯過了，便在新伯福住了幾晚。主角也提到，儘管新伯福逐漸成為壟斷捕鯨業的大城，但南塔基特島的重要性也不可小覷，「是美洲死鯨沖到沙灘上的地點，而那些捕鯨的紅皮膚土著居民最先登上獨木舟去追捕海洋裡龐然大物的，不都是從南塔基特動身的嗎？」，事實上，南塔基特島也是埃塞克斯捕鯨號（The Essex, an American whaleship）主要的停泊港。1820 年，該船遭抹香鯨（sperm whale）在大西洋攻擊而沉沒，是另一段成為故事靈感的真實事件。現在在南塔基特有一座南塔基特捕鯨博物館（the Nantucket Whaling Museum），該博物館由南塔基特歷史協會（the Nantucket Historical Association）所經營，來到這裡不能錯過精采的導覽行程；而隔壁還有歷史悠久的蠟燭工廠（the candle factory），那裡的柱子長年積累沾染抹香鯨油，天氣炎熱時會散發溫暖的香氣。《白鯨記》與人、自然有關，講人對大自然的剝奪、剝削，像是取得抹香鯨油來獲取利益。大自然、海洋是深不可測的，就樣這段引言所說，有看不見的可怕生物潛伏其中，人類必須要學會懂得尊敬大自然的力量，切莫忘了大自然也會有反撲的一天。本引言與稍後的文學經典重現（英文部分）取自 new American library, 1892 所出版的 *Moby Dick*。

PART 1 歐洲篇

PART 2 美洲篇

PART 3 亞洲篇

 揭開序幕小對話

Alisa and Carlos are always the best partners for each other for the overseas trips. If one day you found out they are in an exotic land, you don't have to be surprised. Traveling abroad is as normal as going to a coffee shop for them. Inside the Nantucket Whaling Museum, Alisa and Carlos are watching the giant skeleton of a sperm whale.

愛麗莎與卡洛斯互為彼此最好的旅遊伴侶，如果有一天你發現他們人在國外，你一點也不需要驚訝，對他們來說，出國旅遊就像去咖啡廳一樣稀鬆平常。在南塔基特捕鯨博物館裡，艾麗莎與卡洛斯正在觀賞一座巨大的抹香鯨骨骸。

Alisa: The huge bone reminds me of *Moby Dick* written by Herman Melville.

愛麗莎：這巨大的骨骸讓我想到赫曼‧梅爾維爾的《白鯨記》。

Carlos: Melville created Moby Dick, an undefeatable and threatening whale for every whaler. Moby Dick is the incarnation of evil.

卡洛斯：梅爾維爾創造了莫比迪這個角色，一個對每位捕鯨人來說無法摧毀並令人懼怕的大白鯨，莫比迪根本就是邪惡的化身。

Alisa: I know. And Ahab, a captain and a whaler, lost his leg and sought revenge on Moby Dick. Besides the story itself, the author also provided detailed information about whaling. That's why I love this book so much, very informative.

愛麗莎：我知道這個故事，亞哈船長，同時也是位捕鯨人，失去了一條腿，並向莫比迪尋仇。除了故事情節之外，作者在故事中也提供了關於捕鯨的詳細知識，這是我喜歡這個故事的原因，有很多資訊在裡頭。

Carlos: "Consider how subtle the sea is; how the most dread creatures swim under it, not seen and treacherously hidden beneath the loveliest tints of azure." This is my favorite quote from the novel.

卡洛斯：「想想這大海的存在多麼微妙，多少看不見的可怕生物悠游其中，狡猾地藏匿在美麗的深藍色裡。」這是我最喜歡書中的一句話。

Alisa: Nice quote. I like the idea of danger in disguise.

愛麗莎：引言引得不錯，我喜歡暗藏的危機這個概念。

（While Alisa and Carlos are talking about life philosophy, a group of elementary students is approaching and a guide is explaining how whaler hunts whales for meat, oil, and blubber to make profit and is trying to raise concern about environment protection.）

（當愛麗莎與卡洛斯大談人生哲理時，一群小學生往他們靠近，有一位解說員正在解說捕鯨人為了取得鯨肉、鯨油、鯨脂以取得利益而獵捕鯨魚，並試著提高環保意識。）

Alisa: How about we follow those kids?

愛麗莎：我們要不跟著這些孩子們逛吧？

Carlos: Why not? How can we miss the free guide?

卡洛斯：當然，我們怎麼能錯過免費的導覽呢？

好好用單字、片語

1. exotic *adj.* 異國的

2. giant *adj.* 巨大的

3. skeleton *n.* 骨骼

4. undefeatable *adj.* 無敵的

5. whaler *n.* 捕鯨者

6. incarnation *n.* 化身

7. informative *adj.* 資訊豐富的

8. disguise *n.* 偽裝

9. remind of *phr.* 使回想起。mind *v.* 注意、留心，英文意思為 think、be concerned，思考或在乎的意思。字首 re- 有重複之意。兩者合一，remind 有提醒，也就是讓否人回想起已經提過的事情。

    例 ❶ It's ridiculous that you remind me of something you never told me in the first place.

    你提醒了我你從沒告訴我的事情很可笑。

    ❷ The terrible relationship between my family and I reminds me of my own fragility.

    跟家人糟糕的關係讓我想起自己的脆弱。

10. seek revenge on somebody *phr.* 對⋯復仇。Making somebody suffer because they did the same to you，由於某人曾經加害於你，因此決定復仇。對話中的 sought 為 seek 的過去式。

➤ 類似的片語：seek revenge against someone/ take revenge on somebody.

    例 ❶ If the King is not killed, he will seek revenge on you.

    如果國王沒有死，他會向你復仇。

    ❷ The spirit cursed princess is too disabled to seek revenge on them even in the afterlife.

    那位被詛咒的公主的靈魂已經傷得太重，無法對任何人復仇，甚至連來生也沒法了。

文學佳句怎麼用

Consider how subtle the sea is; how the most dread creatures swim under it, not seen and treacherously hidden beneath the loveliest tints of azure.

想想這大海的存在多麼微妙,想想這海裡有多少看不見的可怕生物悠游其中,狡猾地藏匿在美麗的深藍色裡。

強烈情緒的表達法:how 的使用

表達驚訝(surprise)、驚喜(pleasure)等較為強烈的情緒時,使用 how,標點符號可以使用驚嘆號(!),常見的句型有:

1. [How＋形容詞]

   How amazing!多麼美麗啊!

   How ridiculous!太可笑了!

2. [How＋形容詞＋主詞＋動詞]

   Imagine how brutal and violent the enemies are!

   想想我們的敵軍是多麼殘忍又暴力!

   How subtle the sea is.

   大海真微妙啊。

3. [How ＋主詞＋動詞]

   秘訣:只要將 **How** 直接加在一般句子前就可以表示你的強力情緒了。

   How I wished I hadn't been there!

   我真希望我從沒有到那裡。

   How the most dread creatures glide under it

   這海裡有多少最令人懼怕的生物悠游其中。

強烈情緒的表達法：使用形容詞最高級

表達驚訝或驚喜之情時，除了使用 how 來加強語氣，若在句子中加上「形容詞最高級」，句的強度又更一上層樓了。試比較下列例句，感受情緒強度的差別。

 ❶ How expensive the designer handbag is.

這款設計師的手提包實在太貴了

❷ How the most expensive designer handbag is displayed in window.

最高貴的設計師的手提包竟然就這樣陳列在櫥窗中。

 文學經典重現 🄯 Track43

Consider the subtleness of the sea; how its most dreaded creatures glide under water, unapparent for the most part, and treacherously hidden beneath the loveliest tints of azure. Consider also the devilish brilliance and beauty of many of its most remorseless tribes, as the dainty embellished shape of many species of sharks. Consider, once more, the universal cannibalism of the sea; all whose creatures prey upon each other, carrying on eternal war since the world began. Consider all this; and then turn to this green, gentle, and most docile earth; consider them both, the sea and the land; and do you not find a strange analogy to something in yourself? For as this appalling ocean surrounds the verdant land, so in the soul of man there lies one insular Tahiti, full of peace and joy, but encompassed by all the horrors of the half known life. God keep thee! Push not off from that isle, thou canst never return!

想想這大海的存在多麼微妙，多少看不見的可怕生物悠游其中，狡猾地藏匿在美麗的深藍色裡。想想這些美麗又危險的生物、那些雄偉壯觀的鯊魚；再仔細想想這海裡的肉食生物，牠們視對方為獵物，展開永無止盡的爭搶。然後再看看綠油油柔軟溫和的大地，再把大海和路地拿來比比，你沒發現這兩者間相似的地方嗎？

這塊大地周圍是這嚇人的海洋，人們的心中都有座平靜和樂的大溪地島，然而四周卻瀰漫著對未知生命的恐懼。上帝保佑，別離開這座島，因為你可能永遠都回不來了。

單字小解

1. .tint *n.* 色彩
2. .azure *n.* 蔚藍色
3. .cannibalism *n.* 食肉
4. .analogy *n.* 比喻
5. .appalling *adj.* 嚇人的
6. .verdant *adj.* 翠綠的

來到美國麻州必看必去

　　延續第 23 單元波士頓必看必去的景點，來到麻州還要看看鱈魚角（Cape Cod）、瑪莎葡萄園（Mathar's Vinyard），還有普羅溫斯敦（Provincetown）；其中鱈魚角的地形特殊，從地圖上看起來像是勾起的尾巴，在歷史上也有特殊的第位，1602 年，巴塞洛繆·戈斯諾德（Bartholomew Gosnold）將此地命名為鱈魚角；這裡是美國唯一僅存且是排名第九古老的英國地名；之後塞繆爾·尚普蘭（Samuel de Champlain）於 1614 年將這泥沙淤積的地方繪製城地圖，亨利·哈德遜（Henry Hudson）則在 1609 年底達此地。約翰·史密斯（John Smith）在 1614 年，於其地圖標示出這個地方，最後讓英國清教徒（the Pilgrims）進入這座港口，當時那些清教徒就是搭乘五月花號（Mayflower）在此登陸的。另外到了瑪莎葡萄園附近，可以好好欣賞港口上的小帆船風光，也要去看看觀光客最常拜訪的奧克布拉夫斯（Oak Bluffs）和愛德鎮（Edgar Town），前者的商店餐廳很多，看得到小鎮獨特的特色。普羅溫斯敦（Provincetown）是有名的同性戀村，在這的許多店門口都會插上六色彩虹旗，表達他們支持和歡迎同性戀的客人，是此地的特色之一。

Unit 26 南美洲 阿根廷布宜諾艾利斯
Buenos Aires, Argentina, South America

 Track44

波赫士《歧路花園》 *The Garden of Forking Paths*

> *Before unearthing this letter, I had questioned myself about the ways in which a book can be infinite. I could think of nothing other than a cyclic volume, a circular one.*

—— Jorge Luis Borges *The Garden of Forking Paths*

在發現這封信之前,我曾問我自己:一部書在什麼情況下才能成為無限。我認為只有一種情況,那就是循環不息,周而復始。

—— 波赫士《歧路花園》

文學景點巧巧說

　　一本書的無限（an infinite book）？迷宮（labyrinth）、書和迷宮的關係？本次引言（取自 *Labyrinths* 一書，出版社：New Direction，出版日期為 2007 年，5 月17日）帶讀者來到南美洲阿根廷首都：布宜諾艾利斯（Buenos Aires），也就是作者波赫士（Jorge Luis Borges）的出生地。波赫士是一位博學多才的人物，常將真實事件混合虛幻的敘述，讓人分不清真假，這種奇幻超寫實的風格以《虛構集》（*Fictions*）與《阿萊夫》（*The Aleph*）兩部短篇集為代表，其中常見的主題是：夢、迷宮、虛構的作家、宗教等，本引言就是取自《虛構集》，篇名為《小徑分岔的花園》（*The Garden of Forking Paths*）的短篇故事，內容描述一個一戰時，住在英國的中國人俞尊（Yu Tsan），受雇德國人擔任間諜，將秘密資訊傳給德國的同時，他知道英國上尉理查馬登（Captain Richard Madden）已查到他的同伴魯伯納格（Viktor Runeberg）的住處，不久就會輪到他被逮捕了。為了在逮捕前完成任務，俞尊前去拜訪漢學家（sinologist）史蒂芬艾伯特（Stephen Albert），此人正好對俞尊的先輩崔本（Ts'ui Pên）的作品頗有研究，兩人在討論虛實難分的花園、迷宮、小説中錯綜複雜的時間觀時，俞尊藉故要求再看一次崔本的信，趁學者背對他時，殺了他，只因為這位學者的姓"艾伯特"也是俞尊最後想要提示德國應該攻擊的城市名。波赫士巧妙地將寫實的情境敘述，融合小說中無限迴圈的時間與虛實共存的特性，花園不是花園，它可能是一種虛幻的象徵。故事最後還留下一道「謎」，而答案就在名字裡。來到這裡不能錯過聖特爾莫區（San Telmo）前身為國家圖書館（the National Library）的國家音樂中心（the National Center of Music），波赫士曾在此工作。或是到聖馬丁廣場（Plaza San Martin），順道看看波赫士的故居（old apartments）。還有還有，位於太平洋拱廊購物中心的（Galerias Pacifico）波赫士文化中心（Centro Cultural Borges），來這可以了解波赫士的生平背景，感受波赫士宇宙般（cosmic）的宏觀氣魄吧。

揭開序幕小對話

Carlos didn't spend much time to grow up with his sister, Kate, because he left home to pursue higher education since he was eighteen.

卡洛斯並沒有花很多時間與姐姐，凱特一起長大，因為他在 18 歲時就離開家裡求學去了。

This Saturday, Carlos and Kate went back home for the Chinese New Year. Carlos actually enjoyed hanging with Kate because she is blunt and funny. She is a good listener and is good at giving advices.

這個週六，卡洛斯與凱特都回家過新年。卡洛斯其實喜歡跟姐姐聚在一起，她是個說話很直，幽默有趣的人，同時也是很好的聽眾，也很會出主意。

Kate: Carl, still working on being a great writer?

凱特：卡兒，還在努力成為一位大作家嗎？

Carlos: Of course. I will be a writer of distinction.

卡洛斯：當然，我會成為超棒的作家。

Kate: I still haven't heard of your name from any books or magazines. Is there any progress?

凱特：但是我還沒有在任何書籍或雜誌上聽說你的名字啊，最近有什麼進展嗎？

Carlos: A great writer is also a passionate reader. That's me. A great writer knows his readers' preference, like how to use five senses to intrigue them. I do go through the five senses. Most importantly, I had questioned myself about

卡洛斯：偉大的作家常常也熱愛閱讀，我就是這樣的。好的作家知道讀者的喜好，例如，在文字中喚起讀者的五種感官去吸引他們，而這些技巧我也用了。最重要的是，我一直問

the ways in which a book can be infinite.

自己，一部書在什麼情況下才能成為無限。

Kate: Sounds cool. How do you put these big ideas into practice?

凱特：聽起來很酷，那你要怎麼運用這些理想？

Carlos: I could think of nothing other than a cyclic volume, a circular one.

卡洛斯：我認為只有一種方法，那就是循環不息，周而復始。

Kate: Wow, my little brother is now a grownup and has his own thoughts.

凱特：哇，我家弟弟現在是個成熟的大人了，也很有自己的想法。

Carlos: Actually I got the inspiration by reading Jorge Luis Borges' work, the Garden of Forking Paths. People consider Jorge Luis Borges the most important writer of the 20th Century.

卡洛斯：事實上，這個靈感來自於閱讀波赫士的作品《歧路花園》，世人公認波赫士是二十世紀很有影響力的作家。

Kate: I am not a bookworm like you, but I do know Jorge Luis Borges. When I was on a business trip in Argentine, I paid a visit to National Library of Argentina, and there is a statue of him.

凱特：我這麼不愛讀書的人，我都聽過波赫士呢，我之前在阿根廷出差時，我有去那裡的國家圖書館看看，那裡還有他的雕像呢。

Carlos: I am not surprised. Argentine is the great writer's hometown. His old apartment is also well-preserved in Plaza San Martin.

卡洛斯：聽你這麼說我不意外，阿根廷是這位偉大作家的家鄉，他的故居在聖馬丁廣場被保存了下來。

Kate: I believe he is and will always be the most influential writer now and forever.

凱特：我相信他對以前的、未來的作家都將非常有影響力。

 好好用單字、片語

1. pursue *v.* 從事、追尋
2. higher education *n.* 高等教育
3. blunt *adj.* 直白的
4. distinction *n.* 突出的
5. intrigue *v.* 激起…的好奇心
6. bookworm *n.* 喜愛讀書者
7. influential *adj.* 具有影響力的
8. grownup *n.* 成年人
9. is good at *phr.* 擅長於

    例 ❶ Being good at communication is one of the important traits for a leader.

    擅長溝通是領導者的重要特質之一。

    ❷ Most of football players are better at one skill, but Danny is good at all skills.

    大部分的美式足球員在技巧上都有特別突出的地方，但是丹尼卻是全方位地出眾。

10. hear of *phr.* 聽說過，英文意思為 be told about something，也就是聽別人說某某消息之意。

    例 ❶ Have you ever heard of the economic depression in 1930?

    你有聽過 1930 年的經濟蕭條時期嗎？

    ❷ Derek felt sorry to hear of his cousin who died young in an accident.

    德瑞克聽說自己的表親年紀輕輕死於意外，他感到遺憾。

文學佳句怎麼用

Before unearthing this letter, I had questioned myself about the ways in which a book can be infinite. I could think of nothing other than a cyclic volume, a circular one.

在發現這封信之前，我曾問我自己：一部書在什麼情況下才能成為無限。我認為只有一種情況，那就是循環不息，周而復始。

介係詞 before 的用法

Before *prep.* 在⋯之前，在引言中，before 當作介系詞使用，表達動作的在⋯時間之前，相反詞為 after (prep.) 在⋯之後，介系詞後面需接動名詞，句型為 before/after doing something。

例 ❶ After mopping the floor, the housemaid went to clean the bathroom.

拖完地後，管家去洗浴室。

❷ To help kids maintain healthy toileting patterns, parents should encourage them to empty the bladder before going to sleep.

為幫助孩子維持健康的上廁所習慣，父母應該要鼓勵孩子在睡覺前去上廁所。

PART 1 歐洲篇

PART 2 美洲篇

PART 3 亞洲篇

介係詞 before 表達位置的先後

例 Please put the files in an alphabetical order, for example, D should come before E.

請把檔案以字母的順序排列，例如，字母 D 需在字母 E 之前。

before/after 也可以當連接詞，表達事件發生的時間先後順序

例 <u>Before I unearthed this letter</u>, <u>I had questioned myself about the ways in which</u>

             (a)   (b)

<u>a book can be infinite</u>.

(a) 表達時間先後的副詞子句

(b) 主要句子

    比較 after/before 當連接詞或介系詞的用法表達「我搬出公寓後，我就必須再找新的室友了。」的語意，可以有兩種說法：

(1) 使用 after 當作連接詞，形成修是主要句子的副詞子句。

    <u>After I moved out of the apartment</u>, I will have to find a new roommate.

(2) 使用 after 當作介系詞，形成副詞片語，修飾句子。

    <u>After moving out of the apartment</u>, I will have to find a new roommate.

來到阿根廷布宜諾利斯必看必去

阿根廷布宜諾斯艾利斯（Buenos Aires）有熱鬧的街頭表演、世界最寬的七九大道與建城紀念碑，你還能在這看到由劇院改建成的世界第二美書店，劇院舞台特有的挑高簾幕，遠看特別壯觀，看戲的包廂也特別保留下來，讓逛書店也感受得到特有的莊嚴氛圍，有機會一定要來逛逛啊。

MEMO

加拿大 多倫多愛德華王子島
The Prince Island National Park, Toronto, Canada

 Track45

蒙哥馬利《清秀佳人》 *Anne of Green Gables*

" *Isn't it splendid to think of all the things there are to find out about? It just makes me feel glad to be alive-it's such an interesting world. It wouldn't be half so interesting if we know all about everything, would it?* "

—— Lucy Maude Montgomery, *Anne of Green Gables*

這樣我覺得活著真是太好了，覺得這世界太有趣了。如果什麼事都知道了，趣味也會減半吧，不是嗎？

——蒙哥馬利《清秀佳人》

PART 1 歐洲篇

PART 2 美洲篇

PART 3 亞洲篇

文學景點巧巧說

　　想像力無限奔放、人與人間溫暖的互動和美麗的平原、森林、湖景風光是《清秀佳人》（也稱《紅髮安妮》、《綠色屋頂之家的安妮》）的代名詞，由加拿大小説家（novelist）蒙哥馬利（Lucy Maude Montgomery）所寫，曾改編成電視劇和卡通，其中 1985 年所拍的電視劇最讓人印象深刻，當年 17 歲的女主角梅根法蘿（Megan Follows）演技自然清新，完美詮釋書中的活潑、熱情、充滿想像力的安妮，至今依然留在無數影迷的心中。引言描述安妮對領養家庭的期待，前往新家一路上她説個沒完，一下説孤兒院的生活，一下説自己知道不可以隨便批評事情，讓來自領養家庭的大叔馬修（Matthew Cuthbert）都不知道該怎麼回話才好，可心裡卻對這個小女孩產生好感，最後成為安妮最親密的大朋友。蒙哥馬利自小在愛德華王子島（Prince Edward Island）長大，這裡是加拿大東部海洋三省之一，也是故事中綠屋（Green Gables）的所在地，來到這裡一定要來夏洛敦市（Charlotte-town），看看位於愛德華王子島國家公園內（the Prince Island National Park）的綠色小屋，認識作者長大的地方，她創作的靈感，以及她在國家與歷史上所扮演的角色，美國文豪馬克吐溫曾這麼盛讚蒙哥馬利：「她創作了自《愛麗絲夢遊仙境》的愛麗絲以來，最可愛、最討人喜歡的小説人物。」（Back in 1908, upon the publication *of Anne of Green Gables* (and with reference to Lewis Carroll's *Alice in Wonderland*), Mark Twain had written to Montgomery, saying that 'Anne is the dearest and most moving and delightful child since the immortal Alice.'-from *After Green Gables: L.M. Montgomery's Letters to Ephraim Weber, 1916-1941*）；本引言與稍後的文學經典重現(英文部分)出自Simon and Schuster, 2001所出版的 *Anne of Green Gables*。

揭開序幕小對話

　　It's Austin and Fiona's habit to go for a walk around the neighborhood they live in after dinner. Sometimes they change the route in order to find some new things. Under a clear sky with twinkling stars, Fiona no-

ticed a house with a green roof.

晚餐後到住家附近散步，是奧斯丁與費歐娜的習慣，有時候抱著發現在新奇事物的可能，他們會改變路線。在一個星斗滿天的澄淨夜晚，費歐娜注意到一座綠色屋頂的小屋。

Fiona: Could that be the Green Gables from *Anne of Green Gables?*

費歐娜：那個不就是《清秀佳人》裡的綠色屋頂之家嗎？

Austin: Are you saying a tongue twitter?

奧斯丁：你在說繞口令嗎？

Fiona: Austin! Don't make fun of me. Look at the house at the end of the street. It looks like the Green Gables in Prince Edward Island. It is where the Montgomery grew up and got inspired for the popular story.

費歐娜：奧斯丁！不准嘲笑我，你看街尾的那棟房子，很像就是愛德華王子島的綠色屋頂之家。那裡就是蒙哥馬利成長，並創作《清秀佳人》的地方。

Austin: Are you talking about the red-haired orphan named Anne who is very talkative and always energetic?

奧斯丁：你在說那個愛講話的、充滿活力的紅髮孤兒安妮嗎？

Fiona: That's right. The novel is an immediate success. Then Montgomery later created a series of sequels with Anne as the central character.

費歐娜：沒錯，這部小說一出版就廣受歡迎。後來蒙哥馬利繼續創造一系列以安妮為主角的小說。

Austin: I see. The Green Gables is now a historical landmark in Charlottetown,

奧斯丁：了解，那個綠色屋頂之家不是夏洛敦市的歷史地標

Canada. I wonder who would duplicate a house with a green roof here?

Fiona: Here comes another new thing that arouse your curiosity about the world. **Isn't it splendid to think of all the things there are to find out about? It just makes me feel glad to be alive-it's such an interesting world. It wouldn't be…**

Austin: It wouldn't be half so interesting if we know all about everything, would it?

Fiona: How do you know what I am going to say?

Austin: Cause I am your husband, your best friend, and your soul mate.

Fiona: Austin, I am greatly flattered.

Austin: Of course. Let me take you to the Charlottetown Festival where we can watch the famous musical of *Anne of Green Gables* and check out every site and shop about the beloved character, Anne.

嗎？怎麼會有人在這裡複製了一個一模一樣的？

費歐娜：今天又遇到激起你對世界好奇的新事物了，想到總有事情等著去探索不是很棒的嗎?這樣我覺得活著真是太好了，覺得這世界太有趣了。如果…

奧斯丁：如果什麼事都知道了，趣味也會減半吧，不是嗎？

費歐娜：你怎麼知道我接下來要說什麼？

奧斯丁：因為我是你的老公、你最好的朋友、你的靈魂伴侶。

費歐娜：奧斯丁，你真的讓我很開心。

奧斯丁：當然，我帶你去夏洛敦市的音樂節吧，我們可以看《清秀佳人》的音樂劇，然後到處看看關於可愛的安妮的所有景點跟商店吧。

好好用單字、片語

1. route *n.* 路

2. tongue twitter *n.* 繞口令

3. orphan *n.* 孤兒

4. talkative *adj.* 多話的

5. energetic *adj.* 有活力的

6. sequel *n.* 續集

7. duplicate *v.* 複製

8. flatter *v.* 奉承、使高興

9. make fun of *phr.* 取笑，英文意思為 to laugh at someone or something。

   例 ❶ The humorous host of Saturday Night Live is famous for making fun of famous people.

   那個周末直播節目的主持人以開名人玩笑而有名。

   ❷ The children never made fun of Tom who constantly fell asleep in class anymore because they learned that he stayed up most of the night helping taking care of his grandfather's illness.

   孩子們不再取笑湯姆了，那位總是上課睡覺的男孩，因為他們得知湯姆總是熬夜照顧患重病的爺爺。

10. arouse one's curiosity *phr.* 激起…的好奇心。arouse *v.* 激發，英文意思為 to make somebody have a particular attitude，也就是引起某人對某些事情的想法。arouse 後面一般常接的名詞有 arouse one's suspicion（激起…疑心）、arouse one's attention（引起…的注意力）、arouse one's interest（引起…的興趣）。

    註：如果引起的情緒沒有特定指人，不一定需要加上 one's，直接加上名詞也可以，例如：arouse interest.

    例 ❶ Finding some human artifacts on the higher strata arouses the archeologist's curiosity.

    在較高的地層中發現人工製品激起了那位考古學家的好奇心。

❷ Create a slogan that will arouse curiosity and interests of our potential customers.

創造一個會引起潛在顧客的好奇及興趣的廣告標語吧。

 文學佳句怎麼用

Isn't it splendid to think of all the things there are to find out about? It just makes me feel glad to be alive-it's such an interesting world. It wouldn't be half so interesting if we know all about everything, would it?

想到總有事情等著去探索不是很棒的嗎？這樣我覺得活著真是太好了，覺得這世界太有趣了。如果什麼事都知道了，趣味也會減半吧，不是嗎？

虛主詞的使用方式

(1) It 為「代名詞」，功能是代替前述的名詞片語或是一整句話，本單元介紹的 it 「放在句首當作虛主詞」，真正主詞的內容在「句尾的片語」中。

(2) 中文翻譯時，真主詞要先翻譯。

(3) It 為虛主詞的句型需搭配「形容詞」使用，對說話的人來說，「可以表達對事情的看法」，常見句型有：

　(a) It is＋形容詞＋to＋動詞（不定詞片語）

　(b) It is＋形容詞＋動詞 ing（動名詞片語）

例 ❶ It is splendid to think of all the things there are to find out about. 結構：虛主詞＋形容詞＋不定詞片語

想到總有事情等著去探索是很棒的。

❷ It is impossible preventing bad things to happen. 結構：虛主詞＋形容詞＋動名詞片語

預防壞事的發生是不可能的。

疑問詞的形成

(1) 若要將上述的肯定句改成疑問句時，需將句子（肯定句）的字序倒裝，形成「動詞＋主詞」的句型，注意要在句尾加上相應的標點符號，問號「？」。

> **例** It is splendid to think of all the things there are to find out about.（肯定句）
>
> Is it splendid to think of all the things there are to find out about?（Yes No 問句）
> 想到總有事情等著去探索不是很棒的嗎？

(2) 由「Is it...?」為首的問句又稱為「是否問句」或是「Yes No 問句」。因為當說話者這樣問時，他想聽到的回答是 Yes 或是 No，而不是想知道更多時間地點的資訊。

(3) 由「Isn't it...?」開頭的「Yes No 問句」，則有激問法的意味，中文翻譯雖與「Is it...?」相同，但是說話者的態度是有差別的，當故事的的 Anne 這麼說時，她心裡是非常認同自己這項觀點的，在說出這句話時，她在尋求聽話者的認同。Isn't it splendid to think of all the things there are to find out about?（Yes No 問句）

 文學經典重現 Track46

　　Well, that is one of the things to find out sometime. **Isn't it splendid to think of all the things there are to find out about? It just makes me feel glad to be alive-it's such an interesting world. It wouldn't be half so interesting if we know all about everything, would it?** There'd be no scope for imagination then, would there? But am I talking too much? People are always telling me I do. Would you rather I didn't talk? If you say so I'll stop. I can STOP when I make up my mind to it, although it's difficult.

　　我想有天我一定要把這事搞懂，總是有事情等著去探索不是很棒嗎？這樣我覺得活著真是太好了，覺得這世界太有趣了。如果什麼事都知道了，趣味也會減半吧，不是嗎？一點想像的空間都沒有了，不是嗎？對了，我會不會太多話了啊？總

是有人說我話很多，你會希望我別說話嗎？如果你希望如此，我一定會乖乖閉嘴，只要我下定決心，一定會馬上安靜不說話，但其實這真的不容易啊。

來到加拿大多倫多愛德華王子島必看必去

蒙哥馬利自小在愛德華王子島（Prince Edward Island）長大，這裡是加拿大東部海洋三省之一，也是故事中綠屋（Green Gables）的所在地，來到這裡一定要來夏洛敦市（Charlottetown），看看位於愛德華王子島國家公園內（the Prince Island National Park）的綠色小屋，認識作者長大的地方喔。

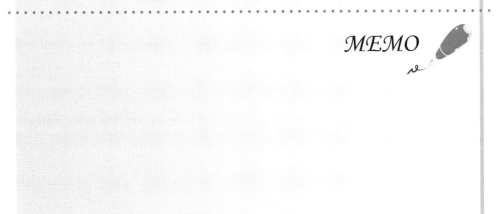

MEMO

美國 紐約哈德遜東岸斷頭谷

Sleepy Hollow, The East Coast
of Hudson Valley, the United States

 Track47

華盛頓歐文《沉睡谷傳奇》 *The Legend of Sleepy Hollow*

"*Another of his sources of fearful pleasure was to pass long winter evenings with the old Dutch wives, as they sat spinning by the fire, with a row of apples roasting and spluttering along the hearth, and listen to their marvellous tales of ghosts and goblins, and haunted fields, and haunted brooks, ... and particularly of the headless horseman, or Galloping Hessian of the Hollow, as they sometimes called him.*"

—— Washington Irving, *The Legend of Sleepy Hollow*

　　他的消遣之一就是和這些荷蘭老太太促膝長談，度過漫漫冬夜，他們會圍坐在火邊，一邊烤蘋果，一邊聽那些鬼故事、鬧鬼的房子和小溪流，尤其是無頭騎士，又叫沉睡谷的奔騰黑森軍，她們有時候是這麼叫他的。

——華盛頓歐文《沉睡谷傳奇》

220

文學景點巧巧說

《沉睡谷傳奇》（*The Legend of Sleepy Hollow*）為收錄於華盛頓歐文（Washington Irving）《見聞札記》（*A Sketch Book*）的短篇故事，同樣收錄於此書的還有著名的《李伯大夢》（*Rip van Winkle*）。《沉睡谷傳奇》故事背景設在哈德遜谷（the Hudson Valley），也就是現在一個叫斷頭谷的地方（Sleepy Hollow），位在美國紐約州威徹斯特郡（Westchester County, New York），東岸有哈德遜河（Hudson River）流經。引言描寫新來的學校教師（schoolmaster）伊克波德（Ichabod Crane）常與村民互動、交換消息，對於村民間流傳的鬼故事特別有興趣。華盛頓藉由《沉睡谷傳奇》與《李伯大夢》，將美國與英國舊時的風俗習慣和純樸的人物如實呈現在讀者面前，同樣地，透過這兩部作品，作者也試圖從前者反諷獨立革命（The Revolutionary War）後，多數民眾的生活並沒有得到改善，並從後者質疑改變與進步是否凌駕於穩定與秩序，作者先是與故事中的女主角卡翠娜（Katrina）站在同一陣線，拒絕伊克波德的追求；另外，儘管伊克波德思維進步，著迷於超自然的力量，還被村民布朗（Brom Bones）用怪力亂神的方式嚇退，似乎是想暗示追求夢想的人（dreamer）始終敵不過務實保守（practical）的思想。《沉睡谷傳奇》曾三度改成電影，最近的一次是 1999 年，由鬼才導演提姆波頓（Tim Burton）所導，男主角強尼戴普（Johnny Depp）在片中飾演斯文纖細，帶點陰柔氣息的年輕警官（police constable）；加上無頭騎士（headless horseman）來去無蹤的兇狠氣勢等服裝設計與場景布置，讓觀眾彷彿身在懸疑鬼魅的氛圍中，可見藝術團隊下了不少工夫，並在 1999 年的奧斯卡（Academy Award）獲得最佳藝術指導獎（Best Production Design）。既然真的有斷頭谷這麼一個地方，喜歡懸疑故事的遊客一定要來看看 1961 年，列為國家歷史名勝（National Historic Landmark）的老荷蘭教堂（Old Dutch Church of Sleepy Hollow），更不能錯過斷頭谷公墓（Sleepy Hollow Cemetery），看看古橋（也就是無頭騎士出沒的地方）的可能遺跡，拍張「超有氣氛」的照片，才不虛此行啦。本引言與稍後的文學經典重現（英文部分）取自 Plain Label Books, 1892所出版之 *The Legend of Sleepy Hollow*。

 揭開序幕小對話

It is a quiet night, Carlos, Isaac, and Austin went stargazing and enjoyed the wonderful night sky on a river bank. While Austin and Carlos are chatting, Isaac was enjoying the crystal-clear view of the sky in silence.

在一個寂靜的晚上，卡洛斯、伊撒克、奧斯丁在河堤上享受看星星的樂趣，當奧斯丁與卡洛斯在聊天時，伊撒克則自己默默的仰望清澈的夜空。

Austin: Do you believe in all supernatural things?

奧斯丁：你相信所有超自然的事情嗎？

Carlos: Ouch! Go away! A mosquito bit me.

卡洛斯：哎唷！走開！有蚊子咬我。

Austin: Are you listening?

奧斯丁：你有在聽嗎？

Carlos: I am sorry. Those Mosquitoes are super annoying. What did you just say?

卡洛斯：抱歉啦，這些蚊子真的超級煩人的

Austin: I recently read Washington Irving's *The Legend of Sleepy Hollow*. Although my wife thought the story is creepy, the spellbinding stories really captivate me. I stayed up the whole night reading it.

奧斯丁：我最近讀了華盛頓歐文的《沉睡谷傳奇》，雖然我老婆覺得這個故事讓人毛骨悚然，不過這引人入勝的故事完全抓住我的心，我還熬夜猛讀呢。

Carlos: I have never read it.

卡洛斯：我從沒看過。

Austin: Those spooky stories are told in countryside like where we are now. You know, those characters, **they sat by the fire, roasted apples and listened to their marvelous tales of ghosts, the haunted brooks, bridges, houses, and particularly of the headless horseman, or Galloping Hessian of the Hollow, as they sometimes called him**.

奧斯丁：那些鬼怪的故事的就是在我們身處的鄉間這樣流傳，你知道嗎，故事中的人物，他們會圍坐在火邊，一邊烤蘋果，一邊聽那些鬼故事、鬧鬼的小溪流、屋子、特別是無頭騎士，又叫來自沉睡谷的奔騰黑森軍，她們有時候是這麼叫他的。

Carlos: I don't feel like talking about it now. It's horrifying.

卡洛斯：我現在不想講這個話題，很可怕。

Austin: All right.

奧斯丁：好吧。

(After a short silence, being unaware of Carlos's loathing reaction to those "scary tales", Austin tried to bring up the conversation again with Isaac.)

（一陣寂靜過後，奧斯丁像是沒有注意到卡洛斯的對鬼怪話題的厭惡，再次把話題提起跟伊撒克討論。）

Austin: Hey, Isaac, have you been to Old Dutch Church of Sleepy Hollow in New York?

奧斯丁：嘿，伊撒克，你有聽過紐約斷頭谷的老荷蘭教堂嗎？

Isaac: No, What's special about it?

伊薩克：沒有，有什麼特別的嗎？

Austin: The author I mentioned earlier with Carlos achieved international fame by writing a scary story with supernatural elements. He was buried there.

Carlos: Austin! Enough Washington Irving! Enough supernatural stories for today! I am leaving.

奧斯丁：剛剛我跟卡洛斯提到的作者靠了寫超自然的恐怖故事在國際間走紅，他死後被埋葬在那裡。

卡洛斯：奧斯丁！夠了，今天不要再説華盛頓歐文、超自然的故事了！我要走了。

 好好用單字、片語

1. go stargazing *phr.* 去看星星
2. bank *n.* 河岸
3. supernatural *adj.* 超自然的
4. mosquito *n.* 蚊子
5. recently *adv.* 最近
6. annoying *adj.* 惱人的
7. creepy *adj.* 令人毛骨悚然的
8. captivate *v.* 使著迷
9. be unaware of *phr.* 沒有意識到，英文意思為 not knowing something or not having knowledge of something，對某事沒有認知的意思。be unaware of 的反義字為 be aware of，注意到、意識到的意思。

   例 ❶ He is too young to be aware of how the older people view events differently.
   她太年輕了沒有意思到年長者看事情的觀點不同。

   ❷ How can't you be unaware of the security issue?
   你怎麼會沒想到安全的議題？

10. bring up *v.* 提出。英文解釋為 start to talk about it，開啟某話題之意。

例 ❶ If you are in a dinner party with nodding acquaintances, don't bring up a subject that may be sensitive.

如果你身在賓客不過是點頭之交的晚宴中，不要提起敏感話題。

❷ It's interesting that you bring up the point that people don't see everything completely. Instead, they see only fifteen percent of what they want to see.

你提出的這點很有趣，人們不會看到事情的全部，他們只會看到事情的百分之十五而已。

 ## 文學佳句怎麼用

    They sat by the fire, roasted apples and listened to their marvelous tales of ghosts, the haunted brooks, bridges, houses, and particularly of the headless horseman, or Galloping Hessian of the Hollow, as they sometimes called him.

他們會圍坐在火邊，一邊烤蘋果，一邊聽那些鬼故事、鬧鬼的小溪流、屋子、特別是無頭騎士，又叫來自沉睡谷的奔騰黑森軍，她們有時候是這麼叫他的。

英文句子組成解析

    學習英語的我們常常會很困惑，為什麼課本教的文法都很簡單，句子短短的，但是看報紙、看書的時候，句子就很長，一句接著一句用「逗號」還有「連接詞」，要怎麼才能把他們好好使用，符合文法之餘又能描述的生動活潑？答案是「模仿」，模仿你看過的英文句子。先來細看佳句中的結構：

They sat by the fire, roasted apples and listened to their marvelous tales of

主詞　動詞片語 1　動詞片語 2　　　　　　　　動詞片語 3

ghosts, the haunted brooks, bridges, houses, and particularly of the headless horseman, or Galloping Hessian of the Hollow, as they sometimes called him.

連接詞＋句子

如何連接動詞片語

1. 先想好主詞是誰，做了哪些動作，若動作有兩個以上，使用 and 來連接動詞片語，營造出豐富的動感。
2. 句型為「A, B, and C」，中文翻譯為「A、B、以及 C」。

如何連接名詞片語

1. 本句中出現三個動詞片語，「動詞片語 1 &2」為基本句型，但是「動詞片語 3」卻很長，技巧是使用「逗號」、「連接詞 and」、以及「連接詞 or」。
2. 句型為「A, B, C, and particularly of D, or E」，中文翻譯為「A、B、C、特別是 D 或 E」。
3. particularly (adv.)特別地。使用副詞來描述一整件事中，說話者想特別指出的。

如何使用連接詞 as

as (conj.) 像…。As 為連接詞時，後面直接加句子，

例：

1. Do in Rome as the Romans do.
   到了羅馬，就做羅馬人做的事（入境隨俗）。
2. She lied to me, as I thought she would.
   她對我撒謊，就像我想的一樣。

注意：從本單元可以看到「連接詞」神通廣大，可以連接動詞、名詞、以及句子，要注意的是，連接詞要用的有「一貫性」，以「A, B, C, and particularly of D, or E」為例，A, B, C, D, E 均應為相同詞性，若是名詞，則都是名詞。

文學經典重現　Track48

Another of his sources of fearful pleasure was to pass long winter evenings with the old Dutch wives, as they sat spinning by the fire, with a row of apples roasting and spluttering along the hearth, and listen to their marvellous tales of ghosts and goblins, and haunted fields, and haunted brooks,⋯ and particularly of the headless horseman, or Galloping Hessian of the Hollow, as they sometimes called him. He would delight them equally by his anecdotes of witchcraft, and of the direful omens and portentous sights and sounds in the air, which prevailed in the earlier times of Connecticut.

他的消遣之一就是和這些荷蘭老太太促膝長談，度過漫漫冬夜，他們會圍坐在火邊，一邊烤蘋果，一邊聽那些鬼故事、鬧鬼的房子和小溪流，尤其是無頭騎士，又叫沉睡谷的奔騰黑森軍，她們有時候是這麼叫他的。他也會跟她們說些巫術的故事，討她們歡心，還有那些康乃狄克郡早期流傳的鬼故事。

單字小解

1. splutter *v.* 聒噪
2. direful *adj.* 可怕的
3. portentous *adj.* 惡兆的

故事背景報你知

　　本段取自《沉睡谷傳奇》描寫新來的學校教師（schoolmaster）伊克波德（Ichabod Crane）常與村民互動、交換消息，對於村民間流傳的鬼故事特別有興趣。

Unit 29 美國 紐奧良
New Orleans, the United States

 Track49

田納西威廉《慾望街車》 *A Streetcar Named Desire*

" *Whoever you are—I have always depended on the kindness of strangers.* "

—— Tennessee Williams, *A Streetcar Named Desire*

不管你是誰，我總仰仗陌生人的慈悲。

——田納西威廉《慾望街車》

文學景點巧巧說

《慾望街車》（*A Streetcar Named Desire*）為托馬斯・拉尼爾・威廉斯三世（Thomas Lanier Williams III），也就是田納西・威廉斯（Tennessee Williams）所寫的戲劇，全劇的舞台設在美國路易西安納州（Louisana）南部的紐奧良法語區（French Square, New Orleans），並從女主角布蘭琪（Blanche DuBois）搭上紐奧良軌道列車（New Orleans Streetcars），抵達新紐奧良的「天堂大道（Elysian Field Avenue）」，投靠自己已婚的妹妹史黛拉（Stella Kowalski）揭開序幕。來自好人家的布蘭琪過慣了富裕的生活，即便破產（broke），還是擺脫不了奢侈的習氣，經常嫌棄妹夫史丹利（Stanley Kowalski）出身低下，日積月累下來，兩人間的嫌隙越來越深，衝突也變得頻繁，最後走向急劇衝擊性的結局。《慾望街車》1951年也曾改編成同名電影，由費雯麗（Vivien Leigh）和馬龍白蘭度（Marlon Brando）主演，主要場景有座階梯，透過這坐階梯，人與人間的緊繃促狹的關係也巧妙地營造出來。到紐奧良除了享受美食，一定要來搭乘「慾望街車」，來趟法語區歷史之旅，看看「慾望街車」劇作的誕生環境，這裡可是紐奧良最古老也最知名的街區呢。本引言取自http://www.imdb.com/title/tt0044081/quotes，為網路資源。

揭開序幕小對話

Back to 2006, New Orleans, a foreign girl stood at the sidewalk of Royal Street, and stared at the map in her hands. From her frowned eyebrow and pouted lips, it was easy to tell that she was confused, probably in trouble. At the mean time, a young French boy just got off a streetcar. It seemed that he was in a hurry. Suddenly they ran into each other.

故事要從西元 2006 年的紐奧良書說起，一個異鄉來的女孩站在皇家大街的人行道上，看著她手中的地圖。從她皺起的眉頭以及嘟起的嘴唇，感覺得出她很困惑，可能遇到麻煩了。同時間，一個年輕的法國小子剛下街車，看得出來他在趕時間。突然兩人就撞上彼此了。

(The girl's map fell down, and the boy tried to help her pick it up.)

（女孩的地圖掉下去了，男孩試著要幫忙撿起地圖。）

Boy: I am sorry. Did I hurt you?

男孩：對不起，有受傷嗎？

Girl: No, I am fine.

女孩：我沒事。

(Glancing at the map, the boy found foreign but familiar characters on the map. He can barely understand the meaning of those words.)

（男孩看著女孩的地圖，發現地圖上充斥著外國的但是又熟悉的字體，他幾乎讀不懂那些字體。）

Boy: Is it Chinese?

男孩：那是中文嗎？

Girl: Yes, it is. You understand Chinese? It's my mother tongue.

女孩：是的，你懂中文嗎？那是我的母語。

Boy: I have studied Chinese for a year. By the way, I am Austin. My place is just one block away from here.

男孩：我曾經學中文一年。對了，我是奧斯丁，我家離這裡不遠。

Girl: Nice to meet you. I am Fiona. I am a student from the University of New Orleans.

女孩：很高興認識你，我是費歐娜，我是紐奧良大學的學生。

Boy: Nice to meet you, too. I have an appointment. See you later.

男孩：我也很高興認識你，我有約，再見囉。

Girl: Wait. Could you please do me a favor? I was supposed to be here with my classmate to interview a successful writer for my class report. The street car was broken on my way to meet my classmates, so I have to get here on my own. Now I am lost, and I just found my cell phone was out of batteries. Today is really not my day…

女孩：等等，可以請你幫我一個忙嗎？我本來要跟我的同學一起來訪問一位成功的作家，但是在我去跟同學會面的路上，街車突然壞了，我就得自己去，只是現在我迷路了，還發現我的手機沒電了，我今天怎麼了…

Boy: All right, where are you heading to?

男孩：好吧，你要往哪個方向去？

Girl: Jackson Square.

女孩：傑克森廣場。

Boy: If my car is with me, I can take you there. But I can still show you how to take the streetcar, it's a convenient option for commuters

男孩：如果我今天有開車，我可以帶你去，不過我還是可以教你怎麼搭街車，很方便的，也上班族的通勤工具。

(At that night, Fiona wrote a diary.)

（那天晚上，費歐娜寫了一篇日記：）

Since I came to America to study, **I have always depended on the kindness of strangers, and whoever he is**, I feel thankful.

自從我來到美國念書，我總仰仗陌生人的慈悲，不管他是誰，我覺得很感激。

PART 1 歐洲篇

PART 2 美洲篇

PART 3 亞洲篇

好好用單字、片語

1. sidewalk *adj.* 人行道

2. frowned *adj.* 皺眉的

3. confused *adj.* 困惑的

4. trouble *n.* 困境

5. pick up *phr.* 撿起

6. mother tongue *n.* 母語

7. appointment *n.* 正式的約會

8. broken *adj.* 損壞的

9. do me a favor *phr.* 幫我一個忙，也就是 help me 的意思。由於是請求別人幫忙的用語，在語氣上會使用助動詞 Could you…？或是 Would you…？的句型，以表示禮貌（例一），但是若是請熟一點的朋友幫忙時或是生氣時，當然也可以使用祈使句（例二）。

   例 ❶ Would you do me a favor and pull over by the gas station?
      可以幫我一個忙，在加油站停一下嗎?

   ❷ You're bothering me. Do me a favor and please leave.
      你干擾到我了，幫個忙，請走開。

10. run into someone/something *phr.* 撞上，英文意思為 crash, collide, hit，有兩者相撞之意。run into 同時也有巧遇的意思。

   例 ❶ Hayley ran into her husband's coworker at the supermarket.
      海莉在超市巧遇她先生的同事。

文學佳句怎麼用

　　Whoever you are-I **have always depended on** the kindness of strangers. 不管你是誰，我總仰仗陌生人的慈悲。

現在完成式

英文的時態用來表示「動作發生的時間」，讓說話者表示「動作發生時間語」與「說話當下時間」的區別。其中現在完成式（Present Perfect Tense），顧名思義，說話者說話的當下，動作已經在過去發生了，並完成了，依照過去式的定義，要使用過去式，但由於這個「動作和現在仍有關連」，為表示過去完成的動作與現在的關連，使用「現在完成式」。

(a) 句型：have/has＋p.p.〔助動詞＋動詞過去分詞〕

(b) 使用時機：當過去發生的動作跟現在有所關聯時，其中關連性可以分成下列幾種情況：

使用時機	例句	文法解析
How long/ duration of time	Austin has left his hometown for ten years.	過去發生的事情，持續到現在。
Present result	Lucy has lost her keys, so she can't get into the house.	過去發生的事情，結果影響到現在。
Life experience	Carlos has been to Paris.	描述過去到現在是否經歷過某事。
Finished or not	Hayley has had breakfast today.	過去開始的動作，現在已經完成了。

來到紐奧良必看必去

一定要欣賞爵士樂和大啖美食！路易斯安那州（Louisana）臨近墨西哥灣（Gulf of Mexico），所以這裡盛產海鮮，來到紐奧良一定要品嚐生蠔（oyster）的鮮美。此外，還要嚐嚐經典的 Cajun 和 Creole 料理，Cajun 的源頭要追溯到 17、18 世紀從法國遷移到加拿大東岸的法國人，當時也有人移民到路易斯安那州，一開始生活相當艱困，經常要獵捕墨西哥灣的海鮮為生，慢慢地這裡的飲食和烹飪手法也融合了法國的特色。Creole 也是移民融合當地食材的特色料理喔，可見美國真的是個大融爐，各種文化的火花都活躍地展現出來了。

美國麻薩諸塞州東部的康科德鎮瓦爾登湖
Walden Pond, Concord, Massachusetts, the United States

 Track50

盧梭《湖濱散記》 *Walden; or, Life in the Woods*

"*Near the end of March, 1845, I borrowed an axe and went down to the woods by Walden Pond, nearest to where I intended to build my house, and began to cut down some tall, arrowy white pines.*"

—— Henry David Thoreau, *Walden; or, Life in the Woods*

　　1845年三月底，我借了一把斧頭，來到瓦爾登湖旁的森林裡，想在附近蓋一間自己的屋子，然後就去砍了一些高大的白松。

—— 盧梭《湖濱散記》

文學景點巧巧說

此次引言取自亨利盧梭（Henry David Thoreau）的《湖濱散記》（Walden; or, Life in the Woods），整部作品皆以盧梭第一人稱的口吻，詳實記下他在瓦爾登湖（Walden Pond）的小屋內，獨自一人經歷的自然野外生活。透過這部有如自我實驗般的作品，盧梭想要傳達獨立（independence）、心靈探索（spiritual discovery）的概念，同時反諷社會（satire），並提倡自力更生（self-reliance）的生活方式。除此之外，他的目標在於透過自我反思，達成客觀看待社會的能力。整部作品富含超驗主義思想（transcendentalist philosophy）（註）。瓦爾登湖旁的小屋其實屬於亦師亦友的愛默森（Ralph Waldo Emerson），鄰近美國麻州康科德鎮（Concord, Massachusetts）。這座湖已列為州保育區（state reservation），備有登山步道（hiking trails），來此也能游泳、釣魚並參觀歷史遺跡（historical site），是麻州熱門的國家公園之一。或是自康科德中心（the center of Concord）出發，沿著瓦爾登湖邊的瓦爾登路，也稱愛默森暨盧梭步道（Emerson – Thoreau Amble），步道自 2013 年開放，全長 1.7 公里，沿途是愛默森與盧梭曾經走過的路線，跟著他們，首先會經過愛默森的故居（Emerson's house），再來是盧梭的小屋（Thoreau's cottage），這也是條自然步道，因此會有多處不平的地方，雨天還會特別泥濘，好在樹木和木板也不少，降低跌倒的可能性。另外若來此地，建議穿防滑耐穿的登山鞋，因為途中也會遇上坡度。瓦爾登湖後因遊客眾多，生態環境受到破壞，違背由盧梭所開啟的生態保育概念（ecology），這是我們不能不檢討的地方。本引言與稍後的文學經典重現（英文部分）取自Princeton University Press, 2010所出版之 *The Writings of Henry D. Thoreau: Walden*。

註：超驗主義（transcendentalism）為宗教與哲學相關的運動，盛行於 1820 至 1830 年代。中心思想為人和自然內的渾然天成的神性（the inherent goodness），認為社會上的組織，特別是有組織的宗教或政治黨派，會腐壞一個人的樸實，而全然自力更生、獨立的生活方式則是提升自我最好的方式。重要代表人物為愛默森（Ralph Waldo Emerson）和盧梭。

PART 1 歐洲篇

PART 2 美洲篇

PART 3 亞洲篇

 揭開序幕小對話

It's the guys' tradition to hang out on Friday night at White Bear bar. Lazily lying at the sofa area of the bar, Austin, Carlos, and Isaac are talking about their traveling experiences.

星期五晚上，那些男孩們總喜歡在白熊酒吧廝混，懶洋洋的躺在酒吧的沙發區奧斯丁、卡洛斯、伊撒克正在討論他們的旅遊經驗。

Isaac: Hayley and I have been to many old castles. We really enjoy to be surrounded by a building with so many historical stories behind. I think Glamis Castle in Angus, Scotland, is the most beautiful one.

伊撒克：我跟海莉去過很多古堡，我們喜歡置身古老建築中，感受背後很多歷史故事的氛圍，我覺得蘇格蘭安格斯區的葛拉米城堡最美了。

Carlos: My choice of a travel destination will be the scenes mentioned in some literary works, for example, the Notre Dame Cathedral in Paris.

卡洛斯：旅遊景點我會選擇文學作品提到的景點，例如巴黎聖母院。

Isaac: Having a trip like that really helps for your writing. You are always so in the zone after you were back from your inspiring and literature-related trip.

伊撒克：這樣的旅遊真的有助於寫作，每次你從文學相關的景點環遊回來後，總是下筆有神，誰都不理。

Austin: Bros, let's not talking about the past. Let's plan for the future? Spring is

奧斯丁：兄弟們，我們不要談過去了，來計畫之後的行程

coming. We should all go camping. How about Yangmingshan National Park?

吧？春天要來了，我們可以去露營，陽明山國家公園如何？

Carlos: I love camping! Alisa and I have been to Walden Pond to experience what Thoreau called, self-reliance, or in other word, a simple life supported by no one. We replicate what the Thoreau's Walden Project about. First of all, **we borrowed an axe and went down to the woods by Walden Pond, nearest to where I intended to build our house, and began to cut down some tall, arrowy white pines…**

卡洛斯：我喜歡露營！我跟愛麗莎曾經去過瓦爾登湖體驗盧梭所說的自給自足，也可以說是一種簡單的自我天地。我們仿效盧梭的瓦爾登湖生活模式，首先，我們借了一把斧頭，來到瓦爾登湖旁的森林裡，想就近蓋一間自己的屋子，然後我們砍了一些高大的白松做為木材…

Isaac: Oh, wait. Someone just said "Alisa and I". What's that all about?

伊撒克：咦，等等，剛剛是不是有人說「我們」，你是不是該解釋一下？

Austin: You two are friends, not a couple, but you act like you and Alisa are….

奧斯丁：你跟愛麗莎只是朋友，不是情人，但是你說的你們好像是…

Carlos: We are just friends.

卡洛斯：我們只是朋友。

Isaac: Austin, do you believe him?

伊撒克：奧斯丁，你相信他嗎？

Austin: My answer is a definite "no".

奧斯丁：我的答案一定是「否定的」。

好好用單字、片語

1. tradition *n.* 傳統

2. lie *v.* 躺、臥

3. surround *v.* 圍繞

4. self-reliance *n.* 自給自足

5. in other word *adv.* 換而言之

6. support *v.* 支持

7. replicate *v.* 複製

8. definite *adj.* 明確的

9. hang out *phr.* 和朋友廝混。英文意思為 Spend a lot of time at a place，常常與朋友相處，就是沒有特定要做甚麼，但是就是相處在一個地方聊天打屁，hang out 就是最適合表示這種朋友間相處的情形，但是要注意，hang out 是很口語並且不正式的用法。

   例 ❶ I really enjoy having you around. We hang out, watch the sunset, and share lives. That doesn't happen to everyone.

   我很喜歡有你在身邊。我們出來廝混、看夕陽、分享生活，並不是每個人都能這樣的。

   ❷ Many people may take it for granted that having a small group of people who accept you to hang out is easy, but I think it isn't.

   很多人也許會認為有一群接受你的朋友出來聚聚是很容易的，但我不這麼認為。

10. in the zone *phr.* 全神貫注做某事。英文意思為 in a state when you can make the best of something，當你在做某件事情，並且感到如有神助的狀態就叫做 in the zone。

    例 ❶ David is in the zone. All he cares is whether he will outstand all the other competitors or not.

大衛全神貫注，他所在意的只有一件事，就是他能不能在其他競爭者中脫穎而出。

❷ When you are in the zone, dancing is the most satisfying thing in the world.

當你全神貫注時，跳舞是世界上最令人滿足的事了。

 ## 文學佳句怎麼用

Near the end of March, 1845, I borrowed an axe and went down to the woods by Walden Pond, nearest to where I intended to build my house, and began to cut down some tall, arrowy white pines.

接近 1845 年三月底的時候，我借了一把斧頭，來到瓦爾登湖旁的森林裡，想就近蓋一間自己的屋子。我先砍了一些高大的白松做為木材。

使用介係詞表示方位

1. by (prep.) 在…旁邊，表示接近、鄰近之意也就是 at the side of something/someone。

2. 介係詞 by 放在句子中，可用來修飾名詞，

   例 ❶ I borrowed an axe and went down to the woods by Walden Pond.

     我借了一把斧頭，來到靠近瓦爾登湖旁的森林裡。

   ❷ Let's book a hotel room by the mountain.

     我們來預定一間山林旁的旅館吧。

3. near (prep.) 在…附近，表是距離上的相近，也就是 a short distance of something/someone。在使用 near 當介系詞時，若要表達再靠近一點使用 nearer，而要比達最靠近時，使用 nearest。

   例 ❶ I don't have to commute because I just live near here.

     我不需要通勤，因為我就住這附近。

❷ It's freezing. Go and sit near to the fire.
好冷喔，往火堆靠近一點吧。

❸ I borrowed an axe and went down to the woods by Walden Pond, nearest to where I intended to build my house.
我借了一把斧頭，來到瓦爾登湖旁的森林裡，想就近蓋一間自己的屋子。

其他常見介系詞

1	At＋名詞 在...場所	See you at the theater after school. 放學後在電影院見。
2	In＋名詞 在…場所內	Do you see the blonde girl in the gym? 你有看到體育館裡的金髮女孩嗎？
3	From＋名詞 從...起	Where do you come from? 你的家鄉在哪？

註：介系詞後面通常接「表地方的名詞」當做介系詞的「受詞」，而在例 3 中，由於問句需倒裝，因此 from 的受詞 where，置於句首。

 文學經典重現 Track51

Near the end of March, 1845, I borrowed an axe and went down to the woods by Walden Pond, nearest to where I intended to build my house, and began to cut down some tall, arrowy white pines. ...On my way home, its yellow sand heap stretched away gleaming in the hazy atmosphere, and the rails shone in the spring sun, and I heard the lark and pewee and other birds already come to commence another year with us. They were pleasant spring days, in which the winter of man's discontent was thawing as well as the earth, and the life that had lain torpid began to stretch itself. ...It appeared to me that for a like reason men remain in their present low and primitive condition; but if they should feel the influence of the spring arousing them, they would of necessity rise to a higher and more ethereal life.

1845年三月底，我借了一把斧頭，來到瓦爾登湖旁的森林裡，想在附近蓋一間自己的屋子，然後就去砍了一些高大的白松。…回家沿途的路上是連綿一片的黃色沙丘，在朦朧的空氣中發著亮光；鐵路在春陽下閃耀著；我聽見雲雀、京燕和其他鳥兒啁啾，和我們一起展開新年。這是美好的春日，人們在冬日感到的不適和大地同時退去冰霜，冬眠的生命開始舒展。…我想也是這個原因，人們還過著低層次、原始的生活，但人們若能感受到喚醒他們的春天，生命必定可以提升至境界更高的地方。

單字小解

1. arrowy [ˈærəwɪ] *adj.* 箭狀的
2. commence *v.* 開始
3. thaw *v.* 融化、解凍
4. primitive *adj.* 原始的
5. ethereal [ɪˈθɪrɪəl] *adj.* 非人間的

來到康科德鎮瓦爾登湖必看必去

瓦爾登湖已列為州保育區（state reservation），有登山步道（hiking trails），來此也能游泳、釣魚並參觀歷史遺跡（historical site），是麻州熱門的國家公園之一。或是自康科德中心（the center of Concord）出發，沿著瓦爾登湖邊的瓦爾登路，也稱愛默森暨盧梭步道（Emerson – Thoreau Amble）走；步道自 2013 年開放，全長 1.7 公里，沿途是愛默森與盧梭曾經走過的路線，跟著他們，首先會經過愛默森的故居（Emerson's house），再來是盧梭的小屋（Thoreau's cottage），這也是條自然步道，因此會有多處不平的地方，雨天還會特別泥濘，好在樹木和木板也不少，降低跌倒的可能性。另外若來此地，建議穿防滑耐穿的登山鞋，因為途中也會遇上坡度。

Part **03**

亞洲篇

日本京都宇治
Uji, Tokyo, Japan

紫式部《源氏物語》 *The Tale of Genji* Track52

> *A commotion means the end of everything. She should be quiet and generous, and when something comes up that quite properly arouses her resentment she should make it known by delicate hints. The man will feel guilty and with tactful guidance he will mend his ways.*

—— Murasaki Shikibu, *The Tale of Genji*

騷動就是結束。女人若遇上讓她憎恨的事，應冷靜、有大度，且不著痕跡地表達不滿。如此男人才會有罪惡感，自然地調整他的行為。

——紫式部《源氏物語》

文學景點巧巧說

　　本此引言取自《源氏物語》（*The Tale of Genji*）第二回帚木（*The Broom Tree*）。《源氏物語》為日本女作家紫氏部（Murasaki Shikibu）於西元十一世紀所寫的長篇小說，故事背景為平安時代，不少人認為《源氏物語》可能是全世界第一部小說，但此說法仍然頗具爭議，但其在日本文學史上的重要性不言可喻，波赫士曾說亞瑟韋利（Arthur Waley）所譯的《源氏物語》渾然天成，充滿魔力，吸引他的地方不是異國色彩（exoticism），而是人與人之間的情感（human passions）。因此也有人說《源氏物語》是一部細膩寫出人性的小說，且人物關係繁複，背景時代設定深遠，日本文學史的高峰也透過此作品達成。引言描述主角光源氏（Shining Genji）和頭中將（To-no-Chujo）等朋友評論當時女性的過程，如女性的地位、如何才是理想的女性等，如當面對丈夫或愛人有不忠時，要懂得不為所動，如此才能讓對方感到慚愧。從討論中可一窺平安時代（Heian）女性的角色，其重要性再次呈現在世人面前。2000 年，《源氏物語》的一幕與作者紫式部出現在日幣 2000 元的紙鈔背面，為的是紀念第 26 屆的 G8 高峰會於大阪舉行，同時也慶祝千禧年的到來。紙鈔上的人物取自依《源氏物語》故事所繪的插畫卷軸，該卷軸收藏於名古屋的德川美術館（Tokugawa Art Museum）；另外關於作者的圖象，則來自五島版的《紫式部日記繪卷》，收藏於五島美術館（Gotoh Museum）。喜歡這部作品的讀者或許可以到這兩座博物館看看卷軸本尊。另外，京都宇治市還有源氏物語博物館（The Tale of Genji Museum），要深入了解源氏物語當時的時代背景，還有其與京都附近各地點的淵源，就不能錯過來此拜訪的機會。本引言(英文版)取自 http://ebooks.adelaide.edu.au/m/murasaki-shikibu/tale-of-genji/index.html，為網路資源，英文版譯者為Edward G. Seidensticker。

PART 1 歐洲篇

PART 2 美洲篇

PART 3 亞洲篇

 揭開序幕小對話

Every time Carlos read a novel, he took up a fleeting interest in visiting the scene mentioned in the book. Although everyone thinks he is crazy about traveling to those destinations, Alisa always holds opposite opinions. She believes it is what a great writer should be like— a man with passion and curiosity of everything in the world. In front of the Gotoh Museum, Carlos and Alisa are about to explore the places and collections related *Genji Monogatari*.

　　每當卡洛斯讀了一本小說，他就三分鐘熱度地想去拜訪小說中提到的景點，儘管大家都覺得卡洛斯這樣太瘋狂了，艾麗莎卻不是這麼看他，她相信這是一個大作家該有的樣子，一個對世界充滿好奇與熱情的人。在五島美術館前，他們正開始要探訪關於《源氏物語》的一切。

Carlos: I can't wait to see the national treasures about "*The Tale of Genji*" in this museum. Can you imagine that they are relics of the first novel of the world!

卡洛斯：我等不及要去看博物館收藏關於《源氏物語》的東西，你能想像那些日本國寶可是世界第一本小說《源氏物語》的相關遺跡啊。

Alisa: Look at you! How special you are! Most people agree that museums are not exactly fun these days, but you are always so excited about going there and see the value of them.

愛麗莎：你看你就是這麼特別，現代很多人覺得博物館一點也不有趣，可是一到博物館你就如此充滿熱情及活力，就是你才看得到它的價值。

Carlos: Alisa, you are being ironic! Try not to imply that I am a weirdo.

卡洛斯：你別諷刺我了，愛麗莎！不要暗示我是怪胎。

Alisa: You are wired, but in a good and cute way though.

艾麗莎：你的確是個怪了，但是怪的很可愛，也沒什麼不好的。

Carlos: Thanks. Then I will take it as a compliment.

卡洛斯：謝囉，我會把它當作誇獎。

(When Carlos and Alisa move inside the museum, there is a couple *having a fight.* People in the museum try hard to *ignore* them but many of them can't help looking on them.)

（當卡洛斯與艾麗莎往博物館內移動時，有一對情侶在吵架，博物館內的民眾雖然盡量忽視，卻無法無視他們。）

Carlos: Didn't the couple read "The Tale of Genji"? A famous quote goes like this "A commotion means the end of everything."

卡洛斯：那對情侶沒讀過《源氏物語》嗎？裡面説：「騷動就是結束。」

Alisa: Do you mean the woman should be quiet and generous, and when something comes up that quite properly arouses her resentment she should make it known by delicate hints.

愛麗莎：你是指女人一旦遇上令她憎恨的事，她應該不著痕跡地表達不滿，表現要冷靜有大度。

Carlos: Exactly. **Then the man will feel guilty and with tactful guidance he will mend his ways.**

卡洛斯：沒錯，如此男人才會心生罪惡，自然修正自己的行為。

PART 1 歐洲篇

PART 2 美洲篇

PART 3 亞洲篇

247

Alisa: Well, no matter what the couple has been through. It's easier said than done.

愛麗莎：嗯，不管這對情侶經過什麼，說的總比做的容易。

 ## 好好用單字、片語

1. fleeting *adj.* 稍縱即逝的
2. opinions *n.* 意見
3. treasure *n.* 珍貴的事物
4. relic *n.* 遺跡
5. ironic *adj.* 嘲諷的
6. weirdo *n.* 怪人
7. compliment *n.* 讚美
8. ignore *v.* 忽視
9. have a fight with somebody *phr.* 跟…起爭執，fight *n.* 爭吵，英文意思為 have an argument or disagree with someone，跟某人在意見上不何而起爭執。

   例 ❶ The drunk teenager had a fight with his dad as soon as he arrived.

   那個酒醉的青少年一到家就跟爸爸吵了一架。

   ❷ Try not to break your promise, unless you want to have a fight with your wife again.

   試著不要再違背你說的話，除非你想再跟你的太太吵架。

10. be crazy about *phr.* 對某人迷戀或對某事熱衷，英文意思為 deeply in love with somebody，對某人瘋狂的迷戀，或是 passionate about something，對某事熱衷的意思。

    例 ❶ Rachel is crazy about Ben, and she believes they are meant for each other.

    瑞秋非常迷戀班尼，而且她相信他們是天生一對。

❷ Nathan is crazy about soccer; he will never miss any games on TV.

❸ 耐森對足球很熱衷,他絕對不會錯過任何一場電視轉播的球賽。

 文學佳句怎麼用

A commotion means the end of everything. She should be quiet and generous, and when something comes up that quite properly arouses her resentment she should make it known by delicate hints. The man will feel guilty and with tactful guidance he will mend his ways.

騷動就是結束。女人若遇上讓她憎恨的事,應冷靜、有大度,且不著痕跡地表達不滿。如此男人才會有罪惡感,自然地調整他的行為。

字詞解析

本段引言,在建議女性在婚姻中若對男人有所不滿,不應該有強烈的情緒(strong feelings)甚至是動怒引起騷動,而應該機智的運用暗示,不著痕跡的表達。引言中所使用的英文解析如下:

憤怒的強烈情緒	女人應採取手段	預期達到的目的
Commotion (n.)騷動 Resentment (n.)憤慨	delicate hint (phr.) 靈敏的暗示 tactful guidance (phr.) 圓滑的引導	feel guilty (phr.) 感到愧疚 mend his ways (phr.) 修正自己的行為

使用情態助動詞 should 表示建議

「助動詞」通常會搭配「動詞」使用，助動詞的使用目的在「表達說話者的觀念或判斷」，should，即表達說話者的建議、價值觀、或是預期發生的狀況。

表達說話者的對事情的看法或價值觀

A woman should be quiet and generous.

一個女人應該要嫻靜並且慷慨。

表達說話者對事情的建議

When something comes up that quite properly arouses her resentment, she should make it known by delicate hints.

女人一旦遇上令她憎恨的事，她應該不著痕跡地表達不滿。

表達說話者預期事情發生的狀況

Jackson and his friends left the party an hour ago. They should get home by now.

傑克森跟他的朋友一小時前就離開派對了，他們現在應該到家了。

注意：助動詞後面永遠接「原形動詞」，助動詞「不會因為主詞的單複數而有所變化」。

來到京都宇治必看必去

　　京都是個古色古香的城市，這裡有古寺、有奈良大佛，隨處可見美景和列為世界遺產的建築；到了宇治，就不能錯過源氏物語博物館、宇治上神社…等，也別忘了看看紫氏部的頭像和宇治川，眺望一下宇治川的美景，真是美不勝收啊。

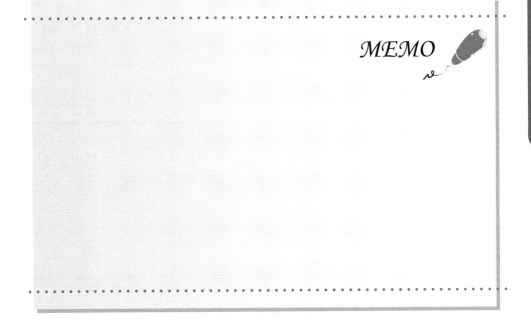

MEMO

Unit 32

日本 京都文化博物館
The Museum of Kyoto, Japan

 Track53

上田秋成《雨月物語》 *Tales of Moonlight and Rain*

" *He trembled with fear and felt faint, thinking that he was about to be taken. Someone emerged from behind a folding screen, saying, 'Master, why do you fret' so* "

—— Ueda Akinari, *Tales of Moonlight and Rain*

他全身發抖，就要昏厥，心想自己的命就要不保了。屏風後方出現了一個人，說道：「主人，您在煩惱什麼？」

——上田秋成《雨月物語》

文學景點巧巧說

本次引言（取自 *the Asian Classics*，由 Anthony H. Chambers 所翻）要帶讀者道京都文化博物館的映像情報室（The Museum of Kyoto, Kyoto Film Archive）觀賞電影，也欣賞文學。本引言取自上田秋成（Ueda Akinari）的《雨夜物語》（*Ugetsu Monogatari; Tales of Moonlight and Rain*），其中的《蛇性之淫》（A Serpent's Lust）篇。故事描述出生富有漁家的兒子，豐雄（Toyoo），一次在雨中愛上一神秘女子，女子還借傘給豐雄後而衍生的故事。她叫做真女子，並向豐雄坦承自己曾是某位當地達官的遺孀，希望豐雄能夠取她為妻，並贈送昂貴的劍做為禮物；豐雄回家後，家人發現這把劍原來是竊取自鄰近寺廟的贓物，而豐雄也因此入獄。當警官前去真女子（Manago）的宅邸調查時，他們發現宅邸根本是座廢墟，真女子則跟著閃電一同消失。這時豐雄才恍然大悟，自己是被幻化為人的蛇妖給迷住了，便向親姊求助，可惜真女子還是跟著他不放。最後，豐雄靠法海師父，終於降伏蛇妖，可惜他的妻子富子（Tomiko）也一命嗚呼。故事和中國故事《白娘子》頗有異曲同工之妙，的確，上田採納中國明末清初作家馮夢龍之《警世通言》（*Jingshi Tongyan; Stories to Caution the World*）中《白娘子永鎮雷峰塔》的元素，如歷史事件、人物描述等，並將之融合日本的歷史背景與特色，而寫出這部作品。《雨月物語》同《警世通言》，也有透過故事導正社會風氣的意涵。1953 年，由溝口健二（Kenji Mizoguchi）改編的《雨月物語》（*Ugetsu*）電影上映，《蛇性之淫》就是其中納入改編的故事之一，而電影中的場景配置、鏡頭等安排，則突顯了這部電影與導演在日本電影界的重要性。京都文化博物館的映像情報室有時也會播放溝口健二等大導演的電影，對電影有興趣的讀者，或許能進來看看，來趟藝術文化之「視覺」饗宴。

 揭開序幕小對話

After their trip to Gotoh Museum, Carlos and Alisa are heading north to Tokyo , the capital of Japan. They traveled around the city by Japan

Metro and on their feet. On their way to the well-known Museum of Kyoto, they stopped at a mystical shrine.

　　繼五島美術館的拜訪，卡洛斯與艾麗莎繼續往日本的北方，抵達東京，日本的首都。他們利用日本的地鐵走遍整座都市，在他們去京都文化博物館的路上，他們發現一座神秘的神社，停留了一會兒。

Alisa: Look, there is a group of Japanese worshipping.

愛麗莎：看，一群日本人在拜拜。

Carlos: I believe It's a ritual practice of Japanese religion. I heard that the function of a shrine is to keep ancient sacred objects.

卡洛斯：我想應該是日本宗教的一種儀式吧。我聽說日本神社的功能是用來保存聖物。

Ailsa: Let's get into the shrine.

愛麗莎：那我們進去看看吧。

Carlos: I would love to.

卡洛斯：當然好。

(In a small room, Alisa noticed a bronze sword on a wall. She touched it and fainted right away. Carlos tried to keep her from falling. Ten minutes later, Alisa opened her eyes.)

（在小屋中，愛麗莎發現牆上有一把青銅劍，她上前碰觸它，竟然立刻昏倒了，卡洛斯上前將她扶住。十分鐘後，愛麗莎再度張開眼睛。）

Carlos: Are you ok?

卡洛斯：你還好吧？

Alisa: What happened?

愛麗莎：發生什麼事了？

Carlos: I have no idea. I guess you might release the ancient power from the sword by touching it.

卡洛斯：我不知道，我猜你應該在碰到劍身時同時釋放了古老的力量。

Alisa: Don't scare me. Before I lost conscious, I only remembered that **I trembled with fear and felt faint, thinking that I was about to be taken. And then, someone emerged from behind a folding screen, saying, "Lady, why do you fret so?"**

愛麗莎：別嚇我了，在我失去意識之前，我只記得我全身發抖，就要昏厥，心想自己的命就要不保了。然後，屏風後方出現了一個人，說道：「女士，您在煩惱什麼？」

Carlos: That's weird. Let's not explore Japanese culture here. It's too dangerous.

卡洛斯：那也太奇怪了吧。我看我們不要在這裡體驗什麼日本文化了，太危險了。

Alisa: We should better explore the culture at Museum of Kyoto, which is more modern and providing interactive exhibitions or souvenir shops, rather than a place like this.

愛麗莎：我們還是去京都文化博物館吧，比起這裡，那邊比較現代，還有互動展覽跟紀念品店。

 好好用單字、片語

1. capital *n.* 首都
2. well-known *adj.* 有名的
3. mystical *adj.* 神秘的
4. worship *v.* 敬拜神

5. religion *n.* 宗教

6. shrine *n.* 聖地、神殿

7. sacred *adj.* 神聖的

8. exhibition *n.* 展覽會（品）

9. lose consciousness *phr.* 失去意識，consciousness *n.*意識，英文意思為 being able to understand things around you with your mind and thoughts，也就是能夠理解、感知周遭發生的事情。

例 ❶ Little Willy was frightened when he saw a man lose consciousness with all color draining from his face.

當小威利看到一個男人失去意識並且臉色全失時，他嚇壞了。

❷ Some of the patients who suffer from nerve disorders will lose consciousness when changing from sitting to standing position.

有些患有神經失調的病人會在改變坐姿到站姿時失去意識。

10. be about to *phr.* 正要，表達你即將要做某事，英文意思為 be going to do something。當你在朋友家，想表達你即將要離開時，可以這麼說：

例 ❶ I am about to leave.

I am going to leave.

以上兩句都可以表示「你馬上要離開」的意思。

❷ It is when I am about to break up with my girl friend, she says she is pregnant.

當我正要跟女友分手時，她告訴我她懷孕了。

文學佳句怎麼用

He trembled with fear and felt faint, thinking that he was about to be taken. Someone emerged from behind a folding screen, saying, "Master, why do you fret so?" 他全身發抖，就要昏厥，心想自己的命就要不保了。屏風後方出現了一個人，說道：「主人，您在煩惱什麼？」

分詞構句的使用 part II

A. 當你想要表達兩個連續的動作時，

例 ❶ He trembled with fear and felt faint.

❷ He thought that he was about to be taken.

❸ Someone emerged from behind a folding screen.

❹ He said, "Master, why do you fret so?"

B. 使用「連接詞 and」，將兩個「前後發生」的合併，使用連接詞連接的句子又稱為「子句」：

He trembled with fear and felt faint, <u>and he</u> thought that he was about to
　　　　　　　　　　　　　　　　　　子句

be taken.

Someone emerged from behind a folding screen, <u>and he</u> said, "Master,
　　　　　　　　　　　　　　　　　　　　　　子句

why do you fret so?"

C. 為求句子的精簡，將句子中「重複的主詞」以及「連接詞」刪除，並將「子句」的動詞改成分詞的形式，若是主動就使用「現在分詞 Ving」；反知若是被動就使用「過去分詞 Vpp」。

判斷技巧：子句中「he thought⋯」以及「he said⋯」為「主詞＋動詞」的主動行式，因此使用「現在分詞 Ving」。

He trembled with fear and felt faint, <u>thinking that he was about to be</u>
<u>taken.</u>

Someone emerged from behind a folding screen, <u>saying, "Master, why do</u>
<u>you fret so?".</u>

到京都文化博物館必看必去

　　看完電影，從京都文化博物館出來後也差不多累了吧，那麼就去看看也在京都的 Hello Kitty 茶寮喝茶、看看 Hello Kitty 放鬆心情吧，Hello Kitty 茶寮是京都觀光會議局推薦的景點，於去年底開幕，相信很快就會變成京都最新的熱門景點吧。

PART 1 歐洲篇　PART 2 美洲篇　PART 3 亞洲篇

日本京都浦島太郎神社、鹿兒島 JR 指宿至手箱號
Urashima- jinja Shrine in Kyoto and JR Ibusuki no tamatebako in Kagoshima, Japan

無名氏《浦島太郎》 *Urashima Tarō* Track54

> 'That name's from a legend I heard as a child—a boy who rode off on a turtle one day some three hundred years ago, some people say.' What? Three hundred years ago! How could that be?

—— Anonymous, *Urashima Tarō*

．．．．．．．．．．．．．．．．．．．．．．．．．．．．．

「這是我還是孩子的時候從傳說聽到的名字啊，聽說 300 多年前，有個少年坐上烏龜走了。」什麼？已經 300 年了，這怎麼可能？

——無名氏《浦島太郎》

文學景點巧巧說

　　《浦島太郎》（*UrashimaTarō*）中的主人翁在某次偶然中，救了一隻被孩童欺負的烏龜，沒想到這烏龜住在海底的龍宮裡，為了報答太郎（Taró）的救命之恩，便邀請太郎來龍宮做客。嚮往海底龍宮生活的太郎當然不能錯過這個機會，於是乘著烏龜，前往龍宮。海底龍宮金碧輝煌，放眼望去盡是貌美的侍女，但最耀眼的還是龍宮公主乙女姬（Otohimesama），她特地前來向太郎感謝他拯救了烏龜，烏龜的弟妹剛好是乙女姬堂表兄弟的妻子。接著龍宮還舉行盛大的歡迎會，會上有佳餚美酒與表演，當乙女姬也在太郎眼前隨著音樂翩然起舞時，太郎也不禁愛上了美麗的公主，雖然公主曾說太郎可以隨時回去，只是時間一久，太郎想回去的念頭一天拖過一天，若不是有天突然夢見他在人間的父母，可能還無法下定決心回去。回去之前，乙女姬交給太郎一個寶盒（也叫玉手箱（Tamatebako）），告訴他有了這個寶盒，他將青春永駐，他隨時都能帶著這個盒子回來娶她為新娘，但條件是千萬不能打開盒子。回到陸地的太郎，發現人事已非，過去住的地方也不復在，攔了路上老人才知道，人間已過了 300 年的時間。太郎驚奇不已，這 300 年的時間竟有如夢幻泡影，他的父母也早就離開人世。這種恍若隔世之感，在美國與中國都有相似的故事，前者是《李伯大夢》，後者則是《南柯一夢》，都有浮生無常的意涵，最重要的，還是要把握當下。《浦島太郎》於 15 世紀的室町時代（the Muromachi period）問世，和以圖文呈現的御伽草子（*otogizōshi*）為相同的文體（genre），但故事最早的源頭要追溯自 8 世紀的奈良時代。京都丹後半島西岸有座浦島神社（Urashima–jinja Shrine），據說為了讚揚浦島家族的成就，而建於西元 825 年。神社中收藏有浦島卷軸（the Urashima Scroll），上有詳述浦島太郎的故事，是非常重要的文化資產，同時可能也是日本年代最久遠的卷軸。九州的鹿兒島（Kagoshima）還有往返於鹿耳島中央至指宿的「JR 指宿玉手箱號」（JR Ibusuki no tamatebako，簡稱 Ibutama），車廂還設計成黑白兩色，靈感就是來自《浦島太郎》，像是太郎開了寶盒後，轉瞬間由黑變白的頭髮，車廂一開還有白煙冒出，和故事打開寶盒時的白煙相呼應，非常有巧思，有機會一定要來搭搭看。本英文版之引言取自講談社出版《うらしまたろう》（*Urashima and the Kingdom beneath the sea*）一書，英譯為麥卡錫（Ralph F. Mc Carthy）所翻。

PART 1 歐洲篇

PART 2 美洲篇

PART 3 亞洲篇

 揭開序幕小對話

Carlos and Alisa's Japan adventure continued. Now, they were ready to go on board of "Ibusuki no Tamatebako", a sightseeing limited express train designed from the famous Japanese folk tale "Taro Urashima". As the train running, they are both observing everything went by.

卡洛斯與愛麗莎的日本行持續著,現在正準備搭乘「指宿之玉手箱」,一個根據日本有民的民間故事《蒲島太郎》所設計的觀光限定快捷列車。隨著列車行駛,他們都在觀察附近的景物。

Alisa: The decoration inside is cozy. That's very different from the modern design of the train which is in black and white. How special.

愛麗莎:列車裡面的設計蠻舒適的。這跟列車外觀黑白的現代感設計差很多,很特別。

Carlos: The black and white design indicates that Taro Urashima's hair turned from black to white in a second when he opened the treasure box given by the princess of the sea.

卡洛斯:列車的黑白設計目的是要呈現蒲島太郎打開公主給他的寶盒時,頭髮瞬間從黑轉白的情景。

Alisa: What story are you talking about?

愛麗莎:你在說哪個故事啊?

Carlos: Taro Urashima, our graduate performance in high school, don't you remember?

卡洛斯:我們高中的畢業公演《蒲島太郎》,你忘了嗎?

Alisa: I do remember the story. My

愛麗莎:我記得這個故事,是

grandmother told me the story before. **That name is from a legend I heard as a child-a boy who rode off on a turtle one day some three hundred years ago.** But I don't remember anything about the graduate performance…

我奶奶告訴我的。這是當我還是孩子的時候從傳說聽到的名字啊，聽説 300 多年前，有個少年坐上烏龜走了。但是我不記得什麼畢業公演。

Carlos: How can you not remember? How could that be? All right, never mind.

卡洛斯：你怎麼可以不記得？怎麼可能？算了。

Alisa: Sorry, I was just too tired yesterday. I didn't sleep well, either.

愛麗莎：抱歉，我昨天太累了，也沒有睡好。

Carlos: Why don't you take a nap?

卡洛斯：那你要不睡個午覺吧？

Alisa: I think I should.

艾麗莎：我真的該休息一下。

(When Alisa falls asleep on the train, Carlos looks at Alisa's sleeping face. He loses in his thought. After the mysterious accident happened in the shrine, he kinds of felt like they were committed to each another in some strange ways. It feels a little awkward, but there was one thing he was sure about－he cared about her and didn't want anything bad happen to her again.)

（卡洛斯看著艾麗莎在列車上睡著的睡顏，沉思了起來。自從在神社發生的神秘事件後，他開始有點覺得他們對彼此有一種莫名的羈絆，雖然有點奇怪，但有件事情他很確定，他很在乎她，也不希望再有壞事發生在她身上了。）

PART 1 歐洲篇

PART 2 美洲篇

PART 3 亞洲篇

好好用單字、片語

1. sightseeing *adj.* 觀光的

2. express *adj.* 快速的

3. folk tale *n.* 民間故事

4. run *v.* 行進

5. observe *v.* 觀察

6. performance *n.* 表演

7. take a nap *phr.* 午睡

8. awkward *adj.* 困窘的

9. in black and white *phr.* 黑白顏色的…。當你想表達物體的顏色時可以這麼使用，通常表達某人衣服的顏色，一位穿黃衣服的女孩，例如：A girl in yellow。black and white 可以替換為其他顏色。

   例 ❶ Do we really have to decorate the wall in black and white patterns? It looks like a prison decoration.
   你真的要把牆壁布置成黑白的樣式嗎?看起來很像監獄的布置。

   ❷ My friends think I look pretty somber all in black and white, but I think it's'classy.
   我朋友認為我全身黑白色調很憂鬱，但我覺得這樣經典又別緻。

10. be committed to *phr.* 對某事感到堅定的、盡心盡力的。英文意思為 devote your time and energy into something。

    例 ❶ There are still thousands and millions of people that are committed to democratic reform in the world.
    世界上還是數以千計的的人民致力於民主改革運動。

    ❷ The principle promised that all the teachers and staffs are committed to offering every students a dynamic learning opportunity.
    校長保證全體教職員都會為學生多元的學習機會盡心盡力。

文學佳句怎麼用

That name's from a legend I heard as a child - a boy who rode off on a turtle one day some three hundred years ago, some people say." What? Three hundred years ago! How could that be?

「這是我還是孩子的時候從傳說聽到的名字啊，聽說 300 多年前，有個少年坐上烏龜走了。」什麼？已經 300 年了，這怎麼可能？

限定詞的用法

常見的限定詞（determiner）有 a purse（一個錢包）, the purse（這個錢包）, my purse（我的錢包）, some purses（一些錢包），「限定詞」用來指定特定或不特定的名詞。

(1)「不定冠詞 a」，指一個、一支、一位等不特定的事物。例如: 當你在公園裡見到一隻鳥時，你會先說 a bird，當你要再將範圍縮小到「指定那隻樹上的鳥」時，就使用「定冠詞 the」。

Carlos: Look! There is a bird.

Alisa: Which bird?

Carlos: The one on the tree.

(2) 這時你可能會有疑問，在浦島太郎的引言中提到的 a legend, a child, a boy 明明都是在指浦島太郎的傳說以及浦島太郎本人，應該要使用「定冠詞 the」，但是要注意的是，「語言的本質是溝通」，也就是 A 說給 B 聽這樣的關係，引言中說話的老人家，認為對方並不知道這個傳說，因此使用「不定冠詞 a」來描述一個傳說。

"That name's from a legend I heard as a child - a boy who rode off on a turtle one day some three hundred years ago, some people say."

(3) 簡單來說，當你要使用 the bird 的時候，你必須確定你前面已經跟對方說過 a bird 了。下面舉一個「錯誤的」例子，句中的限定詞使用錯誤，讓人摸不著頭緒，這樣讀者應該更可以體會「不定冠詞 a」跟「定冠詞 the」的使用時機了。

Carlos: Look! There is the bird.

Carlos: 看啊！那裡有一隻鳥。

Alisa: What?

Alisa: 什麼？

(4) 「數量限定詞 some」，中文意思為「一些」，在引言中，some people 指在「人」的群集中，「有一部分」的人這麼說過，也就是「數量」的概念。

(5) 雖然這些「限定詞」放在名詞前面，但不要跟形容詞搞混了，形容詞是有等級的，例如：Fiona is smart, but Alisa is smarter than her. In fact, Hayley is the smartest. Fiona 很聰明，但 Alisa 比她更聰明。不過事實上，Hayley 是最聰明的。

📷 來到京都鹿兒島 JR 指宿手箱號必看必去

京都鹿兒島 JR 指宿手箱號除了外觀設計為黑白色外，內部的車廂也有很多不同的設計，色彩鮮豔豐富，真的非常有趣；到鹿兒島也一定要體驗砂浴，是真的會讓熱熱的粗砂覆蓋在身上，只剩下頭的砂浴喔，砂浴有助於舒緩肩膀僵硬，但記得時間不要過長，免得肌膚灼傷；另外也別錯過拜訪龍宮神社，來這把願望寫在貝殼上，聽說滿靈驗的。

MEMO

PART 1 歐洲篇

PART 2 美洲篇

PART 3 亞洲篇

台灣 台灣文學館 & 齊東詩舍
National Museum of Taiwan Literature and Qi Dong Poetry Salon Taiwan

王鼎鈞《一方陽光》　*A Patch of Sunlight* Track55

" *If at that time someone would have asked my mother what she liked best, she would most likely have replied that it was that patch of sunlight inside our door during a sunny winter day.* "

—— Wang Ding Jun, *A Patch of Sunlight*

如果當年有人問母親：你最喜歡什麼？她的答覆，八成是喜歡冬季晴天這門內一方陽光。

——王鼎鈞《一方陽光》

文學景點巧巧說

在王鼎鈞《一方陽光》（*A Patch of Sunlight*）裡，讀者彷彿感受得到作者與母親相處的溫暖時刻，還有母親最愛的那塊有陽光照射的天地，那樣的溫度，好像也能透過文字傳達出來。《一方陽光》透過母子之間的關懷與互動，也傳達作者記憶中的家園，透過細膩的敘述傳遞出濃厚的思鄉氣息。王鼎鈞，1925 年生，「是一個經歷中國內戰的塊肉餘生」，他曾說：「若把平生行程再走一遍，這旅程的終站，當然就是故事。」（王鼎鈞，2000），足見他對故鄉的懷念不曾消減。自去年七月底開始，國立臺灣文學館（National Museum of Taiwan Literature）將典藏的詩人手稿或其他文類的詩作手稿，在濟南路齊東詩舍（Qi Dong Poetry Salon）展出，雖然王鼎鈞的詩作並無在此次展覽中展出，但他仍為此次展覽做出評論，他說：『詩歌是心聲，書法是心畫，聲和畫可以互相詮釋，從書法中可以體會詩人寫作時的呼吸，脈搏，心境，可以窺見詩人的性格，閱歷，修養。我一直喜歡蘇東坡的寒食詩，直到見了《寒食帖》以後才對這首詩更了解、更感動。…大體上詩是「密語」，詩人的手跡洩漏更多的秘密，一如台灣文學館所說：「引領觀展者在手稿的字裡行間走入詩人的內觀世界。」』（王鼎鈞，2014）（取自《聯副電子報》http://paper.udn.com/udnpaper/PIC0004/272728/web/ "）所以有空來看看走走這裡吧，日式風格的建築曾經做為官舍，設計與歷史都別有一番特色。本英文版之引言取自天下文化出版《中英對照讀台灣小說》由Nicholas Koss 所翻的《一方陽光》。

揭開序幕小對話

A workshop of Taiwan Poetry is held at Qi Dong Poetry Salon today. The workshop is established to revitalize Taiwan's literature development. It's a big event for passionate writers like Carlo and he would never miss it. It was a warm sunny afternoon and, Carlos and Alisa decided to go there by walking. The bustling Jinan Road, where the Qi Dong Salon located, was packed with students who were on their way home after school. Carlos caught sight of a blue sweater on a short, skinny little boy in dis-

tance.

　　齊東詩社今天有一場台灣詩作的工作坊，為復甦台灣文學發展而創立，是一個盛大的活動。對卡洛斯這位充滿熱情的作家來說，這樣的大活動他是不會錯過的。天氣暖和的下午，卡洛斯與愛麗莎決定走路去那，齊東詩社位在熙熙攘攘的濟

Carlos: I have a blue sweater that looks exactly like the little boy's.

卡洛斯：我有一件跟那個男孩一模一樣的襯衫。

Alisa: Which boy?

愛麗莎：那個男孩？

Carlos: The boy with an orange hat who is standing in front of the traffic light.

卡洛斯：在紅綠燈前戴著橘色帽子的男孩。

Alisa: Oh, I see him and his blue sweater. What about it?

愛麗莎：我看到他跟他的藍色毛衣了，怎麼了嗎？

Carlos: It reminds me of my grandmother who always knitted sweaters or scarves for me.

卡洛斯：他讓我想到我的奶奶，總是幫我織毛衣跟圍巾的奶奶。

Alisa: That's very sweet. It's the first time you mentioned your grandmother to me.

愛麗莎：真窩心。這是你第一次跟我提到你奶奶呢。

Carlos: It has been four years since we lost her. I really miss her.

卡洛斯：自從她去世已經四年了，我真的很想她。

Alisa: I am sorry to hear that.

愛麗莎：我真為你感到難過。

Carlos: It's fine. My nanny used to spend all the afternoon knitting, while I was doing homework. We kept each other company.

卡洛斯：沒關係，以前奶奶常常會花一整個下午的時間織毛衣，那時我就在旁邊寫功課。我們以前就這樣伴著彼此。

Alisa: You guys are adorable. I can tell your granny loves you very much.

愛麗莎：你們好可愛，感覺你奶奶一定非常愛你。

Carlos: I do love her as much as she did. **If at that time someone would have asked her what she liked best, she would most likely have replied that it was that patch of sunlight inside our door during a sunny winter day.**

卡洛斯：我愛她也像她愛我一樣多，如果當年有人問奶奶：你最喜歡什麼？她的答覆，八成是喜歡冬季晴天這門內一方陽光。

Alisa: I believe the patch of sunlight is special for her because you were there by her side.

愛麗莎：我相信那門內的一方陽光對她來說是無價的，因為你在她身邊。

南路上，路上充滿著放學回家的學生，卡洛斯注意到一個穿著藍色毛衣的瘦小男孩。

 好好用單字、片語

1. revitalize *v.* 使復興
2. bustling *adj.* 車水馬龍的
3. in distance *phr.* 在遠處
4. traffic light *n.* 號誌燈
5. sweater *n.* 毛衣

6. scarf *n.* 圍巾

7. adorable *adj.* 可愛的

8. granny *n.* 奶奶，亦稱 nanny 或 grandmother。

9. catches sight of *phr.* 偶然看見、匆忙瞥見。Sight 也就是眼睛所能見到視野，英文意思為 the act of seeing。

   例 ❶ Walking around the lake, I caught sight of a group of Korean tourists holding cameras in hands.

   在湖邊散步，我看到一群拿著相機的韓國的觀光客。

10. by one's side *phr.* 在…身邊，side *n.* 在旁邊，英文意思為 a position near to someone or something，by one's side 除了表達空間上鄰近的意思，更引申為在…身邊支持他或陪伴他的意思。

    例 ❶ The social worker comforts the victim by saying "we are all with you, and you still have people by your side."

    社工人員安慰受難者，他說：「我們都會幫你的，而且你還有這麼多人陪在你身邊。」。

文學佳句怎麼用

If at that time someone would have asked my mother what she liked best, she would most likely have replied that it was that patch of sunlight inside our door during a sunny winter day.

如果當年有人問母親：你最喜歡什麼？她的答覆，八成是喜歡冬季晴天這門內一方陽光。

假設語氣 if

If (conj.) 如果，if 為「連接詞」，if 所連結的句子又稱為「條件子句」，表示說話者對未來或是過去的假設，表達「如果…那就…」的語氣。我們接下來以情境來舉例子：

情境一

當 Carlos 跟 Alisa 在決定要怎麼到齊東詩社時，Alisa 提出他的想法：

If we take MRT, we will arrive at the Salon quickly.

如果我們搭捷運，我們會很快的抵達詩社。

情境一解析

Alisa 說話的時候，還沒去搭捷運，也還沒抵達目的地，整個情境都是「對未來的假設」，「主要子句」使用「未來式」，「條件子句」使用「現在式」。

註：條件子句的形成需注意「動詞的時態」，需按照事情在過去或現在的真否判定。

情境二

當 Carlos 假設如果以前有人問她奶奶最喜歡甚麼時，奶奶可能的回答：

If at that time someone would have asked her what she liked best, she would most likely have replied that it was that patch of sunlight inside our door during a sunny winter day.

情境二解析

Carlos 說話時，奶奶已經過世了，他所假設的事情，從來都沒有發生，也就是「過去不真實」的情況，使用「過去完成式 had＋p.p.」來表達。引言中使用「情態助動詞 would」，用來表是對過去的推測，因此在本句的「主要子句」及「條件子句」的動詞都受「助動詞」的影響，而使用「原形動詞」，變化成「現在完成式 have＋p.p.」。

來到台灣文學館&齊東詩社必看必去

關於齊東詩社社位於臺北市濟南路 2 段 25 號，近金山南路，附近有中正紀念堂、捷運有古亭站，這裡一直是台北人文匯聚的寶地之一，美食、特色小店也不少，古亭近師範大學那邊有夜市美食，吃得到好吃的波蘿包；中正紀念堂附近則有非常有名金峰魯肉飯，店外經常看得到大排長龍的國內外遊客；不遠處還有南門市場、牯嶺街，每到一處都是一個驚喜，週末值得來這逛逛，度過悠閒的午後。

中國上海徐志摩與陸小曼故居
Xu Zhimo and Lu Xiaoman Former Residence, Shanghai, China

徐志摩《偶然》 *Chance* Track56

" *You on your way, I on mine.*
Remember if you will,
Or, better still, forget
The light exchanged in this encounter. "

—— Xu Zhimo, *Chance*

你有你的
我有我的方向
你記得也好
最好你忘掉
在這交會時互放的光芒。

——徐志摩《偶然》

文學景點巧巧說

「悄悄地我走了，正如我悄悄地來。」一提到徐志摩，腦海中似乎就會回蕩這詩句，眼前彷彿看得到康河，古色古香的英式學院建築，還有在河上搖槳的船夫，與船上悠閒自在的乘客。康河，又做劍河，主要流東英格蘭的劍橋，為大烏茲河（Great Ouse）的支流，全長 64 公里，可讓平底船、小船和賽艇通行。但這次我們不看英國劍橋，我們要來看徐志摩與陸小曼的故居，徐志摩一生追求愛戀，還沒和元配張幼儀離婚前，就愛上了林徽音，但林徽音並沒有接受他的追求；後來徐志摩才和陸小曼在一起，他在感情上是勇敢的，那一份未果的等待滋味恐怕也是他最為熟悉的感受吧。徐志摩與陸小曼（Shanghai Xu Zhimo and Lu Xiaoman Former Residence）的故居位在上海四明村，門牌號為延安中路 913 弄，在這看得到兩人過去生活的環境如書房、庭院等，泰戈爾曾來徐宅做客呢。本英文版引言取自己網路資源，原譯者不明。

 揭開序幕小對話

Inside a mall, Hayley and Fiona were taking a break at a coffee place after they were done with the clothing shopping. To describe their friendship, there was a saying goes "Birds of a feather flock together. More precisely, beautiful and smart ladies band together. This is how Fiona and Hayley starts their friendship since they were little. With time goes by, they grow old and grow closer.

在購物中心裡，海莉及費歐娜剛買完衣服，正在咖啡店裡休息。如果要描述這兩個人的友誼，大概就屬「同類相吸」這句話了吧，或是更精確地說，漂亮的女孩總是聚在一起，海莉跟費歐娜兩人的友誼就是這樣展開的，隨著時間流逝，兩人的感情越來越深厚。

Fiona: Hayley, do you remember this song?

費歐娜：海莉，你記得這首歌嗎？

Hayley: I do. It is when we were at Austin's party. Wow, we were so young and were curious about everything in a foreign land.

海莉：我記得，這是我們在奧斯丁的派對上聽到的歌。哇，那時候我們還這麼年輕，並且對異國個所有事情都如此好奇。

Fiona: Oh, America, I miss our dorm, the ice cream place and all the old friends there.

費歐娜：喔，美國啊，我真想念我們的宿舍，我們總是去吃冰淇淋的地方，還有所有的老朋友們。

Hayley: I do, too.

海莉：我也是。

Fiona: Don't you think that music is like a magic? It's like…

費歐娜：你不覺得音樂很神奇嗎？就好像是…

Hayley: The melody and the lyric of the song took us back to those beautiful times.

海莉：歌曲的旋律與歌詞把我們回到那些美麗的回憶中。

Fiona: It's truly a great memory. And it is where I met my husband.

費歐娜：這真是一段相當美好的回憶。在那裡我遇見了我先生。

Hayley: Haha, you reminded me of his crying face on the day you left America at the airport.

海莉：哈哈，你讓我想起來我要離開美國那一天，奧斯丁在機場哭花的臉。

Fiona: And I read the poet of Xu Zhimo to him.

費歐娜：那時候我念了徐志摩的一首詩給他。

You on your way, I on mine. Remember if you will, Or, better still, forget The light exchanged in this encounter.

你有你的，我有我的方向，你記得也好，最好你忘掉，在這交會時互放的光芒。

Hayley: Then he didn't want to break the connection with you and be forgotten. He flew to you a year later, and had become obsessed with Oriental culture and a fan of Xu Zhimo.

海莉：然後，他不想要與你失去聯繫甚至被忘記，他在一年後飛來台灣，還開始對中國文化著迷，並成為徐志摩的大忠粉。

Fiona: He is such an affectionate and crazy person. I remembered we went to Shanghai Xu Zhimo and Lu Xiaoman Former Residence, and he proposed to me in front of the courtyard where Xu Zhimo and Lu Xiaoman used to spend their time together.

費歐娜：他真的是一個感情豐沛又瘋狂的人。那時候我們還造訪了上海市徐志摩與陸小曼的故居，他竟然還在過去徐志摩與陸小曼談情說愛的庭園中跟我求婚。

PART 1 歐洲篇

PART 2 美洲篇

PART 3 亞洲篇

好好用單字、片語

1. feather *n.* 羽毛

2. flock *v.* 聚集

3. band *v.* 聚集

4. friendship *n.* 友誼

5. curious *adj.* 好奇

6. leave *v.* 離開，過去式為 left。

7. airport *n.* 機場

8. connection *n.* 聯繫

9. become obsessed with *phr.* 開始對…著迷。英文意思為 having the same feeling idea, or image repetitively in your mind，也就是持需想著某事情。Become obsessed with 經歷某事情後開始對某事著迷的意思，而 be obsessed with 則只有單純描述：

   例 ❶ After Jill tried the muffins from the Mary's Pastry, she became obsessed with baking muffins.

   在吉兒嘗試瑪莉糕餅店的馬芬蛋糕後，她就開始熱衷自己做馬芬蛋糕。

   ❷ An excellent garden designer said it's fortunate to for him to be obsessed with plants.

   一位優秀的園藝設計師説他很幸運他對植物是著迷的。

10. propose to *phr.* 提出建議，也常用來指求婚。propose *v.* 提出建議，英文意思為 offer an idea or a suggest for consideration，也就是提供建議的意思。

   例 ❶ Isaac made up a special crossword in order to propose to his girlfriend.

   伊薩克發明了一個特別的字謎要來跟女朋友求婚。

   ❷ Real science takes money, so I proposed to find some sponsors for our study.

   科學實驗需要經費，所以我建議為我們的研究找一些贊助。

文學佳句怎麼用

You on your way, I on mine.

Remember if you will,

Or, better still, forget

The light exchanged in this encounter.

你有你的

我有我的方向

你記得也好

最好你忘掉

在這交會時互放的光芒。

〔如果你願意，If you will.〕

If you will 是「表示讓步」的一個句子，will 在此「不表示未來的時間」，而是「表示意願」的情態助動詞，中文意思為：如果你願意…的話。

例 ❶ Put on a new dress, or performed, if you will.

穿上新洋裝、或擦點香水，如果你願意的話。

❷ Let's go to the sport bar for some fun, if you will, we call it a playground for adults. 我們到運動酒吧找點樂子吧，如果你願意，我們都稱他為大人的遊樂場。

PART 1 歐洲篇

PART 2 美洲篇

PART 3 亞洲篇

〔如果你願意做某事，If you will do something〕

在「If you will＋動詞」的句型中，will 一樣表示說話者的「意願」，後面接的動作為說話者「禮貌地要求對方做的事」。

例 ❶ If you will forgive me for interrupting your conversation with your boss.

如果你願意原諒我打斷你跟你老闆的談話。

❷ I would love to share my food with you, if you allow me to add my food to yours.

我很樂意分享我的食物，如果你願意的話，我可以把食物分給你。

〔引言解析〕

Remember if you will,

Or, better still, forget

1. 引言中的使用了動詞 remember，用意在「建議或命令」讀者，這樣只使用一個動詞的句型，又稱為「祈使句」，以「動詞」做為開頭，省略了主詞「你」，祈使句用來「提供建議」、「命令對方」、或「提出要求」。

2. 整句來看，Remember if you will，「祈使句的用法」搭配「表示讓步的 if you will」，表現出作者希望讀者一定要記得，又不好意思用命令的語氣，中文翻譯為：如果你願意的話，記得也好，或者忘記也好。

來到上海必看必去

上海臨近海港，是一座過去到現在都非常活躍的城市，來這裡除了感受文學氣息，其實很多地方都相當值得逛逛走走，從古色古香的朱家角水鄉古鎮、蘇州河畔的郵政博物館，到世博月亮館與環球金融中心觀光廳，好好體驗上海這裡傳統、現代、超現代風格並蓄的街頭和文化。

MEMO

Unit 36

中國 北京大觀園
Grand View Garden, Beijing, China

 Track57

曹雪芹《紅樓夢》 *The Dream of Red Chamber*

" *Here I am fain these flowers to inter; but humankind will laugh me as a fool. Who knows, who will, in years to come, commit me to my grave!* "

—— Cao Xueqin, *The Dream of Red Chamber*

儂今葬花人笑癡，他年葬儂知是誰？

——曹雪芹《紅樓夢》

文學景點巧巧說

《紅樓夢》（*The Dream of Red Chamber*）是部奇書，關於時代背景，特別是人物的描述、人物間的互動關係，實在讓人印象深刻。關於故事裡的建築、庭園、家具擺設與人物的服裝、配飾都極為講究，讓人驚嘆。關於那時代大戶人家的恩怨情仇，各樣細節舉凡人物間的上下從屬關係，應對進退，在曹雪芹的筆下，枝節錯綜繁雜，就像一個自成一格的世界，與外界隔絕。許多人將《紅樓夢》（*The Dream of Red Chamber*）和馬奎斯的《百年孤寂》與普魯斯特的《追憶似水年華》來比較，然而不管如何比較，三部作品都呈現了一種超越時空背景的宏觀，這些作家透過創作，把世界寫了下來，讓數百年後的人們細細品味其中的況味，領悟虛實難以界定，但又能從閱讀中，了解人生無常也無限的宇宙觀。在《紅樓夢》的大觀園裡，生活看似豐碩無虞，稍有一些變化就讓人感慨萬分，引言取自林黛玉葬花時，有感而發的《葬花詞》，賈寶玉在一旁靜靜聽了，也不禁悲痛年少的美和青春都是短暫的，那樣身不由己的無力感似乎也預告著賈家的衰敗與沒落。講到大觀園，當然也要來真的大觀園，一探究竟。本引言(英文版)取自http://ebooks.adelaide.edu.au/m/murasaki-shikibu/tale-of-genji/index.html，為網路資源，英文版譯者為Edward G. Seidensticker。

PART 1 歐洲篇

PART 2 美洲篇

PART 3 亞洲篇

 揭開序幕小對話

As a big fan of Chinese culture, Austin would never missed the annual ancient costume parade at Beijing Grand View Garden. Now Austin and Fiona are in Grand View Garden, watching the costume parade. They were attracted to a classy pavilion when they were following the crowd.

身為至中國文化的粉絲，奧斯丁絕對不會錯過每年北京大觀園舉辦的古典服裝遊行，奧斯丁跟費歐娜現在正在大觀園中觀賞服裝遊行，走著走著，他們被一座典雅的涼亭吸引。

Fiona: This place is huge. I can't walk any longer. I am taking a rest at this beautiful pavilion.

費歐娜：這個地方也太大了，我無法繼續走了，我要在這個涼亭休息一下。

Austin: Sure. I am thrilled to watch so many people wearing the traditional costumes.

奧斯丁：好啊，看到這麼多人穿著傳統服飾在遊行實在太令人興奮了。

Fiona: It's definitely worth a visit.

費歐娜：的確值得到此一遊。

Austin: The Grand View Garden is 12.5 hectares, and has 40 attractions. It's impossible to see them all within a day by walking. I hope we could stay here one more day.

奧斯丁：大觀園總共有 12.5 公頃，其中有 40 個景點，實在不可能一天就把所有景點逛完。我真希望可以多待一天。

Fiona: We could, if you find a place to stay.

費歐娜：我們可以啊，如果你找到地方住的話。

Austin: Ok, let me check if there are still hotel rooms available nearby. Wait for a second. Yes, I just found one.

奧斯丁：好，讓我找找附近的旅館。等我一下，太好了，我找到一間。

Fiona: We are lucky. Then we can go moon watching tonight.

費歐娜：我們真幸運，那麼我們今晚可以去賞月了。

(After Austin and Fiona took enough rest, they are ready again to admire the land-

（待奧斯丁及費歐娜休息後，他們又可以去欣賞富有造景的

scape with elegant design of hills, stones, and trees, manifesting the tradition of Chinese culture. They stopped at another pavilion by a tree. A stone tablet stood on the ground. Austin were approaching it and reading the lines out.)

Here I am fain these flowers to inter; but humankind will laugh me as a fool. Who knows, who will, in years to come, commit me to my grave!

Fiona: This is definitely from Lin Daiyu, a well-educated, intelligent, and affectionate young woman.

山丘、石頭、及樹木的風景，這些都展現了中國文化的精華。走著走著，他們在另一座涼亭停了下來，那兒有一座石碑。奧斯丁走向前，並把石碑上的文字朗讀出來。）

今葬花人笑癡，他年葬儂知是誰？

費歐娜：這一定是出自有教養、聰穎、感情豐沛的林黛玉之口。

 好好用單字、片語

1. annual *adj.* 每年的

2. parade *n.* 遊行

3. pavilion *n.* 涼亭

4. thrilled *adj.* 非常興奮的

5. nearby *adv.* 在附近

6. landscape *n.* 風景

7. manifest *v.* 顯示

8. well-educated *adj.* 受過良好教育的

9. be attracted to *phr.* 被…吸引。attract *v.* 吸引，英文意思為 like someone or be interested in something，也就是喜歡某些人或事物，因此產生興趣。

例 ❶ Churchill once said, " Smoking cigars is like falling in love; first you are attracted to the shape; you stay for its flavor; and you must always remember, never, never let the flame go out. "

邱吉爾曾說：「抽菸就像談戀愛一樣，剛開始你喜歡它的外型，再來是著迷它的味道，但你要記著，千萬千萬不要讓火焰熄滅。」

❷ People are usually be attracted to someone who can do something that you can't.

人們常常會被那些，能做到自己做不到的人所吸引。

10. take a rest *phr.* 休息。rest *n.*休息，英文意思近同 relax，也就是在活動後放空、休息之意。

例 ❶ After twelve hours working, Fiona really needs to go home and take a long rest.

經過十二小時的工作後，費歐娜真的需要回家好好的休息。

❷ Mark is not quitting; he is just taking a rest for a few months.

馬克沒有要辭職，他只是休了幾個月的假而已。

文學佳句怎麼用

　　Here I am fain these flowers to inter; but humankind will laugh me as a fool. Who knows, who will, in years to come, commit me to my grave!

儂今葬花人笑癡，他年葬儂知是誰？

疑問句的使用

Jane saw an car accident.

珍看到一場車禍。

〔提出疑問〕

■ 當你想知道「動作的執行者」是誰時，直接將「主詞」替代為「疑問詞 who」。

Who saw the car accident?

誰看到了那場車禍?

- 引言中林黛玉丟出「疑問」，想知道未來會是「誰」將她埋葬，我們先從肯定句來做變化，再將「疑問詞 who」放在主詞的位置：

例

A stranger will, in years to come, commit me to my grave.

Who will, in years to come, commit me to my grave?

〔表達時間的副詞〕

- 英文中，表達時間的副詞通常放在句尾，「時間副詞」可以放在句首、句中、或句尾，端看說話的人想把他那一句話的重點放在哪裡。

例

Jane helped me with my homework last week.

珍上禮拜幫忙我完成回家功課。

- 引言中的時間副詞，in years to come (phr.) 未來幾年，置於句中，說話者的目的是要強調那些「未來的時間」。

Who will, in years to come, commit me to my grave?

- 再看下列兩個例句，你會發現當時間副詞被置於句首時，說話者在「強調動作發生的時間」。

例 ❶ Perhaps in years to come the young poor man will be a million-aire. Who knows?

也許將來這個年輕的窮小子會變成百外富翁呢。誰知道呢?

❷ I am sure I would remember that beautiful smile in years to come.

我很確定將來我還會記得那抹美麗的微笑。

📷 來到北京大觀園必看必去

北京大觀園位於西城區菜園街，為了拍攝《紅樓夢》而於 1984 年建成。園內完全是照著原著為設計藍圖，小說內的各角色的居所如怡紅院、瀟湘館、蘅蕪苑、稻香村…等都一一呈現出來，好像真的到了一個真實的世界一樣，忘了這也只是一場「夢」啊。

285

中國 北京魯迅博物館
Beijing Luxun Museum, China

 Track58

魯迅《阿 Q 正傳》 *The True Story of Ah Q*

66 *Ah Q would stand there for a second, thinking to himself, "It is as if I were beaten by my son. What is the world coming to nowadays...." There upon he too would walk away, satisfied at having won.* 99

—— Luxun, *The True Story of Ah Q*

阿 Q 在原地逗留了一會兒，心想：「我竟然被兒子打了，這是什麼世界呀…」想著想著，他也心滿意足帶著勝利走了。

——魯迅《阿 Q 正傳》

文學景點巧巧說

「精神勝利法」（winning a psychological victory）是《阿 Q 正傳》（*The True Story of Ah Q*）的核心思想，作者魯迅藉由阿 Q 這個角色，寫出中國人的精神和靈魂來，反諷中國皇室走向沒落境地時，儘管受強國欺壓，卻依然固守成規，缺少面對問題的覺悟。就像阿 Q 只願活在自我欺騙的世界裡，在失敗面前裝做一副自命不凡的樣子。作者魯迅出身浙江紹興，曾到日本留學，主修醫科，後來對西方文學與哲學產生興趣，讀了不少尼采、達爾文等人的作品；《阿 Q 正傳》也融合中西方的長處，被公認為中國現在文學史上的經典作品。若想要了解魯迅的生平，就要親自去一趟北京魯迅博物館，這裡看得到魯迅的臥室間工作室、故居小院；這裡的館藏豐富，包括魯迅的手稿、舊物等，像是阿 Q 正傳的手稿、魯迅為北大設計的校徽等，最後，還能逛逛魯博書屋，回到過去體驗魯迅當時的生活，以及魯迅憂國憂民的精神。本英文版引言與後頁文學經典重視取自"Marxists Internet Archive"。本引言與稍後的文學重現(皆英文版的部分)取自Marxists Internet Archive，為網路資源。英文部分由Yang Hsien-yi and Gladys Yang所翻；中文部分取自金楓印行1988年所出版之《阿Q正傳》。

 揭開序幕小對話

After Austin and Fiona's trip to China, Austin became even more obsessed with expanding his knowledge in Chinese culture. His best friend is Google. Now, Austin is surfing the net about Luxun, the father of modern Chinese literature.

自從奧斯丁跟費歐娜的中國之旅後，奧斯丁更加著迷於研究中國文化，在這件事上，他最好的的夥伴是 google，現在他正在網站上搜尋關於現代中國文學之父－魯迅的事蹟。

Austin: Fee, I just learned that Lu Xun's former residence has become a museum in Beijing where his manuscripts are collected and art exhibitions are held.

Fiona: Don't tell me you have made plans for the next trip to China, you said that we are going to Korea on our next vacation.

Austin: Calm down, Fee fee. I haven't mentioned a word of "going to China."

Fiona: Sorry, I am being too sensitive. It is because the tourist destinations in China are always too crowded for a relaxed vacation.

Austin: I see, then we won't do that again. You have my words.

Fiona: Thanks. And we were talking about Luxun, right? He created Ah Q, the idiot?

Austin: Yes, he did. But I won't call him an idiot. I would say he is smart in taking

奧斯丁：菲，我剛剛才發現魯迅的故居現在已經變成北京的一棟博物館了，裡面有收藏他的手稿還有一些藝文展覽。

費歐娜：不要跟我講你已經計劃好下次去中國的行程，你不是說過我們下次要去韓國的嗎？

奧斯丁：菲菲你冷靜點，我可是一個字都沒有提到「去中國」。

費歐娜：抱歉，我最近太敏感了。因為中國的旅遊景點實在太多人太擁擠了，一個放鬆的假期不是這樣的。

奧斯丁：我了解，下次我們不會再去了，我保證。

費歐娜：謝啦。我們剛剛再討論魯迅吧？他創造了那位傻子，阿 Q 對嗎？

奧斯丁：是沒錯，但是我不會叫阿 Q 傻子，我反而覺得他很

care of his own emotion.

Fiona: Still an idiot.

Austin: Well, that's a point. Once when Ah Q was knocked down, **he and there for a second, thinking to himself, "It is as if I were beaten by my son. What is the world coming to nowadays..." There upon he too would walk away, satisfied at having won.**

Fiona: When Ah Q is unfairly treated, he finds a way to make himself feel better. A man who isn't aware of himself being a loser.

Austin: Yeah, very typical reaction of Ah Q, the spirit of winning a psychological victory.

Fiona: I like his philosophy. Life is hard; life is short. You can choose to be an angry complaint, or you can think on the bright side and make yourselves feel happier.

Austin: I do agree. But if you go extreme, you might turn out to be a pathetic loser who doesn't even know you are one.

會照顧自己的情緒。

費歐娜：這樣還是傻啊。

奧斯丁：嗯…你説的也沒錯。有一次阿 Q 被打倒在地，他在原地逗留了一會兒，心想：「我竟然被兒子打了，這是什麼世界呀…」想著想著，他也心滿意足帶著勝利走了。

費歐娜：當阿 Q 受到不公平的對待時，他總會找到方法讓自己好過些，實在是一個連自己的失敗都不知道的人啊。

奧斯丁：這的確是阿 Q 著名的「精神勝利法」。

費歐娜：我喜歡他這個態度，人生苦短，你可以選擇當一個總是生氣的抱怨者，或是你可以選擇樂觀並讓自己保持愉悦。

奧斯丁：我同意，但如果在某方面太過極端，你真的會成為一個可悲失敗者，甚至連自己是失敗者都不自覺。

289

好好用單字、片語

1. expand *v.* 拓展

2. surf the net *phr.* 瀏覽網站

3. exhibition *n.* 展覽

4. idiot *n.* 笨蛋

5. spirit *n.* 精神

6. pathetic *adj.* 可悲的

7. You have my word. 我向你保證。本句話雖跟「I promise you 我承諾」類似，但是使用時機不同，當你使用 "You have my word." 時，表示你在之前已經有做過承諾了，功能為「加強自己曾經做過的曾諾」。

   例

   Sister: I can borrow 100,000 dollars from you?

   Brother: Of course.

   Sister: Really? Mom said you were running out of money.

   Brother: Don't worry. I have You have my word.

   姐：我可以跟你借十萬元嗎？

   弟：當然好。〔弟弟答應了，也就是給了承諾。〕

   姐：真的嗎？媽説你沒錢了。

   弟：不用擔心，我保證可以借你錢。〔弟弟再次保證會履行承諾的。〕

8. knock down *phr.* 擊倒，英文意思為 hit somebody or something, and make them fall to the ground，也就是將某事或某物擊倒在地，也可以將受詞放在片語之中：knock somebody/something down *phr.* 將…擊倒，除了表示「身體跌落在地之意」，也可以引申為將某人的生活、或是心靈擊倒。

   例 ❶ The news that his wife had AIDS hit him hard, but did not knock him down.

   得知他太太罹患愛滋病的消息讓他遭受打擊，卻沒有將他擊倒。

文學佳句怎麼用

Ah Q would stand there for a second, thinking to himself, "It is as if I were beaten by my son. What is the world coming to nowadays. . . ." Thereupon he too would walk away, satisfied at having won.

阿 Q 在原地逗留了一會兒，心想：「我竟然被兒子打了，這是什麼世界呀…」想著想著，他也心滿意足帶著勝利走了。

〔疑問詞 what 的用法〕

以 What 開頭的疑問句用來表示「什麼？」，當你問別人問題時，心中一定有一個想知道的答案，疑問詞的形成，就根據「你心中想知道的事情」來決定。

1. 從下列肯定句來舉例，假設你想知道的答案是「那棟建築物是什麼？」

The skyscraper over there is Taipei 101.

那邊的摩天大樓是台北 101。

2. 當你不知道摩天大樓時，並想得知訊息時，使用 what 代替你不知道的訊息。

The skyscraper over there is _____.

3. 疑問句的文法規則為「疑問詞放句首」以及「倒裝」也就是將「主詞＋動詞」的字序改變過來，變成「疑問詞＋動詞＋主詞…？」的句型。

What is the skyscraper over there?

〔引言解析〕

引言中使用 what 為首的疑問句，詢問「現在的世界都變成怎樣了」。

What is the world coming to nowadays?

但是其實答案就在文章中，作者只是使用疑問詞來強調他想說的觀點，我們也可以這樣改寫成肯定句，例句的底線處也可以改成 what，形成疑問句。

The world is coming to a place where a father could be beaten up by his son nowadays.

在看文學經典重現前，我想要說的是，北京的文化背景很豐厚，世代的人們經歷了不少歷史交替，所以也不難想像角色人物的性格千變萬化，阿 Q 正是一個絕佳的例子，他的性格非常鮮明，他很矛盾，因為他內心又想反抗，但實際上卻又不敢："Ah Q could do nothing but rack his brains for some retort: 'You don't even deserve...'" 看他反擊「你還不配…」，他摸著他的頭，原來神氣的樣子，好像把他最忌諱的癩瘡疤當成什麼光榮的象徵："At this juncture, it seemed as if the scars on his scalp were noble and honorable, not just ordinary ringworm." 那既然得意，又為何欲言又止呢？那是他怕犯了自己的禁忌，而且阿 Q 是男人，他絕對不能打破自己承諾："However, as we said above, Ah Q was a man of the world: he knew at once that he had neatly broken the 'taboo' and refrained from saying any more." 藉由魯迅巧妙地描述（a man of the world），又更突顯了阿 Q 荒謬的性格。而外在的人物（idlers），就像是隱喻外在的世界一樣，哪有可能放過阿 Q，一定不會給阿 Q 好過，直到滿意為止，和阿 Q 形成強烈的對比："If the idlers were still not satisfied, but continued to bait him, they would in the end come to blows. Then only after Ah Q had, to all appearances, been defeated, had his brownish pigtail pulled and his head bumped against the wall four or five times, would the idlers walk away, satisfied at having won."。可是阿 Q 也沒那麼脆弱，馬上就給了自己一個說法：「我竟然被兒子打…，這是什麼世界呀…」，好像贏了什麼一樣。深入了解阿 Q 這個角色的性格後，就更要去一趟魯迅博物館了，也或許能對此行更有感觸喔。

文學經典重現　Track59

Ah Q could do nothing but rack his brains for some retort: "You don't even deserve...." At this juncture it seemed as if the scars on his scalp were noble and honourable, not just ordinary ringworm scars. However, as we said above, Ah Q was a man of the world: he knew at once that he had neatly broken the "taboo" and refrained from saying any more. If the idlers were still not satisfied, but continued to bait him, they would in the end come to blows. Then only after Ah Q had, to all appearances, been defeated, had his brownish pigtail pulled and his head bumped against the wall four or five times, would the idlers walk away, satisfied at having won. **Ah Q would stand there for a second, thinking to himself, "It is as if I were beaten by my son. What is the world coming to nowadays...." Thereupon he too would walk away, satisfied at having won.**

阿 Q 卻得意洋洋的說：「你還不配…」彷彿他頭上的癩瘡疤是光榮的象徵。不過，話只說了一半又吞了回去，恐怕再講下去自己也會犯了禁忌。那些無賴哪裡肯這麼輕易的放過阿 Q，他們不斷用毒辣的言語刺激他，後來還揪住他的辮子，在牆壁上用力撞四五個響頭，才心滿意足帶著勝利的姿態離去。阿 Q 在原地逗留了一會兒，心想：「我竟然被兒子打了，這是甚麼世界呀…」想著想著，他也心滿意足戴著勝利走了。

單字小解

1. retort *v.* 反駁
2. refrain *v.* 限制
3. idler *v.* 無賴

來到北京必看必去

故宮（The Palace Museum）（舊稱紫禁城（Forbidden City））、長城（Great Wall）、頤和園（The Summer Palace）、天壇（The Temple of Heaven）和天安門廣場（Tiananmen Square）等地，是一說到北京就聯想得到的景點，就連北京大學、清華大學都是值得一去的地方；北京一直是中國歷史悠久的重要城市，有探究不完的文化等著我們去挖掘。

PART 1 歐洲篇 | PART 2 美洲篇 | PART 3 亞洲篇

Unit 38

中國 山東大明湖
Daming Lake, Shandong, China

 Track60

劉鶚《老殘遊記》 *The Travels of Lao Can*

" *At first the sound was not very loud, but you felt an inexpressible magic enter your ears, and it was as though the stomach and bowels had been passed over by smoothing iron, leaving no part unrelaxed. You seemed to absorb ambrosia through the thirty-six thousand pores of the skin until every single pore tingled with delight.* "

—— Liu E, *The Travels of Lao Can*

聲音初不甚大，只覺入耳有說不出來的妙境。五臟六腑裡，像熨斗熨過，無一處不伏貼。三萬六千個毛孔，像吃了人參果，無一個毛孔不暢快。

——劉鶚《老殘遊記》

文學景點巧巧說

　　本引言取自清代作家劉鶚的《老殘遊記》（*The Travels of Lao Ts'an*）第二回「歷山山下古帝遺蹤，明湖湖邊美人絕調」，全篇描述老殘遊大明湖時所看到的景物，引言則為老殘經過戲園子《明湖居》，好不容易掙了一張椅子，和眾人一起看表演的情形，接著便是王小玉出場唱詞，老殘描述她的嗓音「有說不出來的妙境」。魯迅曾將《老殘遊記》譽為晚清四大譴責小說代表作之一，胡適也對此部作品讚賞不已，特別是描述王小玉嗓音的這段，老殘將無形的音樂具體化了，他說：「劉鶚先生在這一段裡連用了七八種不同的譬喻，用新鮮的文字，明瞭的印象，使讀者從這些逼人的印象裡，感覺那無形象的音樂的妙處，這一次的嘗試總算是很成功的了。」這部作品也有俄文、捷克文、日文與英文的版本，英文譯文的部分以謝迪克（Shadick）的版本為最佳，而最主要的原因便在於譯文，謝迪克成功地用英文捕捉了老殘的精髓；當然也不能錯過這次的景點大明湖。大明湖位於山東省濟南市，為面積數頃的天然湖，也是濟南第一名勝，景色會依季節變化而有不同的風光。本引言(英文版)取自《中國文學》（*Chinese Literature: Essays, Articles, Reviews (CLEAR)*, Vol. 3, Dec., 1991), p161-163 ），由Harold Shadick所翻。中文部分取自朔雪寒2014年出版的《老殘遊記》，為電子書。

 揭開序幕小對話

　　Fiona's sister, Shelly, is very good at singing. She has won numerous trophies from singing contests since she was only a kindergartner. If the two girls ever hanged out in their parents' place, they would sit on the sofa watching Super Stars, a singing contest held in China. There is one thing special about this TV show－the contests are held in different places around the world every season. This season, it took place outside at Daming Lake, in the city of Jinan, in Shandong, China. Now, the two ladies were watching the show and laid on the sofa, letting themselves become a

lazy couch potato.

費歐娜的姊姊雪莉很會唱歌,從幼稚園開始,她曾經在無數個歌唱比賽中贏得獎盃。如果這對姊妹回父母家時,他們總會在沙發上看超級偶像,一個中國的歌唱比賽節目。這個節目的特色在於每季的比賽都會到世界各地巡迴舉辦,這一季,在中國的山東省濟南市的大明湖舉辦。現在兩個女孩躺在沙發上看比賽,放任自己成為變成懶洋洋的電視迷。

Fiona: My sister, you really should enter the contest. There is no doubt that you will be the award winner.

費歐娜:我的姐姐啊,你真應該參加這個比賽的,你一定會得獎的。

Shelly: I don't think so. I like my life now, simple and happy.

雪莉:我不認為,我喜歡我現在的生活,簡單、幸福。

Fiona: But you have said that you want to be a popular singer when you grew up.

費歐娜:但是你以前講過你長大想要成為流行歌手。

Shelly: Not anymore. I am already busy being a wife, a mom, and your sister.

雪莉:現在不是了,我忙著當人妻、人母、還要當你的姐姐。

(While Fiona and Shelly are chatting, a contestant is singing Way Back into Love, the theme song of Music and Lyrics. They stop their conversation and become all ears.)

(當費歐娜跟雪莉在聊天時,一位參賽者也正在演唱著 K 歌情人中的重回愛情。她們被歌聲震懾住了,停下來傾聽。)

Fiona: It's a heavenly voice.

費歐娜:天籟般的歌聲啊。

Shelly: Her voice is soulful, like an angel

雪莉:她的嗓音很有靈性,就

singing from above.

Fiona: At first the sound was not very loud, but you felt an inexpressible magic enter your ears, and it was as though the stomach and bowels had been passed over by smoothing iron, leaving no part unrelaxed. You seemed to absorb ambrosia through the thirty-six thousand pores of the skin until every single pore tingled with delight.

Shelly: How amazing you describe her voicc like this.

Fiona: Well, watching the contestant singing at the beautiful, ancient garden surrounded by Daming Lake, I thought of a book I read as a child - *The Travels of Lao Can.*

像天堂的天使一樣。

費歐娜：聲音初不甚大，只覺入耳有説不出來的妙境。五臟六腑裡，像熨斗熨過，無一處不伏貼。三萬六千個毛孔，像吃了人參果，無一個毛孔不暢快。

雪莉：你這樣形容的她的歌聲太神了。

費歐娜：嗯，在這樣美麗古老的湖岸花園中看著歌唱比賽，讓我想起了幼時讀過的書，《老殘遊記》。

 好好用單字、片語

1. kindergartner *n.* 幼稚園生
2. couch potato *n.* 電視迷
3. enter *v.* 參加
4. award winner *n.* 獲獎人

PART 1 歐洲篇

PART 2 美洲篇

PART 3 亞洲篇

5. heavenly *adj.* 天堂般的

6. soulful *adj.* 充滿感情的

7. describe *v.* 描述

8. contestant *n.* 參賽者

9. win the trophy *phr.* 贏得獎盃。Trophy *n.* 獎品、獎盃，英文意思為 an object given to the winner of a competition.。

例 ❶ As a starterof your athletic career, do you want to join a team that won trophies or a team that always lose?

身為剛起步的運動員，你想要加入會贏得獎盃的隊伍還是總是落敗的隊伍呢？

❷ Having a new and strict coach really helps the team win the trophy in this season.

這一季，換了嚴格的新教練總算幫助這個隊伍贏得獎盃。

10. take place *phr.* 舉行，英文意思為 to happen。

例 ❶ The funeral will take place on Sunday at Mr. Chang's childhood church.

這場葬禮將於週日，在張先生年幼時去的教堂舉行。

❷ The 2015 Lantern Festival will take place in Taichung. It is estimated that there will be more than 10,000 people in attendance on the coming weekend.

2015 年的元宵燈會在台中舉行，估計本週末將會有一萬人以上的民眾參觀。

文學佳句怎麼用

At first the sound was not very loud, but you felt an inexpressible magic enter your ears, and it was as though the stomach and bowels had been passed over by smoothing iron, leaving no part unrelaxed. You seemed to absorb ambrosia through the thirty-six thousand pores of the skin until every single pore tingled with delight.

聲音初不甚大，只覺入耳有說不出來的妙境。五臟六腑裡，像熨斗熨過，無一處不伏貼。三萬六千個毛孔，像吃了人參果，無一個毛孔不暢快。

〔假設語氣的用法〕

- 假設語氣與一般直述句的差異在於「事件的真實與否」，當你使用「直述句」時，表示你所說的「事件是真實」的，當你使用假設語氣時，你說的「事件與真實相反」，也就是不真實的。
- 中文中表是假設時使用「如果」，而在英文中則是「改變時態」，來傳達事件與真實相反的意思。請比較下列例句。

(1) Danny likes Athena.

　丹尼喜歡雅典娜。

　〔使用現在簡單式來表達習慣或不變的事實，表達真心喜歡。〕

(2) Danny is behaving as though he had a crash on Athena.

　丹尼表現的一副很迷戀雅典娜的樣子。

　〔使用過去式來表達跟現在相反的事實，雖然看似喜歡，但是卻不是如此。〕

〔假設語氣的用法: as if /as though〕

■ As if/ as though (conj.) 假如，as if 及 as though 在文法上擔任「連接詞」的角色，語意上是「表達與事實相反的情形」，在時態上的使用，「不能和事件發生的時間點一致」，因此非事實的描述會使用「過去式」代替「現在式」。

■ 「表達與事實相反的情形」又可分為下列兩個狀況：

(1) 用來表達明明不會發生，確表現出一副會發生一樣的態度。

例：The couple are acting as though nothing had happened.

這對夫妻表現得好像沒事一樣。

〔其實兩人是有心結的，使用過去事表示跟現在相反的事。〕

(2) 用來強調某事的不真實、或是某事即將不會發生。

例：The indifferent attitude the co-worker shows really pissesMiranda off. She said she'd never speak to him again. As if she cared.

米蘭達的同事一副事不關己的態度真的是激怒她了。米蘭達說她再也不會跟同事說話了，好像她在意一樣。

〔米蘭達是不在意的，使用過去事表示跟現在相反的事。〕

來到山東必看必去

　　除了大明湖，來到山東還可以去看看曲阜孔廟（The Temple of Confucius）、山東博物館（The Shangdong Museum），或是和當地人一同歡慶青島國際啤酒節（The Qingdao International Beer Festival）。

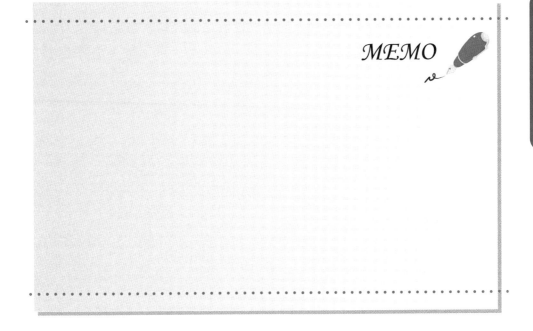

MEMO

Unit 39 中國 山東聊齋園
The Liao-zhai Garden, Shangdon,China

 Track61

蒲松齡《聊齋誌異》 *Liao-zhai's Record of Wonders*

" *A fox still thought to repay a kindness done, even one done through unconscious virtue. Now we can see that the loves of immortals are deeper still than those in the common world.* "

—— Pu Song-ling, *Liao-zhai's Record of Wonders*

一隻狐，因為他人曾經對自己有過恩德，那怕只是無意之中的事，也還在思量如何報答；可見仙人之情比世俗之情要深厚得多！

——蒲松齡《聊齋誌異》

揭開序幕小對話

本引言取自蒲松齡《聊齋誌異》（Pu Song-ling *Liao-zhai's Record of Wonders*）其英文版取自 *An Anthology of Chinese Literatune: Begining to 1911*，全書由 Stephen Owen 所編輯與翻譯。故事描述王太常小時後無意間救了一隻狐，後來狐仙化人來報恩的故事，王太常後來官場順遂，只可惜兒子元豐是個傻子，不好討老婆，很是讓王太常擔心，沒想到有姑娘願意嫁給他，這位姑娘叫做小翠，說也奇怪，小翠雖然老是惹公婆生氣，可她所做的事最後總是能化解某些事的危機，甚至元豐也突然不傻了。其實小翠是狐仙要來報恩的，元豐雖然愛她，可是小翠無法生育，於是便要他娶其他姑娘，元豐答應了，並在娶親鐘太史女兒的那天，驚奇地發現新娘子竟然和小翠的姿態、嗓音和樣子一模一樣，於是想去找小翠來問，但小翠早已不知去向，只從丫鬟那拿出一塊紅巾，紅巾內包著一塊玉玦，元豐暗自明白小翠不會再回來了。小翠到最後還是不忘報恩，她知道元豐會思念她，便先變成鐘家姑娘的模樣。故事裡的狐仙並不可怕，他們懂得報恩，情意比起人世間的人們還要深重。作者蒲松齡的年代，人人想當官，可是官職有限，蒲松齡一直到七十一歲才考到了一個小官職，《聊齋誌異》便是在這樣長年抑鬱不得志的生活中，而孕育出來的；故事除了表達因果報應，也表達其對人與自然萬物的尊敬。聊齋園位於于淄博市淄川區洪山鎮蒲家庄，並以聊齋故事為主題，將人文與自然環境合而為一的大型旅遊區。整個園林占地 30 公頃，興建於 1989 年，園內有蒲松齡藝術館、狐仙園、聊齋宮等景點，具有濃厚的北方藝術特色，文化藝涵也相當豐富。

 揭開序幕小對話

In the *Leaf* coffee shop, Alisa is watching a TV series, *The Fairies of Liaozhai*, which is filmed in Liaozhai Town in Zibo City, China. Meanwhile, Fiona is covering Austin's shift, while he is out for business affairs with new suppliers. Fiona noticed that Alisa isn't paying all her attention on what so ever on the screen. Alisa seems preoccupied, and Fiona is going to check on her.

在葉子咖啡裡，愛麗莎正在看一部電視影集，聊齋傳奇，是在中國的淄博市聊齋園所拍攝，同時，費歐娜正在為去跟供應商談合約的奧斯汀顧店。費歐娜注意到艾莉莎根本沒在看螢幕裡在演什麼，一副心不在焉的樣子，費歐娜決定去看看她。

Fiona: Hello, beautiful. Is the seat available?

費歐娜：嗨美女，對面的位置有人坐嗎？

Alisa: Have a seat.

愛麗莎：坐下吧。

Fiona: Is everything ok with you?

費歐娜：你最近還好吧？

Alisa: How do you know I am upset?

愛麗莎：你怎麼知道我不太好？

Fiona: That's very obvious. I am a good listener, and I will never let the cat out of the bag. You can tell me anything.

費歐娜：你很明顯喔。我是很好的聽眾，而且絕對保密，你可以放心跟我說。

Alisa: I am good, thanks though. By the way, I recommend you an interesting TV series, *The Fairies of Liaozhai*. The story is adapted from *Liao-zhai's Record of Wonders* by Pu Songling. The episode I was watching earlier is about a fox being saved by a mortal, **and the fox still thought to repay a kindness done, even one done through unconscious virtue.**

愛麗莎：不用啦，謝謝你。對了我推薦一部有趣的影集，聊齋傳奇，這是一部根據蒲松齡的聊齋誌異改編的。我剛剛在看的影集是關於一隻狐狸被凡人拯救的故事，一隻狐，因為他人曾經對自己有過恩德，那怕只是無意之中的事，也還在思量如何報答。

Fiona: Then what did the fox do to express its gratitude?

費歐娜：那狐狸是如何報恩的呢？

Alisa: The fox turned itself into a women and became the son of the savior's wife. The plot is kind of complicated, but what the fox does is to help the savior's family.

艾莉莎：狐狸把自己變成女人，並成為恩人兒子的妻子。情節有點複雜，不過狐狸所做的事都是要幫助恩人的家庭的。

Fiona: That's a big return.

費歐娜：那真是大大的回報呢。

Alisa: That's true, **we can see that the loves of immortals are deeper still than those in the common world.**

艾莉莎：真的，這才知道仙人之情比世俗之情要深厚得多。

Fiona: Hey, are we done with the fairy fox topic? Are you ready to tell me what's on your mind?

費歐娜：嘿，狐仙的傳奇故事討論完了吧？你準備好跟我訴訴苦了嗎？

Alisa: Well, I think I might want your advices. Carlos is acting differently after our trip in Japan. I think there will be a "Carlos and Alisa".

艾莉莎：嗯…好吧，我想我想問問你的意見。卡洛斯自從日本行回來之後表現得有點不同，我覺得我們可能真的會成為一對。

Fiona: Finally! Isn't it good news?

費歐娜：終於！這不是好消息嗎？

Alisa: I hope so. I am afraid I might lose him as a best friend.

艾莉莎：我希望如此啊！只是我怕我會失去我最好的朋友。

PART 1 歐洲篇

PART 2 美洲篇

PART 3 亞洲篇

好好用單字、片語

1. supplier *n.* 供應商

2. preoccupied *adj.* 出神的

3. adapt *v.* 改編

4. mortal *n.* 凡人

5. gratitude *n.* 感謝

6. savior *n.* 拯救者

7. return *n.* 報恩

8. done *adj.* 完成了的

9. check on somebody/something *phr.* 關心，英文意思為 to look at someone or something to make sure they are good，確認你不在時某人或某事是否在身體或心靈上呈現安好的狀態。

例 ❶ To take care of our nanny, we take turns and get up in the middle of the night to check on her, making sure she's still breathing.

為了照顧我們的奶奶，我們輪流半夜起床關心她，確認她是否持續有脈搏。

❷ My boss is not the one who fully empowers us at work; she needs to check on our progress almost every day.

我沒有那種充分授權的老闆，她幾乎每天都要確認我們的進度。

10. let the cat out of the bag (idiom) 洩露秘密，英文意思為 tell slip a secret，把秘密講出去的意思。

例 ❶ At a reality TV show, the guest wonderif it's time to let the cat out of the bag?

在真人實境秀的節目中，來賓在考慮現在是否是將秘密講出來的好時機？

❷ Stop her! Hurry! She is going to let the cat out of the bag here. I really shouldn't tell her the truth.

快點阻止她！她馬上就要把秘密説出來了。我當初真不該告訴她實情的。

 文學佳句怎麼用

A fox still thought to repay a kindness done, even one done through unconscious virtue…Now we can see that the loves of immortals are deeper still than those in the common world.

一隻狐，因為他人曾經對自己有過恩德，那怕只是無意之中的事，也還在思量如何報答；小翠等自己恩人的兒子再次完婚，從容而去，這才知道仙人之情比世俗之情要深厚得多！

〔代名詞-part II〕

一個句子中，已經出現過的名詞，單數可以用 that 來代替，複數則使用 those 代替。在引言中作者要表達狐仙的愛（the loves of immortals）以及凡人的愛（loves in the common world），因此「愛 loves」為重複出現的複數名詞，以 those 代替。

Now we can see that the loves of immortals are deeper still than those in the common world.

當你「比較兩件事情」時，大部分是因為這兩件事在某部分上有共通點（share something in common），例如：班上同學小明跟小花的學業表現，重複出現的「名詞」，以代名詞 that 或 those 代替，也就是說，在「比較級的句型中」常常會使用「代名詞」。

Ming's academic performance is better than that of Flora's.

[副詞 even]

Even（adv.）甚至、即使，用來表示令人驚訝（surprising）、不在預期之內（unexpected）、不尋常（unusual）或是極端的事物（extreme）。引言中以 even，表示出狐仙受人恩德，即使是舉手之勞，也要全力回報的世間少有的報恩之舉。

A fox still thought to repay a kindness done, even <u>one done through unconscious virtue.</u> 一隻狐，因為他人曾經對自己有過恩德，那怕只是無意之中的事，也還在思量如何報答。

■ 本引言的副詞不是修飾動作，而是修飾整個句子，也就是整個事件。

例：He doesn't even know that he has a problem.
他甚至不知道自己有問題。

來到山東必看必去

　　山東的青島素有小瑞士之稱，尤其是八大觀，八大觀是青島主要的名勝之一，最能體現青島「紅瓦綠樹、碧海藍天」特色的風景區。這裡的建築物融合了俄、英、法、德、美、日本和丹麥等 20 多個國家的建築風格，所以也譽為「萬國建築博覽會」，八大觀在不同的季節就有不同的景觀，如韶關路春天就開滿碧桃，一片粉紅，也難怪八大觀會成為中國最大的婚紗攝影中心之一。

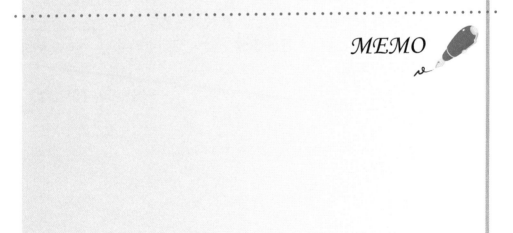

MEMO

中國 江蘇省李汝珍紀念館
Li Ruzhen Memorial Hall, China

李汝珍《鏡花緣》 *Flowers in the Mirror* Track62

Not at all! There are men as well as women, only they call men women, and women men. The mea wear the skirts and take care of the home, while the women wear hats and trousers and manage affairs outside.

—— Li Ruzhen, *Flowers in the Mirror*

　　「唐兄擔心的當然有道理，但是，這個女兒國並不是那個女兒國。這個女兒國也有男人，也是男女配合，和我們一樣。不同的是，男人穿衣裙，作婦人的打扮，主持家裡的事務；女人反而穿靴戴帽，作男人的打扮，處理外面的事情。」

——李汝珍《鏡花緣》

PART 1 歐洲篇
PART 2 美洲篇
PART 3 亞洲篇

文學景點巧巧說

《鏡花緣》（*Flowers in the Mirror*）為清代李汝珍的作品，李汝珍一生經歷清乾隆、嘉慶和道光三朝；於乾隆四十七年（1782 年），十九歲時隨兄到海州（今江蘇連雲港海州區板浦鎮）等地。四十歲時，李汝珍遇上黃河氾濫成災，便毅然到河南踢山擔任治水縣丞。他原本就有管理的能力，又熟讀河渠相關書籍，水患很快就被他治理好，也就是在這段時間，他看盡了大小官吏見錢眼開、為求功名而汲汲營營等醜態，於是一等治河工程結束，便辭官返鄉，從此不再追求功名，這段背景也寫進《鏡花緣》裡，而他一心離開俗世的心境也和書中主角唐敖不謀而合。《鏡花緣》的背景設在武則天時代，秀才唐敖為主角，因為功名仕祿感到厭倦，便隨妻子的哥哥林之洋和多九公出海做生意，途中遊歷數十個國家，親眼目睹了各式各樣奇異的風土民情，這樣遊歷各國的故事，頗有一種東方《格列佛遊記》之感，為的也是諷刺現實的社會人生。旅途中，唐敖等人到了「兩面國」、「翼民國」、「穿胸國」與「女兒國」…，每個國家的描述都是一種情境的評斷，一邊讀一邊有驚奇之感，一邊也不禁覺得現世有多種樣貌，作者這麼寫也是一種抒發，希望能藉由文學帶來一種改革吧。本引言為「女兒國」的描述，先不論這是不是代表女性地位的抬頭意識，但「習慣成自然」則有批判偏見的意味，現在看來也很有道理呢。《鏡花緣》的醞釀和創作都是在江蘇海州完成，因此海州區板浦鎮這裡設有李汝珍紀念館，是深入了解李汝珍與當地風俗民情的地方。本引言(英文版)取自 University of California 所出版之 *Flowers in the Mirror*。中文部分取自城邦文化所出版之《最愛的文學繪本：鏡花緣》，編寫人為張玲玲，原著為李汝珍。

揭開序幕小對話

Running a restaurant is easy, but sometimes it is not that easy. Especially when Austin and Fiona want to take a vacation, they need to have somebody cover for their shift. This is why they are now having interviews with applicants. They decide to hire a person who is trustworthy and shows

311

a sense of responsibility.

　　經營一家餐廳不難，但有時候的確不簡單，特別是當奧斯汀跟費歐娜想要一起去渡假的時候，他們必須要有人代他們的班。這也是為什麼他們正在舉行徵人面試的原因，他們決定要雇用一位值得信任並且有責任感的人。

Austin: Did you just called the girl applicant Mr. Wheeler?

奧斯汀：你剛剛叫那位女孩維勒先生嗎？

Fiona: She looks manly. She wears pants and is with short hair.

費歐娜：她看起來很有男子氣概，她穿褲子又留短髮。

Austin: That's gender stereotype.

奧斯汀：這是性別刻板印象。

Fiona: Well, who doesn't? When I say loving, caring, and compassionate, do you picture a she or a he?

費歐娜：嗯…誰沒有呢？當我講到友愛的、照顧人的、憐憫的，你會想到她還是他？

Austin: I'll say "she".

奧斯汀：我覺得是她。

Fiona: Gender stereotype.

費歐娜：性別刻板印象。

Austin: All right. I admit that I am also under the influence of that. But I thought in modern society, we bear less of it. In Qing Dynasty, the gender's role was more obvious. I recently read a fantasy novel, Flowers in the Mirror by Li Ruzhen. The author actually pointed out the phenomena of gender stereotype.

奧斯汀：好吧，我承認我也受到性別刻板印象的影響，但我想在現代的社會中，我們受到的影響比較少，在清朝男女性別的角色比較明顯。我最近讀了清朝小說，李汝珍的鏡花緣，那時作者就有指出性別刻板印象的影響。

Fiona: Oh really?

費歐娜：喔，是喔？

Austin: He did. The story of the character entered a foreign land and was amazed to see **the men wear the skirts and take care of the home, while the women wear hats and trousers and manage affairs outside. In fact, there are men as well as women, only they call men women, and women men.**

奧斯汀：是啊，故事的主角去到了境外之地，並且震驚的發現男人穿衣裙，作婦人的打扮，主持家裡的事務；女人反而穿靴戴帽，作男人的打扮，處理外面的事情。但是其實，個女兒國並不是那個女兒國。這個女兒國也有男人，也是男女配合，和我們一樣。

Fiona: I see. What's special about it?

費歐娜：了解，有什麼特別的嗎？

Austin: I heard there is a memorial museum about Li Ruzhen in Jiangsu, China. We really should have visited there when we were in China last month.

奧斯汀：我聽說有在中國的江蘇省有一個李汝珍紀念館，我們那時在中國旅遊時應該去那邊看看的。

Fiona: Well, honey, we still haven't reached a conclusion from our last topic. Which applicant should we hire?

費歐娜：嗯⋯親愛的，我們上一個話題還沒有定案呢？我們要雇用哪一個人？

Austin: Sorry. I am too much into Chinese culture lately. Thanks for bringing it up again.

奧斯汀：喔，抱歉，我最近太著迷於中國文化了，謝謝你提醒我。

Fiona: I think the tomboy is a good choice. What do you say?

費歐娜：我覺得那個男孩似的女孩很不錯，你覺得呢？

PART 1 歐洲篇

PART 2 美洲篇

PART 3 亞洲篇

313

好好用單字、片語

1. shift *n.* 輪班

2. cover *v.* 代替

3. applicant *n.* 申請人

4. gender stereotype *n.* 性別刻板印象

5. compassionate *adj.* 憐憫的

6. picture *v.* 想像

7. admit *v.* 承認

8. tomboy *n.* 男孩似的女子

9. point out *phr.* 指出，英文意思為 bring something up to other's attention，也就是把某件事特別講出來。

   例 ❶ Unfortunately, I have to point out that your were wrong about Leo.

   不幸的是，我必須指出你之前誤會里歐了。

   ❷ My sister points out that she feels happy because she chooses to think positively.

   我姐姐說，她會快樂是因為她選擇正面的思考模式。

10. reach a conclusion *phr.* 下結論，conclusion *n.* 結論，英文意思為 the decision you made after a discussion or your second thoughts，也就是經過思考或討論後的結論。

    例 ❶ If you stick to the same approach, you would never reach a conclusion.

    如果你堅持要用這個古板的方法，你是得不出什麼結論的。

    ❷ To ensure the efficiency of our meeting, let's go straight to the details and reach a conclusion.

    為了達到開會的效率，我們直接討論細節並下結論吧。

文學佳句怎麼用

Not at all! There are men as well as women, only they call men women, and women men. The man wear the skirts and take care of the home, while the women wear hats and trousers and manage affairs outside.

「唐兄擔心的當然有道理，但是，這個女兒國並不是那個女兒國。這個女兒國也有男人，也是男女配合，和我們一樣。不同的是，男人穿衣裙，作婦人的打扮，主持家裡的事務；女人反而穿靴戴帽，作男人的打扮，處理外面的事情。」

〔一辭多義：call〕

「call me!」打給我吧！call v. 打電話，是最常見的意思，但是在引言中的 call v.，有「把…稱為…」的意思，請見下列例句：

1. I am William, and you can call me Willy.

   我是威廉，你可以叫我威利。

2. They call men women.

   他們把男人稱做女人。

〔名詞〕

(1) 英文中的名詞，在文法上最常擔任「主詞」及「受詞」的角色，例如：

Normally, the men wears pants.

　　　　男人們　　　　褲子　當主詞當受詞

一般來説，男人穿褲子。

The man is a geek. Who would wear a sweater in summer?

那個男人一件毛衣　當主詞當受詞

那個男人是怪胎，誰在夏天穿毛衣啊?

(2) 名詞分為為「可數」及「不可數」，可數名詞有「單複數」之分，目的為「表達某物的數量」，一般來説，表達「複數」的字根為「字母 s」，例如 a sweater/ sweaters，但是某些名詞的複數為不規則變化，則需特別去記，例如 a man/ men。注意，表達單數時需要加上「冠詞」，表達複數時需在字尾加上 s 或是 es。

(3) 「可數」名詞表複數時的變化

A. 字尾加 s：skirts（裙子）、hats（帽子）、trousers（褲子）、affairs（事務）。

B. 字尾加 es（註）：buses（公車）、dishes（碗盤）、watches（手錶）、boxes（箱子）。

C. 不規則變化：man → men（男人）、woman → women（女人）、tooth→teeth（牙齒）、child → children（小孩子）。

註：當名詞字尾以「嘶嘶音 s, x, sh, ch」結尾時，複數形以 es 結尾。

來到江蘇必看必去

　　南京是江蘇省的省會，過去曾是許多朝代的首都，也是全國政治、經濟與文化中心，來這裡也要看看南京過去身為文化重鎮的面貌，造訪中山陵（Dr. Sun Yat-sen's Mausoleum）、玄武湖（Xuanwu Lake）、南京中國近代史遺址博物館（The Presidential Palace, Nanjing）等地。

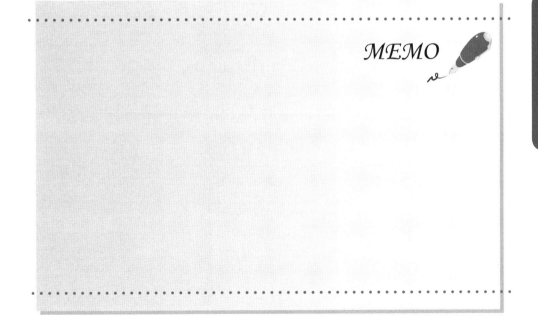

MEMO

英語學習 －職場系列－

定價：NT$349元/HK$109元
規格：320頁/17＊23cm

定價：NT$360元/HK$113元
規格：328頁/17＊23cm

定價：NT$349元/HK$109元
規格：304頁/17＊23cm

定價：NT$360元/HK$113元
規格：320頁/17＊23cm

定價：NT$369元/HK$115元
規格：312頁/17＊23cm/MP3

定價：NT$369元/HK$115元
規格：320頁/17＊23cm

定價：NT$360元/HK$113元
規格：288頁/17＊23cm/MP3

定價：NT$329元/HK$103元
規格：304頁/17＊23cm

定價：NT$369元/HK$115元
規格：328頁/17＊23cm/MP3

英語學習—生活・文法・考用—

定價：NT$369元/K$115元
規格：320頁/17＊23cm/MP3

定價：NT$380元/HK$119元
規格：320頁/17＊23cm/MP3

定價：NT$349元/HK$109元
規格：352頁/17＊23cm

定價：NT$380元/HK$119元
規格：288頁/17＊23cm/MP3

定價：NT$329元/HK$103元
規格：352頁/17＊23cm

定價：NT$349元/HK$109元
規格：304頁/17＊23cm

定價：NT$380元/HK$119元
規格：352頁/17＊23cm

定價：NT$369元/HK$115元
規格：304頁/17＊23cm/MP3

定價：NT$380元/HK$119元
規格：304頁/17＊23cm/MP3

Leader 018

Follow 文學地圖用英語造訪世界 40 大景點

作　　者	趙婉君
特約編輯	瑞塔
封面構成	高鍾琪
內頁構成	菩薩蠻數位文化有限公司

發 行 人	周瑞德
企劃編輯	饒美君
校　　對	陳欣慧、陳韋佑
印　　製	大亞彩色印刷製版股份有限公司
初　　版	2015 年 5 月
定　　價	新台幣 369 元
出　　版	力得文化
電　　話	(02) 2351-2007
傳　　真	(02) 2351-0887
地　　址	100 台北市中正區福州街 1 號 10 樓之 2
E - m a i l	best.books.service@gmail.com

港澳地區總經銷	泛華發行代理有限公司
地　　　　址	香港新界將軍澳工業邨駿昌街 7 號 2 樓
電　　　　話	(852) 2798-2323
傳　　　　真	(852) 2796-5471

國家圖書館出版品預行編目(CIP)資料

```
Follow 文學地圖用英語造訪世界 40 大景點 / 趙
婉君著. -- 初版. -- 臺北市 ： 力得文化,
2015.05
　面 ；　公分. --（Leader ； 18）
ISBN 978-986-91458-8-6(平裝附光碟片)

1.英語 2.讀本

　805.18                              104006907
```